D1051989

He Used to Love Me:

Renaissance Collection

He Used to Love Me:

Renaissance Collection

Dorothy Brown-Newton

www.urbanbooks.net

Urban Books, LLC
300 Farmingdale Road, NY-Route 109
Farmingdale, NY 11735

He Used to Love Me: Renaissance Collection

ISBN 13: 978-1-945855-24-5
ISBN 10: 1-945855-24-X

First Mass Market Printing May 2018
First Trade Paperback Printing December 2017
Printed in the United States of America

10 9 8 7 6 5 4 3 2 1

Distributed by Kensington Publishing Corp.
Submit orders to:
Customer Service
400 Hahn Road
Westminster, MD 21157-4627
Phone: 1-800-733-3000
Fax: 1-800-659-243

He Used to Love Me:

Renaissance Collection

by

Dorothy Brown-Newton

Acknowledgments

First, I have to thank God for giving me the gift that allows me to keep sharing what I love to do. I can honestly say that my dream is now a reality, and I still have a hard time believing that at times.

I want to thank my family and friends who always support me, whether it's sharing my posts, getting the word out, or buying my books when they drop. I just want you all to know that I appreciate the love, and if you haven't heard me say it, I'm saying it now. I love you all, and thanks.

I have to give thanks to my husband, Rodger, who always gives me my space to let me do what I love doing. You always take care of the kids when it's time for me to write or do research, so I just want to tell you thanks, and I love you so much.

Special shout-outs go out to my supporters who have been rocking with me from the time

Acknowledgments

I put out my very first book. This journey hasn't been easy, but I have to say that all the love that has been shown makes it a lot easier. I also want to give a big thank-you to Racquel Williams and everyone on the team. You have all proven that teamwork makes the dream work, and I appreciate every one of you.

Before I go, I have to say thank you to Shawna Brim for always being there when I need you. Thanks for all the feedback, and I'm honored to say that you're my friend, because you have shown me nothing but love from the first day we interacted with one another.

I hope that you all enjoy reading *He Used to Love Me* as much as I enjoyed writing it. I dedicate this book to anyone who has loved and lost or has been betrayed by someone whom you trusted. Just remember that forgiveness is key!

Prologue

I crept slowly out of my bedroom into my daughter's room, trying to be as quiet as possible so as not to wake my husband. Tonight was the last straw, and I was leaving his ass. I had been married to Andris for two years, and lately, it had been hell living with this man. I had really believed him to be a good man, one who would never put his hands on me. At first, he had been disrespectful with his mouth sometimes and a little controlling, but that had been it. But then he had started putting his hands on me.

He had been accusing me of cheating on him for the past six months, and I had no clue what would give him that idea. I didn't even leave the house, because I was home all day caring for our child. You would think that he would use common sense and realize I had no time to cheat. No matter how many times I told him that I wasn't cheating, it just went over his head, because somewhere in his sick mind, I was cheating on him. I hadn't told my family what had been going on in my marriage. If I did, they would only remind me that they had tried to warn me about him. But being young and in love, you saw what you wanted to see. Basically, you were in the relationship with blinders on, acting oblivious to the obvious. But tonight was the last time that I would allow him to put his hands on me.

He had come home intoxicated, wanting sex, and I promise you, I never denied my husband sex, but I'd been nursing my daughter, so all I had asked was that he wait until I was done. He'd hauled off and slapped me without warning, and I'd fallen out of the chair I was sitting on, taking Andrea down with me. He didn't care that she was screaming at the top of her lungs as he picked her up off the floor and placed her on the sofa. He walked back over to me, grabbed me by my hair, and continued to assault me. All I could think about was my baby taking another fall as I pleaded with him to let me go to her, but my pleas fell on deaf ears. He started to kick me, causing me to get into the fetal position, trying to protect as much of my body as I could.

I prayed he got tired, so that I could get to my baby, who was still crying like she was about to choke on her own saliva. After one last kick to my stomach, he screamed at me, telling me that if I ever disrespected him again, he would kill me. Then he ran out of the room. I rushed over to my baby as soon as he was out of sight, and checked to make sure that she was okay. I think she was more upset that I had stopped feeding her than she was about the chaos around her, because, even though I was in pain, I began to nurse her again, and once I put my breast back into her mouth, she quieted down.

Allowing Andris to abuse me was one thing, but I wasn't going to stay around and allow him to abuse our child too. I lifted Andrea out of her crib, and after grabbing her bag, I quietly walked down the stairs. Thankfully, I made it to the garage without incident. I was in so much pain and needed to soak my body in a tub of water, but that would have to wait, as my safety and Andrea's were more important right now.

I put Andrea in her car seat and made sure to strap her in before getting into the driver's seat and pulling out of the driveway slowly. I took a deep breath once I reached the corner, then headed toward the highway, praying the whole way. Andris and I lived in New Jersey, so I had at least a two-hour drive ahead of me to my parents' house in New York. But I knew that once I made it to my parents' house, I would be okay.

Just as I was about to get on the highway, my gas light came on, causing me to cry out in frustration. The last thing I wanted to do was drive to a gas station. I hated pumping gas, so I always waited until my tank was damn near empty before filling up. I would have felt safer if I were now on the highway and knew that I was headed in the direction of my destination. Stopping here meant possibly being caught by my husband, but I had no other choice.

A few minutes later, I pulled up to the gas station on Washington Street, cursing under my breath that I hadn't got gas today after leaving the grocery store, when I noticed that it was extremely low. I looked back to make sure that Andrea was okay once I pulled into the gas station. She was okay, but I wasn't, as I saw my husband's car pull up behind my car. This motherfucker must have put a fucking GPS locator on my car, because there was no way he could have figured out I was on Washington Street. I quickly locked the doors and prayed that he would just leave me alone. I scanned the area and not a soul was in sight, which caused me to panic, in fear of my life.

He climbed out of his car and approached my window. "Open the fucking door, Cydney," he shouted, hitting the window, causing me to jump and Andrea to start crying.

He had this crazed look in his eyes as he threatened that if I didn't open the door, he was going to kill me. I knew if I opened the door, I was as good as dead—I could tell that he wasn't going to spare my life for disobeying him. My eyes got big as I watched him pull out a gun and point it at the window. I screamed. I heard the gas station attendant asked Andris if everything was okay, saving my life in the process. Andris called me a bitch before walking back to his car and pulling off.

Once my heartbeat returned to normal, I reached over and grabbed my bag to get my debit card so that I could get gas and leave. I thought that Andris might be waiting for me to leave, and that scared the shit out of me. I reached for the door handle and froze when the first bullet struck me. Bullets continued to strike me until my body leaned to the side. I heard my baby's cries until everything went black as I took my last breath.

Chapter One

Jakiyah

I couldn't stop the tears from falling as I got off the phone with my mother. She called to tell me that my baby sister, Cydney, had been found murdered at a gas station not too far from her home. Someone had shot my sister and had left her for dead. My four-month-old niece had been left in the car, unharmed. When they'd found her, she was screaming her lungs out. I was thankful that they hadn't hurt my niece, but it really hurt that they hadn't spared my sister's life as well. My mother told me to wait until tomorrow to travel to New York, since I was just about to leave for work. She didn't want me to travel right away in the state of mind that I was in. It didn't matter if I left now or next week; my state of mind wasn't going to change, so there was no need to delay my departure.

I booked my flight to New York as soon as I hung up with her, and I had a flight that left in a few hours. I called work to let them know that I had a family emergency and that I would keep them updated. I also called my best friend, April, to tell her about my sister's passing, and she offered to go with me, but I told her that I would be fine. I would never ask her to leave her daughter with her mother just to accompany me, even though I knew she would have.

I packed a suitcase and then waited for my cab to arrive to take me to the airport. I lived in Georgia and hadn't seen my family since last year, when they came to visit for the Christmas holiday. They used to visit at least once a month, but after my dad got sick, they stopped making the trips. I kind of felt bad that I hadn't seen Cydney in about two years, but once she married Andris, she kind of distanced herself from the family. None of us really cared for Andris because he had always been a control freak, needing to dictate her every move.

My mom had talked to Cydney and had tried to get her to understand that even though Andris didn't put his hands on her, he was still being abusive. She had explained to her that being controlling, disrespectful, and hurtful all fell into the category of abuse, but Cydney hadn't tried to hear anything my mother was saying. After that conversation, Andris had moved her to New Jersey with him. They'd married six months later, and none of her family members had been invited to the wedding. And when she got pregnant with my niece, we'd wanted to be there for her, but she shut us out once again. She really hurt my mother, but it didn't make us love her any less; we just had to love her from afar.

The detective whom my parents spoke to when they went to identify my sister's body told them that Andris was wanted for questioning. The police wanted to know why my sister was even at the gas station at that time of night and not at home with him. I swear, if he was responsible for killing my sister, I was going to jail for killing him. I grabbed my suitcase when I heard the cab outside. The cabbie was laying on his horn, annoying the hell out of me. His ass just blew his tip, and I didn't care if he helped with my suitcase. He wasn't getting shit but the fare.

I arrived at the airport and boarded the plane, trying to prepare myself mentally to be strong for my parents and my brother, Tyhiem. My sister was only twenty-five years old and didn't deserve to be gunned down the way that she was. Cydney was a good person, a little stubborn, but still a good person. She would have given up her last dollar, so I knew in my heart that this wasn't a robbery, which was what my dad had suggested, trying to give Andris the benefit of the doubt. Cydney would have protected my niece, without question, so I knew she would have given a potential robber whatever he demanded to save her daughter. I had to admit that even before my mother mentioned that the detective said Andris was wanted for questioning, my first thought was that he was a suspect. I hadn't trusted him before this happened, and I wasn't about to trust that he didn't kill my sister.

After departing the plane and getting my baggage, I walked over to Avis to get my rental car so that I could head to my parents' home. I called my father to let him know that I had arrived and would be there soon. He said that Tyhiem wanted to pick me up, but I told him that I had already rented a car when I booked my flight.

I pulled into my parents' driveway about thirty minutes later and said a silent prayer, asking God for strength. I had promised myself that I would be strong, but I needed some assistance with this one. I felt the tears trying to fall already, and I hadn't even gotten inside yet. I walked inside and gave my mom a hug, holding her tight and not wanting to let her go as my tears fell. Trying to be strong went out the window as soon as I saw my mother. It really hurt that I had stayed away from my family for so long because of my own selfish reasons. I let her go and went and hugged my dad. I'm not going to lie. I was a daddy's girl. My tears continued to fall. He told me that it was going to be okay, but was it really going to be okay? My brother sat quietly, wearing an expression that I couldn't read, but I promise you that he had murder on his mind. I walked over, and he stood to hug me, and I really tried not to cry again but failed miserably because the shit hurt and didn't make any sense.

We all went and sat in the living room, and then we listened to my dad speak about what the officers on the scene reported to the detectives handling the case. He was told that Cydney's body was badly bruised and showed signs of abuse, causing me to see red. He said that until they received a full report from the medical examiner's office, he couldn't say for sure, but if he had to make a guess based on the bruises, he would say that they were inflicted hours before the shooting. Tyhiem got up and walked out of the room, but in that moment, I was having a different emotion. I became upset with my sister because she had said nothing about domestic violence. If she was being abused, why did she say nothing? All she had to do was say something, and my family would have bodied his ass. Now she was gone, and we would never see her again, because she didn't trust her family to have her back.

I now wondered if her being out that late on the night she was killed had anything to do with her leaving him. But by then it was too late for her. She should have left his ass the first time he laid hands on her. I just didn't understand why she'd been so weak for this man. Growing up, we never saw our parents fight, but our mother was never a pushover for my father, either. We were raised with the notion that if someone hit you, you hit their ass back. Cydney was always fighting while she was growing up, whether it was against male or a female, so I didn't understand what he had over her that would cause her to permit him to put his hands on her.

Chapter Two

Jakiyah

My mom and I arrived at Browne Funeral Home to start making arrangements for my sister. I basically handled all the decisions because it was too much for my mother to have to bury her child. I picked out a coral-blue casket with a silver lining. For as long as I could remember, coral blue was Cydney's favorite color. I had to close my eyes briefly and take a few deep breaths before completing the process. My heart was heavy: making the funeral arrangements made it all final, drove home the fact that I would never see my sister again. My mom stepped out for some fresh air, but I knew she didn't want me to see the tears in her eyes. I decided to just wrap it up so that we could leave, because this whole process was overwhelming. I chose to have the viewing and funeral this Friday, and the burial would be on Saturday.

I left the funeral home, not feeling well. We were supposed to go and get the outfit that my sister would be wearing at her home-going ceremony, but I decided to do it another day and without my mother. She looked so broken, and it hurt me that I couldn't take the pain away. The ride back home was quiet, as my mom and I were both lost in our own feelings of losing our loved one. I wanted to talk to her about what her plans were as far as baby Andrea was concerned. I'd be damned if his family got my niece. Both of my parents were retired and probably wouldn't be able to care for Andrea on their own, because Dad had some health issues, and Mom would be basically doing it on her own. I was willing to help in any way that was needed to avoid having Andrea placed with those people. I didn't know if his parents knew that he was a monster, but I was not willing to take any chances by placing her with them.

"Mom, are you okay over there?" I asked her as I saw her wipe at the tears that fell from her eyes.

"I'm not okay, Jakiyah. I can't stop wondering if there was something that your father and I could have done. Maybe we could have called more to let her know that we weren't upset with her leaving. We just let our baby girl move hours away with a man she hardly knew, and we did nothing. We made her feel like we had given up on her, and she didn't have any family support," she cried, breaking my heart into pieces.

"Mom, please don't blame yourself. None of us knew that she was being abused or was even unhappy in her relationship. Cydney always insisted that she was okay when I would speak to her on the phone. Yes, Andris was known for being unfaithful and controlling, but none of us knew that he was putting his hands on her. But trust me, he will be dealt with," I said, getting angry that my mom was hurting.

"Jakiyah, I don't need for you to get into any trouble. Just the thought of losing another child would kill me. Let the authorities handle what needs to be handled concerning Andris," she said sadly.

"Mom, I'm not trying to see his ass in jail, still breathing, when my sister is dead. He didn't care that he was leaving his daughter motherless, so I could give two shits about leaving her fatherless," I cried, letting my emotions get the best of me.

I had to apologize quickly to my mother. I shouldn't have been having this conversation with her, because all it did was upset her more, and I wasn't trying to do that. I was just so angry, and I wanted his family to feel the same pain that my family was feeling right now.

Once we finally made it back to the house and stepped inside, my heart skipped a beat when I saw German sitting in my parents' living room with Tyhiem and my father. German was the last person whom I wanted to see sitting in my mother's living room. German and my brother were best friends, and he was my ex. We'd dated for two years before he broke up with me. He started another relationship when he was still involved with me, but he didn't give me a chance to be mad and end the relationship, because he did it. When I found out he was cheating, I thought he was going to apologize and tell me how much he loved me, but instead, he said that he loved the other woman and that he was leaving me.

He hurt me so bad that I moved to Georgia and hadn't been back home until now. Had my sister not passed away, I would have never stepped foot back in New York. I loved my New York family, but they knew that if they wanted to see me, they had to travel. I tried to avoid looking at him, but it was hard because he was still fine after all this time. German was of Dominican descent. He had that sun-kissed skin that was blemish free, curly hair, which he had cut low, thick eyebrows, and brown eyes. That tatted body of his always put me in a trancelike state when I looked at him, and now was no different. As much as I hated him, I couldn't get my eyes to focus elsewhere. That was until my brother screamed in my face, "Earth to Jakiyah," not only breaking my stare but embarrassing me too.

"You play too much, Ty," I said, punching his ass.

"Ouch, J! That shit hurt. I had to do something. You were making us all uncomfortable with the way you were just staring at German," he joked.

"I wasn't staring. I was just... Anyway, I don't have time for your jokes, bighead," I said, deciding not to put my foot in my mouth.

"How are you feeling, Ms. Smith? I just stopped by to offer my condolences. I'm really sorry for your loss," German said to my mother.

So, he's really not going to acknowledge me? I thought as I low-key watched him from the corner that I was now sitting in. This nigga must have forgotten that I was the one who should have been acting funny toward him. You would think that he would show me some sign of endearment, the same as he had just shown my mother, considering the situation. It didn't take long to figure out why he wasn't trying to show me any love, as his girlfriend descended the stairs. He had the nerve to bring his girlfriend to my mother's house. Seeing her kiss and hug my mother and offer her condolences let me know that this wasn't her first time visiting.

"Jakiyah, this is German's girlfriend, Tamia. Tamia, this is my daughter, Jakiyah," my mom said introducing us.

So, everybody was going to act like they didn't know that this was the female German had left me for? Given the circumstances, I decided not to be petty, even though my sister, Cydney, would have been like, "Fuck that bitch." I spoke to her, accepted her condolences—the ones that German didn't even have the courtesy to extend to me himself. I excused myself for a second as my mother began telling them about the arrangements and showing my father pictures of the casket that I picked for Cydney. I stood in the kitchen, listening to them interact with one another, and I became even more convinced that Tamia was a regular at my parents' home. I wasn't going to lie; I felt some kind of way about it, but what could I really say? After all, I had been gone for two years. It seemed as if my mother had bonded with another female who wasn't me or my sister, and my mother was not to blame, because neither one of us had been here for her.

I walked back into the living room and saw Tamia holding my niece, and I could hear my sister in my ear telling me to take her daughter from the bitch. I laughed at the thought of my sister, who was a no-nonsense chick when it came to females we didn't care for. That was why it was really hard to believe that she been too weak to confront Andris's bullshit. Her ass stayed checking someone, and if she were here right now, she would be checking German and his girlfriend.

Chapter Three

German

I knew that Jakiyah was going to come home for her sister's funeral, but I never thought she would be here so soon. Ty hadn't even given a nigga a heads-up that she was here, even though he knew that I was stopping by with Tamia. I was really caught off guard when I saw her walk in; she was still as stunning as I remembered her. She still wore her hair bone straight, but she was rocking honey-blond highlights in her hair. They were similar to Tamia's highlights. The only difference was that Tamia's hair was in a short hairstyle. Jakiyah was still built like a stallion, causing my dick to get hard, so I did the wise thing and ignored her.

I didn't need Tamia to come downstairs and find me staring at another female, with lust written all over my face. Jakiyah wasn't making it any easier for me by staring at a nigga like she was ready to ride the dick the way she had in the past. Ty's ass was foul for calling her out in front of everybody, but that shit was funny. He was always in joke mode, and I wasn't mad at him, because he did take all of us away from how we were feeling about Cydney—even if it was only for a minute.

"So, was that her?" Tamia asked me after she walked into the room and sat on my lap.

We had just gotten home from Ty's mom's crib, and I'd been sitting in the living room, chilling, while Tamia had been upstairs, doing what she did best. She'd been on the phone, gossiping with her friend Raven, probably telling her about Jakiyah.

"Stop acting like you didn't know that was her, babe," I responded, lifting her off my lap.

"She's pretty, but she doesn't have anything on me," she said, swinging her head from side to side like she had some hair on her head, causing me to laugh.

"You're too much. That girl's not thinking about you." I continued to laugh at her because she was being really comical, showing her insecure side, which I didn't see often.

"I'm not stunting her ass, either," she said, rolling her eyes and jumping on my back as I stood.

I swung her ass around until she was begging me to put her down. I lowered her onto the couch, then lay on top of her and kissed her lips.

"Babe, you don't have to ever worry about another woman, because I'm with the woman I want to be with," I admitted, then kissed her lips again, slipping my tongue in her mouth this time and causing her to moan.

She had just awakened the monster inside of my pants, and I wanted to fuck the shit out of her right there on the couch, but she shut me down.

"German, let me up. I want to get out of these clothes and shower before dinner," she said, pushing me off her, smiling.

"You're such a tease," I joked. I slapped her on the ass before she walked away. She headed upstairs.

I had loved me some Tamia from the first time I laid eyes on her. She had been working downtown, at the Westin Hotel that she managed, and I'd been there for a luncheon that my job was having in one of the conference rooms. I had stepped out to take a call from Jakiyah, and that was when I saw Tamia and quickly ended my call. I walked over to her, then asked her a stupid question. I believe it was something along the lines of where the men's room was. It just so happened that we were standing right across from the sign that read RESTROOMS. She smiled and asked me if that was the best that I could come up with, causing us both to laugh. We spoke only for a few more minutes, as I had to get back to the luncheon. She gave me her number, and we talked later on that night, agreeing to go out that following weekend.

Tamia was a few years younger than I was, but she was great at communicating. I found myself wanting to talk to her every chance that I got. I knew that I was wrong for seeing her behind Jakiyah's back, but I started to fall for her, to the point where I got careless, and Jakiyah found out. I had never meant to hurt Jakiyah, because I did love her, but I had fallen in love with Tamia, which led me to choose her. Jakiyah was so hurt that she moved away a month after I broke things off and never returned—until now.

After the breakup, my relationship with Ty was strained for a few months, but we got over it and were back like we had never fallen off. Tamia didn't know that I was still with Jakiyah when I first started seeing her; she just knew that Jakiyah was my ex. I let her think that Jakiyah and I had dated in high school. I fudged the details about the relationship that I had with Jakiyah only because I didn't want Tamia to know that I was that type of dude. Seeing

Jakiyah again had stirred up some old feelings, but I would never take it there. Tamia was the woman whom I wanted to be with. If I didn't, I would have never left a relationship to be with her.

After Tamia showered and we had dinner, we called it a night, but not before I put that ass to sleep by banging her back out. I hopped in the shower before she awoke the next morning because I had to be at work early. I worked as a technician for Time Warner Cable, so I started in the field as early as six most mornings. Tamia's ass ended up waking up when I turned on the water, and she joined me in the shower and we had round two.

Chapter Four

Jakiyah

We were now leaving the funeral home where my sister's funeral had been held to go to the church for the repast. My heart was heavy, and I just wanted to go back to my mom's house, get in bed, and cry. I knew that I couldn't go home. I needed to be there for my parents. Even though my mom was doing okay, I knew that she was just being strong for everyone else. I had to say that my sister was loved as I looked out at all the friends and family who had shown up today to pay their respects.

As I got in the back of the limo, I tried to remember the last conversation I had had with my sister, but I couldn't remember as the tears fell. In the past week, I must have called her phone a million times, just to hear her voice on her voice mail. No one had shown up from Andris's family, but his mother had reached out to my mother, offering her condolences. In return, my mother had pleaded with her to tell her son to turn himself in. She insisted that her son didn't kill Cydney, and she felt it was best that they didn't attend the funeral. I wished I'd been home when that call came in, because I would have offered her a few choice words about her and her son.

The limo pulled up to the church, we all got out, and I took my mother's hand as we walked inside together, with my dad and Ty following. It felt good to see that my friend April had shown up after I told her that it was okay not to attend, given that she had the baby, but once again, she was here for me, as always. She wasn't able to stay for the entire repast, and I understood. I hugged her and told her to call me when she landed safely. After helping my mom serve everyone, I was ready to go home, but my parents wanted to stay for prayer, so after thanking everyone for coming, I accepted Ty's offer of German dropping us off.

German and Ty spoke among themselves, as I was lost in my own thoughts once again. I considered whether I would return to Georgia or stay in New York. Although I did have a life in Georgia, I was feeling some kind of way about going back to that life and leaving my family again. I didn't even realize that we had reached my parents' place until I heard Ty calling my name and saw German staring at me from the rearview mirror.

"Thanks," I said as I got out of the car.

"Call me if you need me, sis," Ty called after me, but I didn't answer.

I went inside, climbed in the bed, and cried for my sister. I wished that I could tell her one last time that I loved her, and that I was sorry that she felt she couldn't tell me what she was going through. Just as I was about to get out of my clothes and take a shower, my phone alerted me that I had a text message. I ignored it at first because today was my day of mourning, and I didn't feel like entertaining anyone. I had to remind myself that I needed to respond to all the people who weren't able to attend the service, and most of them had sent their condolences through social media or via text messages. I looked at the phone and saw that it was April, letting me know that she had landed and telling me to give her a call if I needed to talk. The tears started to fall again because I just felt so angry inside, and I knew that the feeling wouldn't get any better until the man responsible for my sister's death was six feet in the ground.

No, it wasn't going to bring my sister back, but knowing that he paid for what he had done to my sister would take some of my anger away. I responded to April's text message, letting her know that I would be okay and thanking her for coming to my sister's home going. Then I took my shower. I didn't even know if I had the strength to watch my baby sister being put in the ground tomorrow.

Sometimes, when you were the strong one in the family, no one thought that you needed a shoulder to cry on. I just wanted to be held and to be told that it would be okay, but I didn't have that special someone in my life to catch me when I fell. I hadn't dated anyone since the breakup with German. It wasn't because I wasn't trying to; it was just that no one measured up to him. Yes, he had cheated on me and had left me, like he had never loved me, but before this female had come into the picture, he was the perfect man for me. I guessed that I must have been lacking what he needed in his life, so he did what he felt he needed to do to have it. I just wished that if he wasn't happy with me, we could have discussed it before he found comfort in the arms of another woman.

My mom and dad got home soon after I showered, so I took baby Andrea from my mom to get her ready for bed. We let her stay with my grandmother's caregiver. This woman had been caring for my grandmother for about three years, so she was considered family. We had agreed that Andrea shouldn't go to the funeral; she was too young, anyway, so it really wasn't a big deal that she be there. After I gave her a bottle and changed her into her nightclothes, she fell asleep, so I placed her in her crib. Then I went to my room, lay down, and closed my eyes, mentally preparing myself for tomorrow.

We arrived at the Springfield Gardens Cemetery with about fifteen cars following us. I really hadn't expected so many people to attend the burial, but they had proven me wrong. We exited the car, then made our way over to where my sister's final resting place would be. My uncle began handing out flowers to everyone as the pastor prepared to pray over my sister's grave. Just as we were about to bow our heads, my eyes grew wide. I was looking at my sister's husband, Andris, as he approached, walking toward us as if he belonged here.

"Ty, nooo!" I yelled, stopping Andris in his tracks because I saw him reaching for something, which led me to believe he was strapped.

Had it not been my sister's burial, I wouldn't have stopped him, but I couldn't let him do that here. German told Andris to chill as my father calmly walked over to him and got in his face, but not in a threatening manner, out of respect for the pastor and the guests.

"Andris, you need to leave." My father spoke in an even tone, my uncles standing right beside him, probably hoping that Andris would get out of line with my father.

My uncle Tony was nothing to fuck with, and unlike my father, he could care less about who was in attendance today. He would shoot Andris where he stood and would have his ass buried right here in the cemetery, and we all knew it. My mother put her hand on his shoulder in a calming gesture, letting him know that now wasn't the place or time.

"I have every right to be here, just like everyone else," Andris said to my father, with his head down, as if he was mourning like the rest of us.

"I know you heard my pops tell you to leave," Ty barked, stepping up to Andris and letting him see that he was strapped, giving him a final warning to bounce.

Just like the punk that he was, Andris turned to leave. It didn't surprise me at all, because most men who hit females never stepped to a man in the same manner. My blood was boiling by now, and I wished his ass had shown up at the house instead of at my sister's burial. The nerve of his ass, showing up here, but he knew exactly what he was doing, and trust me, he was still going to get two to the head. Every dog got his day, and his days were numbered. I was counting them down.

When it was over and my sister was being lowered into the ground, my mother had a breakdown. She had been strong up until this point. Her breakdown caused me to break down with her. I didn't want to be strong anymore. I wanted my sister back, and I didn't care how I looked to anyone as I sat on the ground and rocked back and forth, crying my eyes out. I felt someone rubbing my back as they helped me to my feet, attempting to calm me. I looked up, wiped my eyes, and I would have never thought that it would be Tamia who had come to comfort me.

"I know this isn't easy, Jakiyah, and I'm not going to say it will get better, because I don't know that it will. But what I will say is that she's in the arms of God now, and she will be okay. You have to be strong for her daughter, whom she left behind," she said, rubbing my back and walking with me over to the limo.

Did her words offer me comfort? No, they didn't, because the fact remained that my sister was gone, and she wasn't coming back. Ty came to help me into the limo. I whispered a thank-you to Tamia before entering the car. The ride back to the house was quiet, other than my mother's cries. My dad was the first to break the silence when he spoke to my brother, but I just laid my head back and closed my eyes, thinking about my sister and how my life as I knew it had taken a drastic turn.

Chapter Five

Tyhiem

Seeing my mom and sister break down at the burial had me feeling like shit. Then this sucker-ass nigga showed up, disrespecting my sister as she was being laid to rest, and I couldn't even put two in his fucking head. I was pissed that he was able to walk away with his life, and the only thing that made me feel somewhat better was the fact that his ass was going to be dead sooner than later, and I put my life on that.

After we dropped Jakiyah off, German drove by Andris's mother's house to see if his ass had bounced to her place, but we sat out there for about an hour, with no movement going in or out of the house, so we bounced. I knew that his ass would be laying low somewhere, but I promise you that I was not going to rest until his ass was dead and stinking.

I didn't want to be alone, so I called up Chanel. She was a chick I'd been kicking it with for over a year now. I wasn't ready to settle down, so I had a few females whom I called up when I wanted to smash, but Chanel was my main chick, and I fucked with her on a regular. When German dropped me at my crib, I dapped him up and thanked him for the ride and for holding a nigga down.

I headed inside and took a shower right away. When I was done showering, I put on a pair of basketball shorts and a beater and then chilled on the couch, watching a *Martin* rerun, while I waited on shorty. I also made sure to call my dad to check on my mom and my sister; he said that they were both sleeping. He told me that he knew I was feeling some kind of way about not being able to handle the earlier situation with Andris, and how right he was. Chanel was at my door, so I told my pops I loved him and ended the call. I really didn't want to talk about Andris, because all it was going to do was piss me off even more.

"What's up, shorty?" I asked as I let her in.

"I'm good. How are you feeling? I wish you would have let me be there for you," she said.

"Chanel, my head space was and still is in a fucked-up place, and at that time, I just wanted to be there for my family. You're here now, so it's all good," I explained, then kissed her lips. "What do you have in the bag?" I asked her after noticing the bag in her arms. I took it from her and headed for the kitchen.

"Just some groceries so that I can bless you with a meal before we chill for the night," she said and smiled.

"Let me find out you've got some skills in the kitchen," I said to her as I placed the bag on the kitchen counter.

"Ty, there's a lot you don't know about me, because for the past year, you haven't been trying to know me on that level. You only reach out when you're in need of some pussy," she responded, seriously causing me to have second thoughts about calling her ass.

Just what I didn't want, and that was to have this same conversation that we always ended up having. Today was really not the day for it, since I had just buried my sister. I knew Chanel deserved more, and I didn't deny that, but I'd been honest with her about not being ready to settle down, so why couldn't she just respect the shit? I wasn't forcing her to accept what I had to offer right now; she wanted to be here, so she just needed to let this shit rock the way it had been rocking.

"I'm sorry, Ty. I didn't mean to be all in my feelings when you've got your own shit going on," she said, apologizing.

"Don't sweat it. It's all good," I replied, walking out of the kitchen and letting her do her thing.

I wasn't going to lie and say that I wasn't feeling shorty, because I was, but these bitches be fake as hell, showing you what they thought you wanted to see, until you wifed the bitch. My ex, Shayla, had really fucked a nigga up as far as trying to wife another chick. She had been everything a nigga wanted until we became exclusive and she started smashing everything moving, just like a nigga would. Had my ass checking to see if I still had a fucking penis the way that bitch was playing me, and I was still trying to be with her. So it was hard trying to be exclusive with Chanel and to make her wifey. She didn't understand, because I had yet to tell her what had happened with my ex that left me with trust issues.

Twenty minutes later, I went back into the kitchen. "You good?" I asked her, walking up on her, grabbing her from behind.

"Just about done. Are you ready to eat?" she asked, turning to face me, with a smirk on her face.

"I'm always ready to eat," I responded, pulling her close, kissing her, and slipping my tongue into her mouth.

I felt kind of fucked up after leaving the kitchen the way that I had. She didn't deserve that, and it was her right to express how she felt. It was just bad timing, but she had apologized, so I shouldn't have been rude. I thought she was going to give me the cold shoulder now, but she didn't. She must have really meant her apology, and that was another thing that I liked about her. She always owned up to it when she was wrong, and she was able to move on, without dwelling on issues. I had gone back into the kitchen to let her know that we were really good and that I accepted her apology.

After a few minutes, she broke the kiss and whined about finishing dinner. She knew that once I got started, dinner was a wrap. I wanted to let her finish cooking, but she had got a nigga's dick hard as hell, so I said, "Fuck dinner." She turned off the stove, and we headed to the bedroom to make it do what it do.

Chapter Six

Jakiyah

One month later . . .

I didn't realize I'd slept so long; I'd been doing that a lot lately. I was sad to say that I had moved back to New York, and for the past month, I had been doing nothing but sleeping. I wouldn't say that I was depressed, but I would say that I didn't have the drive to do anything but sleep, and that would soon need to change. I was still living at my mother's house, sleeping in my old bedroom, when I should have had my own place by now. I really missed living on my own.

After brushing my teeth and washing my face, I walked downstairs and instantly caught an attitude, as I saw Tamia sitting on my mom's beige lounge chair, holding baby Andrea. Tamia had been over here just about every other day, and it was starting to annoy me, really getting on my nerves. Granted, this was something she had done before I moved back, but it was still annoying as hell. However, don't get me wrong; I did appreciate her. She had provided that companionship that my mother didn't have from either of her daughters. I got it, but I was here now.

I continued to the kitchen. I wasn't trying to be rude, but I wasn't in a speaking mood, so I opted out of speaking. Knowing my mother, I should have just spoken, because she followed me into the kitchen, and I really wasn't prepared for the tongue-lashing that I knew was coming.

"Jakiyah, I know you saw that we have company, and that was rude of you not to speak," she said, chastising me.

"I wasn't trying to be rude, but it's kind of annoying that she's always here. I feel like every time I turn around, I'm bumping into her," I argued in my defense.

"Jakiyah, she's here because I invited her. I enjoy her company," she retorted, with a frown on her face.

"Well, I'm here now. Do you really need to have her visiting all the time? I hardly get any time with my niece because she always has her," I said, pouting.

"Are you sure this is about me and not about the fact that she's German girlfriend?" she asked, giving me the side eye.

"No, Mom, this has nothing to do with German. He and I had a conversation, and we're cool. I can honestly say that we are just friends," I responded, the irritation evident in my voice.

"Are you sure?" she repeated, pushing what she believed the truth to be.

"I'm sure," I said, slamming down the pot that I was going to use to boil my eggs.

She just looked at me, shook her head, and exited the kitchen. I hadn't meant to upset her, but she had upset me with her accusations. She needed to tell Tamia that her companionship was no longer needed. Just as my eggs were ready to be removed from the pot, the unwanted guest walked into the kitchen and sat at the table like she had been invited to invade my space.

"Jakiyah, what do you have against me?" she asked, with a roll of her eyes, making me want to punch her ass in the throat.

"Tamia, trust, if I had something against you, I would have no problem addressing it," I responded, with a roll of my eyes too.

"Well, I heard you talking to your mother, and clearly, you expressed that you have a problem with me being here. German is here just about as much as I am, but I didn't hear you mention him being here too much," she spat, getting in her feelings.

"Okay, and you said that to say what?" I asked, confused, because if she had heard what I said to my mother, then she already knew what the fuck the matter was. And if that was the case, what was she mentioning German for? She was sitting there, trying to make it about German, when I was not thinking about German's ass. It seemed as if she wanted to see where my head was at when it came to him, but she could keep shopping, because I wasn't buying.

"Well, whatever your reason is for not wanting me here, the fact still remains that your mother loves my company. Until she tells me otherwise, what you think really doesn't matter."

"Bitch, get your life. Matter of fact, get the fuck out my face, because if it didn't matter, you wouldn't have come in here with the bullshit," I yelled at her.

"Why you mad? Calling me out of my name for what?" She smiled as she walked out of the kitchen, pleased that she had got a rise out of me.

Stupid bitch, I said to myself, upset that I had let her take me there, because that was what she had wanted to do.

I heard the front door open and then close, and I had a feeling she was going to be a problem with her crazy-looking ass. My mother entered the kitchen again, with a displeased look on her face, and honestly, I really wasn't in the mood to hear it right now.

"What happened, Jakiyah? Tamia left out upset, so what did you say? I only sent her in here to get a bottle for Andrea," she said to me.

"She came in here questioning me about what I said to you, and I told her," I answered, getting a little upset with my mother.

"Jakiyah, you may not like her, but not having you or your sister to talk to really put me in a state of loneliness, and Tamia has been heaven-sent over this past year. But if it bothers you that much, I will ask her not to visit so much," she said sadly, as if it was going to hurt her not to see that freak.

"Mom, that won't be necessary. I'm going to be finding my own place, so I won't be here much longer," I said, not addressing my past absence due to the guilt I felt.

"What do you mean, find your own place? Jakiyah, I don't want you to leave. You just got here, and we have more than enough room." She was on the verge of tears, which caused me to feel bad.

"Mom, I'm twenty-seven-years old. I don't need to be still living at home with my parents. I promise that I will find a place not too far from here and will visit as much as I can. That's if your little friend Tamia stops visiting so much," I said.

"Chile, I just told you that I'm going to have her not visit as much, but me wanting you to stay has nothing to do with her. I want you here because I miss you, and you haven't been back long enough to be leaving me so soon."

"I know, Mom, but you do know that I can't stay living with you forever. Eventually, I'm going to start dating again, and inviting a man home to my childhood twin bed isn't going to work," I said and laughed.

"I know, baby. I'm just not ready for you to leave, because you just got back," she repeated, then hugged me before leaving the kitchen and getting back to my niece.

"Jakiyah, I forgot the bottle, and I need for you to come and change Andrea for me," she shouted from the living room a few seconds later.

After I fed and changed Andrea, I put her down for a nap. Then I went upstairs to wash and get dressed because I was meeting up with my childhood friend Yessenia.

Chapter Seven

Jakiyah

I pulled up to Yessenia's house in the rental that I had been driving for the past month. I was supposed to be meeting up with Ty later on so he could take me to a dealership to get a car. Driving someone else's car was for the birds, and paying 198 dollars a week for a car that didn't belong to me wasn't worth it. Yessenia was standing in the door, waiting on me. She hadn't changed a bit; she was still as pretty as I remembered, and looked like a younger version of Zulay Henao. Yessenia and I had been friends since our freshman year of high school. I had really missed her and didn't realize how much until right now.

I climbed out of the rental and walked to her door. "Hey," I said, hugging her before walking inside.

Yessenia had done really well for herself; her place was beautiful. Her living-room walls were a light green, with burnt-orange borders. Now, I would have never mixed those two colors, but she had blended them well with her lime-green living-room furniture and some polka-dot pillows that matched the walls. After admiring her beautiful home, I took a seat on the sofa to get caught up.

"So, how have you been? I'm sorry I wasn't able to make it to the funeral. I really felt bad that I was out of town at the time. Are you settled in?" she asked me.

"Girl, I have yet to do anything. I haven't had the strength. All I've done is let my job know that I won't be returning. And don't worry about missing the funeral. I know that if you had been here, you would have come. And I do apologize for not being up to seeing you until now," I told her.

"So, do you have any idea when you're going back to Georgia to wrap things up?"

"Hell, no, but I'm going to go back soon, because my lease is up at the end of the month. I need to go and put my things in storage and sell my car. I'm going to the dealership today for a new one. Mom is not trying to hear me about finding my own place. I told her that I couldn't live with her forever."

We both laughed, because she knew how my mother was.

"I saw your mom a few months ago with some chick who was acting as if she was your mom's bodyguard when I walked over to say hello."

"That must have been German's girlfriend. Girl, she and I just got into it this morning about her being at my mother's house so much."

"That chick just rubbed me the wrong way, so you better watch her ass," she said.

"I just hope that she's overly friendly when it comes to my mother and is not on no bullshit. As much as I like my freedom, you know how I am when it comes to my family."

"I feel you. Anyway, what's up with German?" she asked me.

"Well, you know how we ended, but we did have a conversation and agreed that there were no hard feelings. He moved on, and I'm still stuck in neutral, but it's all good."

"I thought you and German's ass were going to get married." She laughed.

"Yeah, you and I both, but it wasn't in the cards for us. I wish him all the best, with his stalking my mother-ass girlfriend." I laughed.

"Do you remember Qua from Forest Hills?" she asked me, smiling.

"If you're talking about my high school boo, you know I will never forget his ass." I smiled at the thought of him.

"Well, he's single, and he and Keem started hanging out again. *So*, since you've moved back, let me set something up," she said, putting on the puppy dog face.

Just thinking about Qua had me blushing. He'd been so fine back in the day, and if he was still fine, he could get it. "When you say set some shit up, what do you have in mind?" I asked her.

"Keem and Qua are on their way here. We're just going to get reacquainted," she revealed.

"Yessenia, why didn't you give me the heads-up on the phone? I would have dressed for this damn reunion," I said, brushing my hair down with my hands.

"Girl, you look exactly the same. The only difference is you're stacked now," she joked.

I knew my body, face, and hair were on point. What I meant was I wouldn't have shown up in a Love Pink Victoria's Secret hooded sweat suit with some damn sneakers.

I looked cute, but, shit, when you were seeing an ex after a long time, you wanted to be top-model cute. My nerves were now all over the place as the anticipation of them walking through the door was getting the best of me.

I had to ask Yessenia to get me a drink, just to calm my nerves. I was chilling on the couch, sipping my drink, when Yessenia came running from the window, screaming that they were here. I jumped up so fast and ran up the stairs, almost busting my ass, with Yessenia laughing at me. I went into the bathroom and paced like a damn teenager about to go to her senior prom.

Qua was my first crush in high school, and just like now, my ass had always been scared to approach him, until I had no choice. Back then, Yessenia had tricked me into going with her to Keem's house, saying she was just going to pick up some money. She had said that once she got the money, which she was going to spend on getting her hair done, we would leave, but she'd lied. Qua had been there, waiting on me, because she had told him I was feeling him. I swear, I almost pissed on myself when we walked inside Keem's house and he was sitting there looking fine as hell, still in his basketball uniform. Yessenia had to push me to walk over to him, and truth be told, I expected him to be stuck up, but once he spoke and I started talking to him, I learned that he was nothing like the other players.

He was down to earth, so I relaxed a little and opened up. I really had expected him to kick game just to get in my panties, but he was the complete opposite of his teammates. We dated throughout high school, and it wasn't until about a year and a half after graduation that we broke up. He was away at Davidson College in North Carolina, on a basketball scholarship, and I was still in New York, attending York College. The long-distance relationship wasn't working for either of us, so we agreed to part ways, but the truth was that I agreed only because he had mentioned it first. He didn't get drafted into the NBA because of an injury, and when he returned home, I had already moved on and was in a relationship with German.

"Jakiyah, are you okay up there?" I heard Yessenia yell up the stairs.

I looked in the mirror and made sure my hair looked okay. I was so nervous and really wasn't ready to see him again. I swear, had I been dressed better, I wouldn't be as nervous, but I knew I had to suck it up and take my ass down-stairs. I felt my heart beating fast as I descended the stairs, counting the steps in my head, trying not to fall down them. Qua was still standing when I walked into the living room. He was still as fine as I remembered. The only thing different about him was that he was rocking a goatee. He still had a muscular, thin build. He was wearing sweatpants with a T-shirt, and it looked like he and Keem had just finished playing basketball.

"Hey, stranger. You're still looking good," Qua said, pulling me in for a hug.

Damn, he still wore Dolce & Gabbana Light Blue, and it was still as intoxicating as I remembered. I held on to him a little longer than I needed to.

"Can I get some love?" Keem asked, then laughed as I walked over to him. "How are you doing? I'm sorry to hear about Cydney," he said.

"Thank you. I'm doing somewhat better," I lied.

"How long are you in town?" Qua questioned.

"I have moved back and am staying at my parents' house right now," I answered.

"That's cool. Look, I need to go home and shower, but how about you give me your number so I can give you a call later?" he said, causing me to smile on the inside.

Yessenia's crazy ass was in the kitchen doorway, doing the happy dance, being silly. I put my number into Qua's phone, and he promised to call me tonight. After giving me a hug good-bye, he left. I joined Yessenia in the kitchen, and we were both jumping up and down like we had hit the lottery. Keem just stood there watching us.

"Both of you are crazy. I'm going to take a shower. Good to see you again, Jakiyah," Keem announced, then left us and went upstairs.

I stayed with Yessenia for about another hour before heading back to my mom's house to meet Ty and go to the dealership.

"Adios, amigo," Yessenia said as I was leaving her house.

"Ditto." I laughed.

When I got to my mom's house, German was parked outside, waiting on me, because, as usual, something had come up, and Ty couldn't take me to the dealership.

Chapter Eight

German

"You didn't tell me you had to work late tonight." Tamia hit me with that before I was even through the door.

"I didn't have to work late, Tamia. Ty needed a favor, so I handled it for him," I told her.

"And what might that be?" she inquired with an attitude.

"He needed for me to take his sister to the car dealership," I answered, telling her the truth. I never lied to her, and I wasn't about to start now.

"Are you fucking serious? So, you're fucking that bitch again?" she asked me.

"Tamia, you're bugging. Did you not just hear me say that I did a favor for Ty? How does that equal me fucking his sister again?"

Tamia had been a different person since Jakiyah moved back to New York. No matter how many times I told her that she had nothing to worry about, she would start questioning me and would refuse to believe anything that I told her. It was really starting to annoy me.

"You know what, German? If I find out that you're fucking with her again, I swear, I'm fucking you up. I don't know why you would do a favor that involves that bitch after she basically told me to stay away from her mother," she shouted.

"Tamia, I'm not about to stand here and argue with you about something that happened between women. Now, I told you I did a favor for Ty, and that's it," I said. I then walked upstairs, leaving her to sulk.

I went into the bathroom to take a shower and clear my head. Tamia had my ass pissed. At first, her being jealous was cute, but now it was annoying and was stressing me the hell out. I hated being accused of something I wasn't doing. I just wanted to shower and take my ass to bed because I had to be at work at six tomorrow. As the warm water rained down on me, I felt a draft on my back, so I turned around to make sure the shower curtain was still closed. I saw Tamia's ass getting into the shower, ass naked.

"I'm sorry," she whispered, then got on her knees and took my dick into her mouth.

I grabbed the back of her head, pumped in and out of her mouth, forgetting how pissed I was as she continued to deep throat my shit. I felt my knees buckle when I was on the verge of busting in her mouth. I tried to hold on, but after a few more pumps in her mouth and her sucking the life out of my shit, I busted and she swallowed every drop. After getting my nut, I was going to pay her ass back and not let her get off, but she bent her ass over the tub, and my dick was brick hard in seconds. I wasted no time entering her from behind.

"Ooh, shit, Tamia. Slow down," I moaned, because she was wilding on my dick, and I wasn't ready to cum again just yet.

I grabbed her hips, slowing her movements, and I pumped inside of her at a slower pace, enjoying every inch of her tight, wet pussy.

"German, stop playing and fuck me," she panted, throwing the pussy back.

She wanted me to beat up the pussy, so I showed her no mercy as I pulled out and rammed my dick back inside of her. I was punishing the pussy, and now she was begging me to slow down. All I wanted to hear was my balls slapping against her ass as I deep stroked her.

"You wanted this dick, so shut up and take all this good fucking," I said, continuing to bang her walls until I released inside of her, and she glazed my dick with her juices.

After washing and getting out of the shower, her ass was walking like she had just got finished riding a horse. I had fucked that pussy up. I laughed to myself as I walked right past her ass. She knew I was a beast when it came to my dick game, and that was why I always tried to slow fuck her, but being that she was a freak, she had wanted it rough, knowing she couldn't handle the dick.

After putting on a pair of boxers, I walked back into the bathroom to throw my towel in the hamper and brush my teeth. As soon as I came out of the bathroom, Tamia was standing with the screw face, holding my phone in her hand.

"Why the fuck is Jakiyah texting you at this time of night? Better yet, how did she get your number?" she screamed.

"What did the text say, Tamia?" I asked her, trying to remain calm, because she had no business being all up in my phone.

"Does it matter what she texted you? It's after ten p.m., so she has no reason to be texting your phone. And again, why does she have your number!" she yelled.

"Tamia, I have to admit that you being jealous was cute, but now it's getting aggravating as hell.

I gave Jakiyah my number when she took the car for a test-drive so that if she had any problems, she could call my phone. So, if she's texting me, she probably was just texting to say thank you. So stop the insecure bullshit. . . . It doesn't look cute on you," I said to her, no longer calm at this point.

"If I'm insecure, it's because since that bitch has been back, you have stayed at her parents' house."

"Now I know you're bugging, because you know that anytime I'm over there, it's me stopping through to see Ty. Do you see me checking you about how much time you spend over there? I could say that you're over there hoping to see Ty," I barked at her simple ass.

"Well, if you say it, how wrong would you be?" she asked, with a roll of her eyes.

"Exactly my fucking point, so stop accusing me of shit I'm not doing," I said, shutting the conversation down. I took my phone and left the room.

Chapter Nine

German

I just got up after a bad night, and now I was having a bad morning. It was raining so hard, and I hated being in the field when it rained. Tamia was up early this morning, but as I got ready for work, I didn't say anything to her. We had never gone to bed mad at each other before, and it was bothering me, but I wasn't up for discussing it, because I was still pissed. I had never given her any reason to doubt me, and I had always told her the truth when she asked, so I didn't know why she was letting Jakiyah being back cause problems in our relationship. The worst thing a female could do was stress a nigga out about some shit he *wasn't* doing: this could push his ass right into the arms of the next bitch. Tamia's ass better find some act right, and find it quick, because I had zero tolerance for unnecessary bullshit.

***

I was on my way to return the truck, because my shift was over, when my phone rang. Jakiyah's number showed up on the screen.

"Hey, what's up, Jakiyah?" I asked, answering her call.

"Hey, German. I'm sorry to bother you, but Mom's cable box in the living room went out. We tried to troubleshoot over the phone, but it didn't work, and they don't have an appointment for a tech to come out until next week. My dad is losing it because he's going to miss *Power* tomorrow since we only have Starz on the living-room cable box."

"Say no more. I'll be there in a few." I laughed because her dad was addicted to watching *Power*.

Instead of returning the truck, I headed on over to Jakiyah's mom's house. I knew that getting home late again was going to cause more problems, but I couldn't let the Smith family down. Mr. Smith probably would have a heart attack if he missed his show. *That shit is funny as hell*, I thought to myself as I cruised to my destination.

I pulled up to the house about twenty minutes later, and I saw Jakiyah standing on the stoop, talking to some dude who looked vaguely familiar. She was all blushing and shit up in his face. I didn't even know she had started seeing someone.

I grabbed my workbag and headed to the house, slightly feeling some kind of way.

"Hey, German. Dad is waiting for you inside," she said and smiled.

I waited for her to introduce dude, but she didn't. She went back to her conversation, so I just went inside to do what I had to do. Mr. Smith was waiting for me in the living room, so I walked over to him.

"Hello, German. Thanks for coming out, son. I really appreciate it," Mr. Smith said, patting me on the back.

"No problem, sir. Anything for my favorite family," I responded as I stepped over to the TV to see what the problem was.

By the time I was finishing up, Jakiyah had come inside, still wearing that silly smile on her face. I really didn't have time to kick it, but I was curious as to who dude was. When she went into the kitchen, I followed her.

"Hey," I said, walking up to her as she stood and looked inside the refrigerator.

"Hey, German. Thanks for making it possible for Dad to watch his show tomorrow. That old man is a mess. He's got no business watching *Power*," she said and laughed.

"No problem. Who was ole dude you were talking to?" I threw out there.

"Oh, that was my ex, Quameek," she responded, a smile on her face again.

I remembered the name. He was an ex, the guy that she was with before we started dating. I wondered how she had run back into him, but it was none of my business, I told myself.

"Oh, okay, cool. Well, I'm going to get on out of here. I will talk to you later." I was about to walk out of the kitchen, but she stopped me.

"You know, you could have responded to my text last night," she said.

"You mean the text that had me up arguing and sleeping on the couch last night?" I responded.

"Oh, wow. I apologize. The last thing I need is for her to think I want her man."

"Don't sweat it. It's late. Let me go, because I don't need a repeat of last night. Later."

"Later, and thanks again," she said, hugging me good-bye.

It was already going on 8:00 p.m., and I needed to return the truck. If I had to work the weekend, I would have kept the truck until tomorrow, but I didn't. I thought about calling Tamia to let her know that I was running late, but I thought twice about it. I realized that either way, I was going to be in the doghouse. Ty was having a showcase at his club tomorrow, and we were invited, so hopefully, Tamia wouldn't act up. I was really hoping we would make up, because she wasn't going to want me to go to the club without her.

After dropping the truck off, I got in my car and headed home, still hoping for a peaceful night without all the extra shit. I wasn't going to even front: seeing Jakiyah cheesing over that nigga had me low key hating on him. I wasn't no hating nigga, but I damn sure didn't want her around me with no other dude. Even though we weren't together, I still didn't like the shit. I had no idea why it bothered me so much, but I was thinking it had to do with me never seeing her with another man before.

If Tamia had seen my face when I saw Jakiyah's ass on the porch with dude, I would have never lived that down. That shit took me by surprise, made me realize that I still had some feelings for her. I guessed it had been easy for me until now, given that I hadn't had to see her, but now that she was back, this shit was going to be really hard. I pulled up in our driveway and took a deep breath, praying one more time that Tamia didn't want to argue with my ass about being late again.

Chapter Ten

Tamia

When German walked in last night, I didn't even bother to ask him why he was late. I already knew that he had stopped by Jakiyah's, because her mother had told me. I thought he would offer an explanation, but he didn't, so I left it alone and just continued making dinner for both of us. If I hadn't called Mama Smith to see if she still needed me to take her to her doctor's appointment on Monday, which she declined, I would not have known he was there. I didn't pick an argument, because I had things to handle tomorrow afternoon, before getting ready for the showcase.

The next day I left the house at about 11:30 a.m. and parked down the block from my destination. I had never thought I would be back at this house that I had once called home. I walked into the backyard, making sure my

hood was on my head. I had to be as discreet
as possible and not draw attention to myself. I
knew that Ms. Johnson, who lived next door,
always went to bingo every Saturday afternoon,
so I wasn't worried about her being in the window and being nosy, which she was every day of
the week. I knew she still lived there, because
her old, beat-up red pickup truck still sat in
her yard. The bingo hall was at the church at
the end of the block, so she never drove there. I
prayed that the lock on her back door was still
the same as I put the key in and turned it.

Bingo, I thought when the key unlocked the
door. Yes, I still had the key to the place I used
to call home. I had held on to a lot of things that
I should have just let go. The house was quiet,
but I knew he was inside, since I followed him
here last night. Unbeknownst to German, I had
gotten home just ten minutes before he had last
night. That was why dinner wasn't already
finished when he got home. In fact, I had just
gotten started, and he never questioned why,
and that was cool with me.

I crept up the stairs to the bedroom where he
now lay in our old bed, sleeping peacefully. The
room was the same as I remembered it. The rocking chair that I had purchased when I found out
that I was pregnant was still sitting in the same

spot. Many days I had sat in that chair, rocking and reading to my unborn baby. I had anticipated the day of his or her arrival, which never came. I wiped at a few tears before they fell from my eyes. I walked over and sat in the rocking chair and reminisced about the day that my life was crushed to pieces.

My baby daddy had come home from work that tragic evening and had told me that he needed to talk to me, so I'd stopped what I was doing and met him in the living room, where I took a seat. We had been waiting for him to get a promotion at work, so I just knew tonight would be the night when we opened up the bottle of champagne to celebrate. I was ready to receive the good news because with the baby coming, this promotion would mean everything was going to be okay. But when he started by saying, "Tamia, you know I love you . . . ," with a grim look on his face, I knew the talk wasn't work related.

He went on to say that he had met someone and that they were in love, and so he couldn't be with me anymore. I begged and pleaded with him, asked him how he could leave me when I was pregnant with our child, with no means of support or anywhere for me to live.

He expressed that he was sorry and that he wasn't trying to hurt me. He said that he would be there for his child, but he was done with the relationship. I was devastated that he could walk away from a three-year relationship as if I meant nothing to him. I had had no idea he was unhappy, but he had to be unhappy. Why else would he pursue another woman? He said that he hadn't gone out looking to cheat on me, but that it was something that just happened.

He confessed that he had fallen in love with her and that she was the one he wanted to be with and start a life with. I was so hurt. The tears fell from my eyes, and without thinking, I started to attack him physically where he sat. He blocked the blows, asked me to be an adult about the situation and to stop before I hurt the baby, but I was at a point of no return. He stood and grabbed me by my wrists, pushed me down on the couch, and attempted to walk away. He proceeded up the stairs, with me following him, still begging him to please reconsider, with tears blurring my vision. As I neared the top landing, I missed a few steps and fell down the stairs.

He called 911, an ambulance rushed me to the ER, and while I was in the hospital, losing our unborn child, he left. Upon my release from the hospital, his mother came and handed me an envelope from her son. Inside was a letter telling me that he was moving on, and that I needed to do the same. Months later, I was still depressed about losing my child, and the money he had given me was going to run out in a few weeks, so my depression soon turned into anger. I vowed to make him pay by destroying him and the bitch who had caused my downfall.

Him stirring in his sleep brought me back to the present and to the reason I was here, paying him a visit. He awoke and stood, and his eyes traveled over to where I was rocking back and forth in the chair.

"Tamia?" he questioned, wiping at his eyes, as if he wasn't seeing clearly.

"In the flesh," I responded with a laugh.

"What are you doing here, Tamia? And how did you know I was here?" he asked. He looked like he wanted to lunge at me, so I pulled out the gun and pointed it at him.

Looking like the gun didn't faze him, he started to walk toward me, causing me to fire a warning shot, to let him know that I was serious.

"Andris, sit on the bed, and if you so much as look as if you're up to something, I'm going to shoot your ass," I said to him.

He stepped back and sat on the bed, his arms up, as if surrendering.

"So you thought I was going to let you get away with what you did to me. I would never let you live happily ever after with the bitch who ruined my life. You loved that bitch so much that after all those calls and letters you received about her cheating, you still didn't leave her. Like the weak bitch that you are, you turned into an alcoholic abuser instead of just leaving. I honestly didn't think you had it in you to kill her, but it's all good, because you did me a favor. I was going to kill the bitch, anyway. Oh, and just so you know, your precious wife wasn't cheating on you. She actually loved you," I said, taunting him.

"You crazy bitch—"

I cut his sentence short by shooting him in the shoulder.

"Bitch, you shot me!" he yelled out in pain.

"As much as I would like to sit and continue to entertain you, I have to go. I have more lives to destroy," I announced, then shot him twice in the chest and watched his body fall back on the bed.

I walked over to him and shot him two more times, this time in the head. I put the stolen gun in my pocket and proceeded down the stairs. I wasn't worried about the police, due to the silencer on the gun, and I wasn't worried about prints, because I had on gloves. I went out the back door, making sure not to lock it. Then I punched the glass out at the bottom of the door and left the home quickly and quietly.

I knew in those moments before he died, he probably wondered how I had found his ass, but he could thank his mother for leading me right to him. I knew he was in town because he had shown up at the burial site, and I had made sure he didn't see me once I realized that it was him. I knew that his mother would eventually show at her sister's house: for as long as I'd known them, they had played cards faithfully every Friday. The first few Fridays she'd attended, but there'd been no sign of Andris. That hadn't stopped me from stalking the place, and he just so happened to show this Friday, and it cost him his life.

Chapter Eleven

Tamia

The club showcase was in full effect when German and I arrived. This was the second showcase that Ty had done since he opened up the club a year ago. It was an amateur showcase that was open to anyone who wanted to compete for a 250-dollar prize. It was basically an open mic night. We walked over to the VIP section, where Ty's off again, on again girlfriend Chanel, Jakiyah, some dude she was with, and a couple that I didn't know were sitting. I felt German's body tense as he released my hand. He clearly wasn't happy with Jakiyah being here with dude, and I wanted to know why. I couldn't sweat German right now, as I introduced myself to the unknown visitors. Once they introduced themselves, I learned that Yessenia, Keem, and Quameek were friends of Jakiyah.

German seemed to know the bitch Yessenia, as he said, "What's up?" to her and told her, "Long time no see." I didn't like the way the bitch was looking at me, being that she didn't know me, but then again, she was friends with Jakiyah. I guessed that meant she didn't like me, either. *Isn't that the way it works among friends?* I thought as I excused myself. I told German I was going to the restroom.

After handling my business, I went back upstairs, took a seat, and tried to enjoy the showcase. A woman had just left the stage after singing "No One," by Alicia Keys. She'd sounded okay, but I didn't think she would be taking home the prize money. Ty announced the next talent to the stage, a woman, and she started to recite a poem. I listened. The poem went like this:

> You sit wondering why I don't want to be the flavor of the month.
>
> My mom instilled self-worth in me, so I will never fall victim to your stunt.
>
> What? I didn't hear you. Did you say you love me?
>
> Oh, I apologize, because the line to the prize was too long for me to see.
>
> I'm black and beautiful with a heart of gold.

I will not dismiss my self-dignity and fold.

To have this queen on your pedestal for all to see.

No other woman in the world has to exist but me.

The crowd went crazy when she was done. I mean, the poem was good, but not that good, but you wouldn't know that from the way they were cheering, clapping, and whistling. I looked over at German, who didn't look like he was having a good time. I guessed he was in a funk over the public affection that Jakiyah and Quameek were showing each other. I didn't have time to address what he had going on. I just wanted to sit back, continue to watch the showcase, and wait for the real show to start. Ty was back on the stage now, announcing the next participant, but everyone's attention had shifted to the police officers who were swarming into the club. Everyone started to panic when one of the officers spoke on a bullhorn and requested that the lights be turned on and that no one move.

"Who is the owner of the club?" the same officer asked as soon as the lights were turned on.

"I'm the owner, nigga. What the fuck is going on?" Ty barked from the stage.

"Are you Tyhiem Smith?" the officer asked him.

"Yes, I'm Tyhiem Smith. So again, what the fuck is going on?" he repeated, clearly getting pissed off.

That officer told several officers to start evacuating the club. Jakiyah ran down the stairs to get to her brother, with German in tow. I reluctantly followed behind them, hoping that I didn't get stopped before I made it to the stage. I turned and watched as two officers exited Ty's office and gave a head nod to the officer who had the bullhorn and thus appeared to be in charge. The one in charge walked over and stood in front of Tyhiem, then told him he was being arrested for murder. He then proceeded to read Tyhiem his rights as he was being handcuffed.

All that could be heard was Chanel and Jakiyah crying, but what bothered me was the fact that German was the one who was comforting Jakiyah, and not Quameek, whom she'd come with. Quameek had refused to leave her when an officer told him he had to exit the club, so that alone should have been enough for German to fall back.

"We need to go down to the police station and see what the fuck is going on," Keem said.

"Jakiyah, come with me. I will take you," German said to her.

"No disrespect, but I've got her," Quameek said, taking her by the hand.

That was just what the fuck German got, trying to play Captain Save a Ho, like he didn't see me standing here. I hoped he didn't think that we were going to the police station. I was going to bitch a fit if he even fixed his face to say that we were. I walked to the car with an attitude, not saying two words to his thirsty ass. He hadn't even comforted Jakiyah after her sister passed away, so that told me that his punk ass was jealous and was trying to prove something, but he got his ass checked.

"Before you even fix your mouth to ask, the answer is no. I'm not going to the police station," I said, fastening my seat belt.

"Tamia, don't start no bullshit, like you didn't just see them take my fucking best friend out in handcuffs," he barked.

"No, I didn't see, because you were blocking my view, all hugged up with your ex," I sassed.

"Really, Tamia? You can't be that fucking self-centered."

"Yes, the fuck I can, especially when you straight disrespected me in my face," I yelled at him.

"Wow. You can't be serious right now." He shook his head as he pulled out of the spot we were parked in.

I sat quietly for the rest of the ride: as long as we were going home, there was no need for me to continue arguing with him. When we pulled up to the house, I noticed that he didn't pull into the garage.

"Why didn't you pull into the garage?" I asked him.

"I'm waiting for you to get out of the car. You said that you weren't going to the police station, so I'm dropping you off at home," he responded, like he was annoyed that I was still sitting in the car.

"German, I said that we weren't going to the police station," I said to him.

"Tamia, get out of the car now," he yelled, banging the steering wheel, losing his patience with me.

I got out of the car, saying no more to him. I just stood there, watching to see if he would see things my way, but he pulled off, screeching his tires, leaving me looking stupid as his headlights disappeared as he rounded the corner.

Chapter Twelve

Jakiyah

Qua, German, and I had been at the police station for at least two hours, but no one had told us anything yet. I was so annoyed and was losing my patience with these fucking crackers right about now. I rested my head on Qua's shoulder. I was getting sleepy, but I wasn't leaving until someone came out to tell us something. I hated the 113th precinct with a passion; they were rude and didn't care that we had been waiting this long, with not so much as a word about my brother. I didn't understand how they could come into his place of business, accuse him of murder, and not say who he was supposed to have murdered.

"Jakiyah Smith," I heard and thought to myself that it was about time as I stood.

I walked over to a white officer dressed in a suit. He introduced himself as Detective

Fields from the homicide unit. He led me into a room that I guessed was an interrogation room, because the room contained only a table and two chairs, and it had no windows. I sat and listened to him, and I'd be the first to tell you that these police officers were a piece of work with their bullshit. He hadn't given me any information concerning who my brother was being accused of murdering. All this detective had done thus far was ask me about my brother's whereabouts before coming to the club and about whether he owned a gun.

I might not have a degree in street smarts, but I knew not to answer no fucking questions, especially when this shit was one sided. He didn't answer any of my questions, but he expected me to answer his, and then he tried to threaten me by telling me that my brother was going to go away for a long time if I couldn't provide an alibi for his whereabouts during the crime in question. *Yeah, okay, I must have the word* stupid *tattooed on my forehead*, I thought as I stood to leave, because he was wasting my time. I needed to leave and go home to let my parents know what had happened so that we could make sure that my brother got a lawyer.

"What did he say?" Qua asked me as soon as I walked out of the interrogation room.

"He didn't say much of anything. All he did was ask me questions about Ty's whereabouts and if he owned a gun. He didn't offer me any information about why he was arrested, and I felt as if he was wasting my time, so I walked out," I explained to him.

"This shit is crazy. They be on that bullshit. Come on. Let me take you home so that we can talk to your parents together," German said to me, causing Qua to sigh in annoyance.

I didn't know what was up with German acting like a jealous boyfriend, but he needed to chill out before Qua started thinking we had something going on. I thought that he would leave when Keem and Yessenia left, given that Qua was here with me, but he didn't.

"German, if you're going to the house, you can go ahead. Qua will drop me off. Thanks for offering." I was trying not to show how irritated I was about his antics tonight.

The three of us filed out of the police station and headed to the parking lot.

"I thought you said you and dude broke up?" Qua asked me as soon as we got into his truck.

"Qua, German and I broke up two years ago, and *he* broke up with me, like I told you," I said to him as he drove out of the parking lot.

"Well, he's acting like he has some unresolved feelings for you," he said, briefly turning his eyes away from the road to look at me.

Qua's ass was so fucking handsome, and that mean expression he was wearing now was making my kitty tingle. When we used to date and he got upset about something I had said or done, it was hard to take him seriously, because it always turned me on.

"Qua, trust me, we are just friends. He has the woman he wanted to be with, and she's the same woman that he left me for. If he has any unresolved feelings, I have no idea where they're coming from," I explained to him. "Do you know how cute you are when you're mad?" I asked. I smiled at him, causing him to smile.

"Jakiyah, I'm really feeling you, but you know that I don't like drama," he admitted, with a cute frown.

"Qua, I'm single, and trust me when I say, I have no drama in my life besides what's going on with my brother right now," I promised, then reached over and kissed him on his soft lips.

I swear that if my brother hadn't been arrested, I would be going back to Qua's place with him, because that kiss had my body on fire. I hadn't had sex in eight months, and if I was keeping count based on good sex, I would have to say the last time was when I was with German.

Qua pulled up to my mom's house, and after he put the car in park, he pulled me into his arms and kissed me with so much passion. I had to break the kiss as he was about to start something I didn't have time to finish.

"Qua, I have to get inside," I moaned as his hand massaged the inside of my thigh.

"Call me later," he said. He kissed me before letting me get out of the car.

"Okay, I will." I smiled as I got out.

As soon as I got inside, I discovered that my mother, father, and German were sitting in the living room, waiting on me. I had thought I would have time to go to the bathroom, because my panties were damp, but I knew it had to wait.

"What took you so long to get here? We did leave from the same place," German said sarcastically. I ignored him.

"Jakiyah, your brother called. He said he's being charged with Andris's murder," my mom cried.

"Andris? Mom, Ty didn't kill Andris. Trust me, if he did this, he wouldn't be a suspect right now," I told her.

"He said that they told him that they found the murder weapon in his office at the club," my father added.

"Dad, if anybody knows that Ty didn't do this, you should. You know Ty is not that careless," I said to him.

"Well, your dad called a lawyer, who is going to show for his arraignment. There is really nothing else we can do tonight," My mom announced as she stood. She headed upstairs, and my father followed her.

I knew that Ty didn't do this. He already knew how my mom felt about losing another one of her children. If he had done this deed, it would have been clean, and Andris's body would have never been found.

"You okay?" German asked me.

"Yes, I'm fine, but you know this is bullshit," I said to him.

"Of course I know that, and trust me, he wasn't going to do this on his own. We were watching his mother's house together the other night, and there were no signs of that nigga. I know that if Ty got the drop on him, he would have called me," he said.

"Exactly. So I don't know what the fuck is going on and how they're saying they found the murder weapon in his office." I tried to hold my tears in as he pulled me into his arms. "Thanks for being here, but I need you to go," I said, removing myself from his arms.

Disappointment showed on his face, but what the fuck did he want from me? This was the same man who had left me and hadn't even comforted me when my sister passed. I really couldn't say that I was surprised that he wanted to be all in my space now. After all, it was just like a nigga not to want to be with you until he saw you with the next man.

"Hit me up if you hear anything concerning Ty," he requested, like I would call about something otherwise.

I didn't know what was going on with him and Tamia, but as far as he and I were concerned, there was nothing happening besides us being friends. After he left, I locked the door, headed upstairs, showered, and then stayed up talking to Qua for a bit before taking my ass to bed.

Chapter Thirteen

Jakiyah

Two weeks has passed, and my brother was still locked up. We went on a visit yesterday, and he was stressing. My mother didn't make it any better by crying, after we had all agreed to be strong for him, but I understood that it hurt her to see her son locked up like that. The lawyer was confident that he could get Ty bail at the bail hearing next week, and I was praying that he could, because we all knew it was better to beat a case on the outside.

Today I was on my way to meet Qua at Yessenia and Keem's place. We were going to have drinks and play cards. I really needed this, because sitting in the house, doing nothing, was becoming very depressing. The highlight of my days had been talking or texting with Qua. When I got to Yessenia's house, I parked behind Qua's truck, then checked my hair in the rearview mirror to make sure that not a strand was out of place.

"Hey, girl. Sorry I'm late. I had to put Andrea down before leaving as she was giving Mom a hard time," I explained to Yessenia once I was inside.

"What's up, Keem?" I asked, walking over to him. I gave him a hug.

I then approached Qua and kissed him on the lips. That turned into us sharing a passionate kiss, letting me know that he had missed me just as much as I had missed him.

"Eww, get a room," Keem said, causing us all to laugh.

"Stop hating over here and get the drinks so that we can get this game started. Jakiyah and I want to show you and Yessenia how it feels to get your asses spanked," Qua said to Keem, laughing.

Yessenia put a bottle of Hennessy on the table for the guys and a bottle of Apple Cîroc for us women. I wasn't much of a drinker, but I'd been feeling stressed lately, and I just wanted to let loose tonight and enjoy myself. Needless to say, Qua and I were the ones getting spanked in spades. The shit was hilarious because Qua didn't like to lose, so he was wearing his sexy frown, the one that always had my juices flowing.

I was tipsy, which had my hormones going crazy, and I gave Qua a certain look, letting him know that I wanted to fuck.

"Hold up, Jakiyah. You just reneged. You cut diamonds in the last hand." Yessenia laughed, breaking my nasty thoughts and pissing Qua off even more.

I looked at the last book I took down, and sure enough, I had cut diamonds. As bad as I felt, I couldn't help but to laugh.

"Game over. My partner's drunk and fucking up," Qua said.

"I'm sorry. Do you forgive me?" I said, apologizing. I got up and sat on his lap, wrapping my arms around his neck, and kissed him.

"It depends. Are you coming home with me?" he asked me.

"Only if you're going to make it worth my while," I answered him, flirting.

"Have you ever known me to disappoint?" he responded, placing my hand on his very hard and ready dick.

"Never." I smiled, hopping up to let Yessenia know that it had been real, but we were about to be out.

"Really?" Yessenia said.

"Yes, girl. It's time to go," I said, winking at her.

"Thanks for coming. And, Jakiyah, I will talk to you tomorrow. Oh, and make sure to get up on a room and go half on that baby," she joked.

We always used to joke about getting up on a room and going half on a baby whenever one of us was going to chill at a dude's crib. Her ass was tipsy and was laughing like Kevin Hart had told a damn joke, causing me to do the same. Qua and Keem were looking at us like we were crazy as we walked to the door, holding each other up, still laughing.

"It looks like Jakiyah will be leaving her car here tonight and riding with you," Keem told Qua, laughing.

"No doubt. Her ass isn't about to get behind the wheel tonight," Qua said. We walked outside, and he helped me down the porch steps.

"I got it," I told him as I walked over to his truck.

"Get home safe, and I'll holla at you tomorrow," Keem said, giving Qua dap.

When we got to Qua's condo, I was impressed. I had expected some man cave–type setup, but his place gave off a family home vibe. He had pictures of his family on a living-room wall, and there was a sixty-inch television on the opposite wall. A mantel held his trophies. The furniture matched the cream and black living room decor.

He showed me the kitchen next, and it had all stainless-steel appliances. The dining room contained a china cabinet, and the table and chairs matched the bar that he had set up in a corner of the room. I didn't get a tour of the upstairs, so I just took a seat on the sofa, since I was feeling just a little light-headed. He excused himself and went upstairs, and for some reason, I got kind of nervous at the thought of what was about to go down. I didn't understand why I felt this way, because he was familiar territory.

When he came back downstairs, he was wearing basketball shorts and no shirt, and this sent my kitty into overdrive. I had to cross my legs to calm her down.

"So, you got comfortable, and I have to chill in these jeans?" I asked, pouting jokingly.

He took a seat next to me on the sofa. "I don't have a problem helping you out of those jeans," he retorted, rubbing my thigh.

Just as I was about to tell him that we should take the party to the bedroom, his doorbell rang, and I looked at him with questioning eyes. It was a bit late for somebody to be ringing his bell. I remained on the sofa, and he got up to answer the door. He was at the door for a little longer than I expected him to be, especially since he had no shirt on, so I got up. I wasn't trying to be rude, but he was being rude by standing at the door and having a conversation, knowing I was waiting.

"So, you're just going to leave me standing out here?" I heard a female voice say, and this caused me to two-step faster to the door.

"Hey, is everything okay, Qua?" I asked him, making my presence known.

"Everything is okay, Jakiyah. Just give me a few minutes," he replied.

I really didn't know if I wanted to give him a few minutes. Something wasn't right with the way this chick was looking at me. She was a pretty chick, so that was another reason I was hesitant to remove myself, but given that Qua wasn't my man, I excused myself. I returned to the living room and sat back down the sofa. Fifteen minutes later he came back into the living room, with her walking behind him with a suitcase in her hand. He walked over to me and asked if he could see me in the kitchen. I got up to follow him into the kitchen, knowing I wasn't going to like what he was about to say out of his mouth.

"Jakiyah, remember I told you I was seeing someone when I was away at school? Well, that's her. I didn't know that she was coming, and she didn't know that I was dating. She visited about two months ago, and I was still single then. She apologizes for just showing up, but she needs somewhere to stay, just for tonight. She just drove twelve hours to get here, and I don't feel comfortable sending her back on the road, tired," he explained.

"Why can't she stay the night in a hotel?" I asked him, not caring if I was being inconsiderate.

"I wouldn't feel comfortable sending her to a hotel when she came to visit me," he responded.

"So, you're asking me to leave?" I asked, wanting him to confirm it.

"I'm not *asking* you to leave, but it would be kind of awkward having you both here," he said.

"No problem," I responded, disappointed with him.

I walked back into the living room, where she had made herself comfortable on the sofa that I had just sat on, with her feet up. I looked over at her. She just gave me a look, crossing her legs, as if to say that she was his bitch and had just laid down the law. I pulled out my phone, scrolled through my call log, and hit the call button when German's name appeared. I could have called Yessenia to have her or Keem pick me up, given that my car was at their house, but

I already felt stupid that Qua had put me out. I didn't need to give German any details, so he wouldn't even know what had happened and whose house this was.

"I'm going to make this up to you," Qua promised, walking up on me.

"No need to make it up. I understand," I lied, trying not to show him how hurt I was.

I wanted to show my true feelings, but I couldn't, because, like I said, he wasn't my man, and I would be playing myself. Granted, we had been just about to fuck, but that was the extent of it, so I wasn't going to try to make it something that it wasn't. I had honestly expected more from him, but I guessed people changed. My phone alerted me that I had a text message from German, letting me know that he was outside. I walked outside, closed the door behind me, not offering Qua a good-bye. Walking to German's car, I tried my best not to cry, because crying meant that I would have to explain what had happened. As I got to the car, I sighed deeply when I saw that Tamia was in the car with him. He could have given me the heads-up that his jealous girlfriend was riding with him, I thought as I opened the back door to get in.

"Thanks for coming, German," I said to him once I was in the car.

"No problem. Give me the address where you left your car," he said.

"Hello to you too, Jakiyah," Tamia spat sarcastically.

"Hey, Tamia," I said dryly, not in the mood to entertain her ass.

Chapter Fourteen

Jakiyah

When I got home last night, I was so pissed that I just took a shower and went to bed. That was the only way that I wouldn't have sat up, dwelling on what had happened. Now that I was up this morning, I was trying hard to get rid of this stress headache that sat right in the middle of my forehead. I looked over at the clock and realized that it was no longer morning; it was almost one in the afternoon. I went into the bathroom to wash my face and brush my teeth before slipping on some sweatpants and a tank top. Then I decided to make a cup of tea and a sandwich so that I could take two Tylenols and pray that they worked. I went down the back stairs to the first floor. I didn't feel like talking to anyone right now, as I was still in a fucked-up mood about what Qua had done to me last night.

I opened the refrigerator, pulled out the ham and cheese, and closed the door. When I glanced up, I saw Tamia standing there, leaning against the sink, a glass of water in her hand. She scared the shit out of me, causing me to jump and drop both the ham and the cheese on the floor.

"I'm so sorry. I didn't mean to startle you," she said, taking a drink of her water.

"Why are you even here?" I asked, pissed, as I picked up the ham and cheese off the floor.

"Jakiyah, I'm here visiting, and I'm starting to get annoyed at the way you treat me every time you see me. I just can't put my finger on what it is that you don't like about me," she said, smirking, letting me know that she really didn't care if I liked her or not, and that she was just fucking with me.

"Tamia, do you ever stop to think that the reason you can't put your finger on it is that it doesn't exist? I have no ill feelings toward you. I just don't need any new friends right now," I said, reaching behind her to take the bread out of the bread box.

"I understand," she responded before leaving the kitchen.

This chick was really starting to freak me out, and I didn't understand why German or even my parents didn't see that she had issues. I wasn't trying to judge her—I didn't know her well enough to do that—but something about her ass just rubbed me the wrong way, I thought to myself as I finished making my sandwich. After making a cup of tea, I took the back steps to go back up to my room. Once there, I plopped down on the bed, took a bite out of my sandwich, and took a sip of my tea.

I casually looked at my phone to see if I had any missed calls from Qua or even a text message, but the only text message was from Yessenia, asking me if I wanted to go to the movies later. She had added that Qua said that he would go, which caused me to respond quickly that I would go. She texted back a few minutes later, saying that everyone would be meeting at Loews for the 6:00 p.m. showing so that we could go out for dinner and drinks after. I really shouldn't be hanging out tonight, because my mother's doctor's appointment was tomorrow, and I had agreed to go with her.

Not only that, but it was just so funny that minutes ago, I had been complaining about my headache and feeling some kind of way about what he did to me—and about the fact that I hadn't received a call or text from him—but now I was smiling. As soon as Yessenia said he had agreed to go, here I was, hyped about seeing him.

Before I knew it, I was inside my closet, looking for something to wear, feeling excited about him again, like nothing had even happened last night.

After taking a shower and getting dressed in black jeans, my black and red pullover sweater, and a pair of black four-inch shoe boots that I had purchased from Nine West, I was ready to go. I put on some lip gloss and checked my hair one last time before grabbing my keys, my bag, and my cell phone. I told my mom that I was going to the movies with Yessenia and would be back later. I was glad to see that the psycho had already left and had gone about her business.

I pulled up to AMC Loews Kips Bay movie theater and found a parking spot that didn't require me to pay at a meter, which was a good thing. I walked inside to a waiting Yessenia and Keem, but I didn't see Qua.

"Hey, girl. We're just waiting on Qua to get here," Yessenia said, hugging me.

"So, did you guys decide on what movie we're going to see?" I asked.

"Well, Keem wants to see *Creed*, and I'm guessing that Qua is going to agree with him. I'm trying to see *Daddy's Home*, and the only way we can pull it off is if you ride with your girl," she said and laughed.

"You already know—" I didn't even get to finish my sentence, as I saw Qua approaching with the female from last night. I put my game face on, but my feelings were hurt once again.

"Who the fuck is this, Qua?" Yessenia asked him.

"Yo, chill with all that. This is my friend Tamara, who is visiting from North Carolina," he said.

All I could do was shake my fucking head, because this nigga had said that the bitch would be leaving today. I wanted to show my ass, but I thought about me not being his girl and about not putting claims on a nigga who didn't belong to me.

"What's up, Jakiyah? I didn't know you would be here," he said.

"Clearly," I responded, then walked off. Yessenia followed behind me.

"Girl, I had no idea this nigga was coming with a bitch," she said.

"Yeah, the same bitch that he basically kicked me out for last night to accommodate her ass. He was talking about she's a friend, when he just told me last night that she was his ex-girlfriend," I told her.

"Stop lying." She looked at me like she didn't believe me.

"Yessenia, I had to call German to pick me up and drive me to your house to get my car last night," I said, on the verge of tears.

"No the fuck that nigga didn't, and if Keem thinks that I'm staying to see a movie with the two of them, he's wrong," she said, pissed. She gave me a hug.

"I'm just going to go. I'll call you later," I said, trying to hold on to the tears just long enough to make it to my car.

"Okay, girl." She hugged me again.

I held my head high as I walked out of the theater; I couldn't believe that he didn't come over and say something to me before I headed out. I wasn't saying that he had to come over and stop me from leaving, but he could have come over to tell me that it wasn't what I thought, but he didn't. When I got to the car, the tears just fell. I just didn't understand what it was about me that had niggas always trying to play me. First, it was Qua, who didn't want to continue a long-distance relationship, despite the fact that I didn't feel the same way that he did about this. Then it was German, who left me, with no real explanation, other than he had met someone else. And now this shit.

Just as I was about to start the car, my phone rang. I was hoping that it was Qua, but it was German's number that appeared on the screen.

Slightly disappointed, I decided to answer the call, just in case it was something important.

"Hello," I answered.

"Hey, are you okay?" he asked, triggering something in me that caused me to cry again."-Jakiyah, are you okay?" he repeated after hearing me sniffling on the other end of the phone.

"No, German, I'm not okay," I cried.

"Where are you?" he asked.

"I'm leaving the AMC Loews movie theater on Second Avenue and heading home," I told him in between sniffles.

"I'm going to meet you at your mom's crib," he said.

"Okay," I replied, then ended the call.

No, I didn't want to see him, but I needed to talk to someone, and my brother wasn't here. Maybe I also could get German to tell me what I had done to push him into the arms of another woman. I was really thinking about moving back to Georgia, since this shit just wasn't working for me. I really loved being here with my family and didn't want to leave at a time when my brother was handling those criminal charges, but something had to give. Maybe it was time for me to get back to work. If I did that, I wouldn't have so much time on my hands and wouldn't be going backward with bullshit.

Chapter Fifteen

Jakiyah

Mom and I had just got back from the doctor, and he had put her on a new medication for her high blood pressure. I hadn't known that she was dealing with so many health issues. I'd known that she suffered from asthma, but I hadn't known about her being borderline diabetic and having high blood pressure.

German had come by yesterday, and I had to say that he really had made me feel a whole lot better. I didn't tell him what had happened with Qua; I just asked him some questions about the relationship we had had. He told me that there was nothing that I had done in the relationship, and that it was just him. Like most men, he had got caught up and had believed that the grass was greener on the other side. He also apologized for hurting me, and I accepted his apology for the second time.

After returning from the doctor, I had retreated to my bedroom. Now I heard talking downstairs, so I took the back stairs down to the first floor, staying out of sight, in case it was the psycho visiting again. When I peeked into the living room, I felt my jaw tighten. The psycho standing in the middle of the room, and she wasn't alone. She caught sight of me.

"Hey, Jakiyah," she sang, as if we were friends.

"What's going on?" I asked her, looking at who she had brought into my mother's house.

"I told your mother that my sister was visiting, and she told me to bring her by. Jakiyah, this is my sister, Tamara, and Tamara, this is Jakiyah," she said, introducing us.

"I know her," Tamara said with a roll of her eyes.

"No, you don't know me. You know *of* me, so get it right," I said to her.

"What am I missing here?" Tamia asked her sister.

"She's salty because she was hanging out with my dude, and I shut the shit down," Tamara said.

"Bitch, you didn't shut shit down, and if I'm not mistaken, you were introduced as his friend twice. So miss me with faking the funk for your sister right now," I snapped.

"Trust me when I say I'm more than his friend, and he proved that last night, when he had me screaming his name," she teased.

I knew we were standing in my mother's house and were disrespecting her right now, but I was at a point of no return from her last statement. I spoke no more words as I snatched that bitch by her jacket and started wailing on her ass. She grabbed my hair, pulled my head down, but I didn't stop beating her ass. My mother was telling her to let go of my hair and was even trying to pry her hands off my hair. Once I felt her grip loosen on my hair, I went back to kicking her ass, until I felt Tamia grab me from behind, causing me to turn around and start fucking her up. I didn't know if she was trying to break it up or was jumping in, but at this point, I didn't care.

"Jakiyah, stop it!" my father yelled as he came into the living room. He pulled me back, and this gave Tamara the opportunity to sucker punch me.

I didn't want to disrespect my father, but that bitch wasn't going to sucker punch me and get away with it. I held on to my father and kicked that bitch so hard, she fell back and hit the wall. I heard my mother pleading at this point for Tamia and Tamara to just leave.

"Bitch, I know you heard my mother tell you to leave," I growled, trying to get out of my father's grip so that I could get at Tamia's ass again.

"Jakiyah, that's enough!" my father yelled at me, pulling me into the kitchen.

I heard Tamia apologizing to my mom, which she should have, but when I heard my mother tell her that it wasn't her fault, I got pissed. I pulled away from my father and went up the back steps to my room. I was so pissed that I was pacing back and forth, talking to myself, to try to calm down before I went back downstairs and fucked those bitches up again. I picked up my phone, dialed Yessenia, hoping she was able to answer, being as she was at work.

"Hold on," she said when she answered her phone.

I could hear her moving about, so I figured she had to walk away from her desk.

"What's up?" she asked after getting back on the phone.

"Girl, you're not going to believe who this psycho bitch brought to my mother's house," I said, getting angry all over again.

"Girl, who?" she whispered.

"Qua's so-called friend Tamara, who, Tamia claims, is her sister," I told her.

"Stop fucking lying. Wow, it's a small fucking world. I can believe it, because that bitch Tamara rubbed me the wrong way too," she replied.

"Well, Tamara got out of pocket, talking about I was salty because I was chilling with her dude, and she basically nipped the shit. So, I told her that if she was his dude, he sure wasn't claiming her ass. She went on to say he had her screaming his name last night, and I lost it on her ass. I attacked her, and I don't know if it was because she was disrespecting my mother's house or she hit a nerve. Long story short, Tamia grabbed me, and I didn't know if she was trying to break it up or if she was jumping in, so I turned around and started fighting her ass too, until my dad stopped me," I said, now out of breath.

"Bitch, you're crazy. You know that bitch hit a nerve, talking about your Qua making her scream." She laughed.

"Whatever." I laughed, even though wasn't shit funny about the situation.

"That bitch was fucking with you because the whole time at the movies, his ass was distracted. She kept sweating him, trying to make it more than what it was, being hella creepy," she told me.

"Really?" I smiled with my dumb ass, like this nigga didn't just play me twice.

"Yes, really. Now, calm your ass down and then go downstairs to apologize to your parents. I will call you later, when I get off."

"Cool," I replied, then ended the call.

Chapter Sixteen

Qua

I was trying so hard not to black out on Tamara's ass right now, after my dude Keem called and told me what his girl, Yessenia, had told him about Tamara showing her ass at Jakiyah's mom's house. First off, she had never even told me she had family living here, and now finding out that her sister was the girlfriend of Jakiyah's ex-boyfriend, German, pissed me off even more.

"Qua, I don't understand why you're mad at me. I had no idea that my sister was taking me to Jakiyah's house," Tamara tried to explain.

"When are you going back home, Tamara?" I asked her, because it was time for her ass to go.

"So now I have to leave, after I just told you that I didn't know?" she whined.

"Tamara, granted you didn't know, but why did you get fly out the mouth, lying, talking about I had you screaming my fucking name, when you know I didn't touch your ass?"

"That bitch called you?" she asked with an attitude.

"No, she didn't call me, but does it matter who called? That shit you said shouldn't have been said," I said to her dumb ass.

"She got out of pocket first, so I was just trying to get under her skin, and the bitch attacked me. You're mad at me, but what was I supposed to do? Just let her attack me and do nothing?" she spat.

"Well, by the look of your face, it looks like you did nothing," I told her, because she was talking like she put in work after being attacked.

"Whatever, Qua. If you want me gone, I will call my sister and will stay with her."

"Yeah, call the sister you didn't tell me about, knowing you had somewhere to go, but you lied so that I would let you stay here. You stood on my porch, talking about you weren't from here and didn't feel safe going to a hotel, fucking up what I was trying to have with Jakiyah," I snapped at her ass.

"I don't understand how you were trying to have something with her. The last time I visited, we slept together, and you said we could work it out between us," she stated.

"Yes, I said that shit in the heat of the moment, and it's been two months of me hardly talking to you, so you had to know that shit was just talk."

"Really, Qua?" she said, on the verge of tears.

"I'm just keeping it real," I told her, not giving a shit about her tears. She needed to get her ass up out of here.

I had fucked up. I had believed her ass and had basically kicked Jakiyah out that night, and then her ass had talked me into calling Keem back and telling him that I would go to the movies. She had whined about having to leave the next morning, and she had said that she wanted to go out, being that it was her last night here, but she really had had no intentions of leaving the next morning. I had no idea that Jakiyah was going to be at the movie theater, and I was pissed at myself for letting her walk out of the theater, but trust, if I had known that Tamara had family here, I would have left her ass standing right there in the theater. The whole time during the movie, she was trying to give Yessenia something to take back to Jakiyah, but I wasn't giving her ass no play. When I told Jakiyah Tamara and I were just friends, it was the truth.

"Are you going to call your sister?" I asked her, because she was just sitting there.

"Can I just stay the night? I promise I'll leave at six a.m. to drive back home," she whispered.

This chick really thought that she was running game on me, but I would let her believe what the fuck she wanted. I knew I shouldn't have been trying to show her any sympathy, because her lying ass knew that what she did was done on purpose.

"Tamara, set your alarm for six a.m. I don't want to hear nothing about you overslept," I told her.

"Thank you, Qua," she said, thinking her ass had got over on me. "Do you want to watch a movie and have a few drinks?" she asked me.

"Nah, I'm good," I responded.

"Come on, Qua. I said sorry, and I meant it. This is our last night together, and I'm not trying to come on to you. I just want to chill," she said.

"What do you want to watch?" I asked her, just to shut her ass up.

"You can pick the movie, and I will fix us a drink and something to eat," she said, walking to the kitchen.

I woke up on the couch, barely able to lift my head as I felt the room spinning. I remembered having one drink with my dinner, but that was about it. I sat up slowly and started bugging out when I realized that I didn't have any clothes on. I put my head in my hands, trying to remember what the fuck had happened up in here last night, but I drew a blank. I looked around for my underwear, and it was on the floor, under the end table. I didn't see or hear Tamara, so I put my underwear on and climbed the stairs to see if she was still here so that she could tell me what the fuck had happened. I checked every room, but she was gone, and so was her suitcase. Then it hit me that she had said that she was leaving at 6:00 a.m. Why hadn't she awakened me so that I could lock my door behind her?

I went back downstairs and looked out the window at the street before locking the door and sitting back on the couch in somewhat of a daze. My phone alerted me that I had a message, so I grabbed it off the table and read the message. It was from Jakiyah.

So, you send me a video of you fucking that bitch Tamara?

I texted her back.

Jakiyah, what are you talking about? I didn't send you anything.

I looked at my outgoing messages. I didn't have a video in my phone that I'd sent to her, so she had me bugging right now. Was she pulling my leg? Was she trying to get me to admit to fucking Tamara? I was just about to text her again when another message from her came in. I opened it. I felt my anger rise as I watched myself lying on the couch, Tamara riding my dick, with her hands on my shoulders. It looked like I was moaning and enjoying it, but I swore I didn't remember fucking that bitch. I texted Jakiyah.

Jakiyah, I know you're not going to believe me, but I don't remember anything on that video.

She texted me right back.

You know what, Qua? It's all good. I'm not your girl, so it really doesn't matter. I'm just pissed that it was sent to me.

I sent another text.

Jakiyah, just think about it. Why would I send you a video of me fucking a female? What reason would I have to want to hurt you like that?

I waited for about twenty minutes for her to respond, but she didn't. I tried calling Tamara to ask her if she had sent the video to Jakiyah, but she didn't answer her phone. I knew she had to have sent the video. And now that I thought about it, it dawned on me that she must have put something in my drink. I watched the video a few more times, and it became clear to me that

I wasn't actually moaning. I wanted her off me, but my words were incoherent. I also noticed that she was holding my shoulders down, and not because she was in her zone. She was doing that because I was trying to get up.

I swear, I'm going to kill that bitch, I thought as I called Keem to tell him what this bitch had done.

Chapter Seventeen

Tamia

"You had one fucking job, and you couldn't do the shit. Why the fuck would you fuck that nigga and send a video?" I asked my stupid-ass sister.

"He was coming at me sideways about this bitch Jakiyah, telling me how I fucked up what he was trying to have with her. I wanted to shut down any chances of him being with her by making her hate his ass," she said.

"Tamara, are you listening to yourself right now? You were supposed to give that nigga enough of the drug to kill his ass. So, if the nigga was dead, how the fuck would he have a relationship with Jakiyah?" I asked, shaking my head, not believing how dumb she was.

I really felt like slapping some sense into her ass right now. I had planned this shit with perfection, and she had fucked it up. I swear, if she wasn't my sister, and if I didn't need her to assist me further, I would kill her ass too.

"Sis, I understand that you're upset, but what did Qua do to you that you want him dead? I think what I did was enough, because he wants Jakiyah to be his girl, and I stopped it from happening. You heard him on my voice mail. He's pissed, so that alone should tell you that I didn't fuck up," she said, sounding even more stupid.

"Well, Tamara, it's a good thing that you don't get paid to think, because you would be a broke bitch. You went and fell in love with this nigga, so say that, but don't sit here and insult my intelligence with the bullshit reasons, making excuses for why you didn't just kill his ass." I walked away to take a breather.

"I could say the same about you. You fell in love with German too, because if you didn't, this shit wouldn't have been prolonged," she yelled behind me.

She was right. Yes, I fell in love with German, but it didn't stop me from wanting to seek revenge on them all. I honestly didn't want to tell her why I wanted Qua dead, because she already thought that I was crazy. And it wasn't just her; it was everyone in my family. I had been told that I was crazy my entire childhood, but nobody had sought any help for me. I could admit that the shit had spiraled out of control, but so what? She had to be just as crazy to agree to help me without knowing why I wanted them all dead.

"Are you still mad at me?" Tamara asked after I finally decided to go back into the living room. "Tamia, I think you can get revenge on Qua for whatever he did to you without killing him," she continued.

"And how might that be, Tamara?" I asked, wanting her to enlighten me.

"Maybe you can do something to take everything away from him, causing him not to want to live. I mean, something that would turn his world upside down," she said.

I thought about what she had just said.

"Tamara, I need for you to check into a hotel. You can't be here when German gets home, because I have yet to tell him about you. He's already upset with me, and he's not really speaking to me. He believes everything that bitch told him and has not even given me a chance to explain," I said to her, really needing her to go.

"Well, he knows now, but my question is, why would you be with someone for this long and not tell him you have a sister?" she asked, as if she was offended.

"Tamara, I wasn't ready for him to know just yet, and I really don't have time to have a conversation about why. So, can you please go? I will call you later," I snapped, getting agitated.

"Fine, Tamia," she said, grabbing her suitcase.

"Tamara, you can just stay at the Holiday Inn near the airport," I suggested. That hotel was close to my home.

"Call me when the argument is over," she said sarcastically, then walked out.

I didn't even know if there would be an argument. After all, German had been giving me the silent treatment. It was crazy that we had been together for so long without any issues, but as soon as Jakiyah came back to town, it seemed as if he didn't care for me as much as he claimed. He was mad at me for something that I didn't provoke, and just because I didn't tell him about my sister, it was "Fuck me." I wasn't looking for an argument with him, but he was going to talk to me. I refused to walk around like we were fucking strangers. I decided to make dinner and clean up to kill some time before he was expected home.

German walked in the door at 7:00 p.m., and I watched as he dropped his keys on the table, then walked right past me to the kitchen. He had come home on the same bullshit he had left on, and I wasn't having it. His ass was going to talk to me whether he wanted to or not. I waited for him to come back into the living room, and when he did, he had a Corona in his hand, letting me know that he had had a stressful day today. Such days were the only time he indulged. I didn't want to add to his stress, but fuck that. He was going to talk to me. I wasn't going to let him get up until he did.

"German, we need to discuss why you're just walking around, not giving me a chance to explain my reason for not sharing with you that I had a sister," I said to him.

"Tamia, what reason could you possibly have for not telling me that you have a sister and then failing to tell me that she was visiting? You didn't introduce her to me, but you take her over to Mama Smith's house to introduce her. Why? Could it be that you went over there to rub the shit in Jakiyah's face, being as your sister is the ex-girlfriend of the dude she was trying to get back with?"

"German, it wasn't even like that. You were at work, and since I look at Mama Smith as a mother figure, I wanted her to meet my sister. That's all. I was going to tell you before all this shit went down. It just bothers me that you took that bitch's word and shut me out like I'm not your fucking girlfriend," I replied, getting pissed off with him.

"I didn't take her word for it, Tamia. The shit actually happened, and I'm starting to feel like

I can't trust you. I mean, if you lied about this, what else are you lying about?"

"German, my sister and I haven't been on good terms. We just started talking again about three months ago. I had no ill intentions when I decided not to mention her to you. It's just that I wasn't thinking of her as my sister at the time," I lied.

"Well, you need to let me meet your sister, and both of you owe Mama Smith an apology. No matter the situation, her house shouldn't have been disrespected," he said.

"I have no problem apologizing to Mama Smith, but I need for you never to shut me out again. If we have an issue, we need to discuss it like adults," I told him.

"Tamia, I'm hoping there won't be a next time. And if I find out that you lied to me about anything else, it's over. I refuse to be in a relationship with you lying to me," he said.

I wanted to get fly out of the mouth, but I changed my mind, because he wasn't leaving me until I said that the relationship was over. I called Tamara up, told her that everything was cool, and invited her to come over to have dinner with us so that she could meet German. I went into the kitchen after telling German that my sister was on her way over to have dinner with us. After setting the table, I called Tamara back to see how long it would be before she got back over here. After having two beers, German's ass was now dozing, and I needed to get this shit done tonight so that Tamara and I could get back to what I needed her to do next.

Chapter Eighteen

Jakiyah

My phone rang just as I pulled up to the house the Realtor was showing me today. I had decided to rent a home instead of buying. I honestly didn't think I would be staying long term in New York, like I had originally planned, so renting was the best option for me right now. I ignored Qua's call as I got out of the car to get this over with and to stop delaying my move. Yes, I was no longer upset with my mother, and I had apologized for disrespecting her house, but I was ready to move out and be in my own space. She was not happy with my decision, but it was a decision I needed to make, as I was sure this wasn't going to be the last time we bumped heads about that trick Tamia.

"Hello, Ms. Smith," the Realtor greeted me.

"Hello, Mrs. Walters. How are you?"

"I'm fine. Are you ready for the tour of the home?" she asked, smiling.

"Yes, I'm ready," I responded as she opened the door.

The house was located in Rosedale, off of 148th Road, and I had to say it was a beautiful home. It had three bedrooms—the master bedroom had its own bathroom—a spacious living room, a dining room, and a kitchen with all new appliances. The best part was the wood floors throughout the home. I really didn't need three bedrooms, but when I was searching for two-bedrooms, I discovered that the price wasn't much different than that of three-bedroom houses. After touring the house with Mrs. Walters, I took a few more minutes to do a walk-through on my own. I did want to say yes in haste because she had made the place sound perfect, which it was, and I wasn't going to get all excited in front of her.

I stood in the master bedroom, already decorating it in my head. Next, I went to the bedroom toward the back of the house to look out at the backyard, and I loved it. I wished that there was a pool, but there wasn't, but I could live without a pool. My ass didn't know how to swim, anyway. I knew that I could afford the nineteen hundred dollars a month rent, but I would definitely have to get my ass back to work at somebody's job sooner than later. People might wonder how I was able to afford nearly two grand a month, but it was nobody's business.

"Mrs. Walters," I called out once I got back downstairs.

"I'm here, hon. What do you think of the place?" she asked, coming from the kitchen.

"I love the home. The only complaint that I do have is that the tiles in the hallway bathroom are loose near the tub area," I told her.

"Okay, I can assure you that if you take the place, I will make sure that the owner has that fixed before you move in," she responded with a smile.

"I'm going to take the place, Mrs. Walters."

"Great. You can meet me at my office tomorrow morning with the Realtor's fee, first month, and security."

"No problem, and thank you so much," I said, shaking her hand.

I left the rental house, and since I had about thirty minutes to kill before meeting up with Yessenia for lunch, I decided to stop by the bank to get the money that I needed for tomorrow. Yessenia finally had a day off, so we had decided to meet up to discuss the bullshit that had been going on in my crazy life. Getting my own place made me feel somewhat better. However, I knew that my mother wasn't going to be pleased with me leaving the house, but she would have to accept that I needed my own place.

I loved my mother to death, but she had made me realize why it was so easy for me to leave the first time I left: she wasn't the easiest person to get along with at times. Since the incident at her house, I just felt like she blamed me, even though I had apologized for my part in the fight. Sometimes I wished that my dad would stand up to her and let her know when she was wrong, but he always stayed neutral. I just hoped that she understood that I needed my own space and that me moving had nothing to do with the disagreement that we had. I hated that I would not be there to help with baby Andrea the way that I had been, but I would make sure to help out as much as I could.

When I got to the restaurant, Yessenia was already waiting because I was, like, twenty minutes late. I had no idea where my ATM card was at, so I had had to wait on a teller to get the money and had decided to cancel the ATM card and get a replacement.

"Hey, sorry I'm late," I said, hugging her.

"No worries. It's not like I have anywhere to be," she said before she walked over to the hostess to let her know that her guest had arrived.

"So, what the hell happened over at the Smith residence? I tried calling you back when I got off of work, but you didn't answer," she said when she sat back down at our table.

"Well, like I told you on the phone, all I did was ask Tamia why she had Tamara at my house, and Tamara got out of pocket, so I had to check the bitch. I don't know if I told you, but when it was all said and done, I heard my mother telling Tamia that it wasn't her fault. I took it as her saying that it was *my* fault. So, there's been a lot of tension in the house since it happened, and I'm not feeling it," I said sadly.

"Well, there were three parties involved, so she could have been speaking about Tamara, especially if your mother heard how it all started," Yessenia said, defending my mother.

"Yeah, but even though I apologized, I still feel like she's mad at me. I might just be reading more into it than I should," I admitted.

"Okay, so on to the next issue. Let me see the video that you said Qua sent to your phone. I have to be honest with you, though. I don't think that Qua would send you a video of him fucking another female. This has Tamara written all over it, just like I told you on the phone," she said, still not convinced that it was Qua.

I watched her as she looked at the video, and she was better about it than I was. As soon as I saw that it was a sex video starring Qua and that bitch, I had clicked it off. She, on the other hand, was all into the video, as if it was arousing her ass. This pissed me off just a little, because I wanted her to have the same reaction that I had had.

"Enjoying it, are we?" I asked with a hint of sarcasm.

"Hell no, and trust, his ass wasn't enjoying it, either. That bitch drugged his ass. Look and tell me what man you know that when a bitch is riding him, he's not grabbing her ass or her breasts. Jakiyah, Qua is trying to get the bitch off of him, and she's holding him down," she said, all excited, like she had just solved her first murder case.

I really didn't want to watch the video again, and especially while sitting in the restaurant, but Yessenia kept pushing. She wanted me to tell her I saw exactly what she was seeing. I took a deep breath before lowering the volume, just in case, and starting to watch the video. I felt the anger rise in me as I was looking at what Yessenia had described, and I wanted to beat Tamara's ass all over again. Damn, I hadn't even given him a chance to explain when he was trying to tell me that he didn't send the video.

I fucked up, I thought to myself. This desperate bitch really needed her ass beat, and I swore that if she came anywhere near me again, I was going to be the one beating that ass.

"You need to call him," Yessenia said, bringing me back to the present. She could tell I was really seeing red now.

"Jess, he's not going to talk to me. I've been ignoring his calls and his text messages," I whined, calling her by my nickname for her, which I hadn't used in, like, forever.

"Trust me, he's waiting for his phone to ring," she said, trying to convince me.

"I'm going to wait until later. Let's just take this time to enjoy our meals," I said, knowing I wouldn't be enjoying my meal, because now my mind was elsewhere.

"So, tell me about the place you found and where it is located," she said, trying to get me to focus on something else.

"Girl, the place is really nice. It's a three-bedroom located in Rosedale, right off the corner of One Hundred Forty-Eighth Road, near the store. If you remember where Keita used to live, it's, like, a block from there," I told her.

"Oh, yeah. I know exactly where that is. Did you get a good price?" she asked.

"I got it for nineteen hundred dollars a month."

"Damn, it's a good price for that area, but shit, you're practically paying someone's mortgage."

"I know, girl, but I just can't see myself buying a house right now. I don't know if New York is going to be my final resting place," I said, being honest with her.

"I feel you, but you need to make up your mind because that's a lot of money, and you could be putting it into your own home," she said seriously. "So, if you're basing your sticking around on Qua, you better get his ass on the phone ASAP," she added.

"No, that's not why I'm not sure if I'm sticking around," I lied.

I would love to see where Qua and I could go with a relationship, but I wasn't going to lie. I was scared to death because of the drama that had already started, and he wasn't even my man. My phone rang just as my greedy ass was about to stuff another mozzarella stick into my mouth. I ignored it at first, but then I saw it was my mom calling, so I took the call, praying that everything was okay.

"Hey, Mom. What's going on?" I asked, a little nervous.

"Where you at, bighead?"

"Ty?" I asked, trying not to get excited, since I wasn't sure.

"Who else would it be? Now again, where are you?" he asked me again.

"I'm on my way," I said excitedly. I looked over at Yessenia. "Girl, Ty is home. I have to go, but I promise I will make it up to you," I told her.

"You better stop. We're good. I'll take care of the bill."

"Thanks, sis," I said. I hugged her before rushing out of the restaurant.

Once I got on the road, I had to tell myself to slow down. I was driving too fast, and Lord knows, I didn't need to get pulled over before I made it home to see my brother.

Chapter Nineteen

Jakiyah

I almost tripped on the porch steps from running so fast, trying to get inside the house. As soon as I made it through the front door, I ran into my brother's arms. I wasn't trying to let him go as the tears fell.

"Why are you acting like I've been gone for years?" He laughed.

"I just missed you so much, and I didn't know if I would see you again," I cried.

"I'm out on bond, but I'm sure my lawyer is going to beat this case," he said, sounding convinced.

"Well, I'm just glad you're home. And I pray that this nightmare will be over soon. . . . I know that you didn't do this."

"Nah, I didn't get a chance to handle his ass, but trust, if I had had the opportunity, his ass would not have been found," he whispered to me.

"Baby, are you hungry?" my mom asked him.

"Yes, Mom. The food up in there was horrible." He laughed.

"Okay, baby. I'm going to fix dinner, but in the meantime, I'll fix you a sandwich to hold you over." She turned to me. "Jakiyah, would you like a sandwich too?" she asked me.

"No, thank you. I just finished lunch with Yessenia," I told her. I wondered if I should tell them that I had found a place and would be moving.

My dad had already gone back upstairs to do what he did best, and that was sitting in his recliner and watching the Spike channel. I told Ty about my run-in with Tamia and the sister whom no one ever knew she had. He tried to convince me that Tamia was good people, and she had never disrespected our mother or her house for as long as he had known her. I wasn't trying to knock what he was saying, but I just felt that if her sister was grimy, she was grimy too.

"Who picked you up from the courthouse?" I asked him, trying to change the subject because I had already given them tricks enough of my energy.

"Chanel came and picked me up and drove me by the club to pick up my car. I'm going to go back to the club tomorrow and try to get it open for the weekend," he said.

"Really? So soon?"

"Yes, I missed my family, but I missed my club just as much," he said, laughing. "That shit was crazy, locking me up on some bullshit at my showcase. I didn't even get to finish the show, so I'm going to put that back in rotation and schedule it for next weekend."

"I found a place," I blurted out.

"You found a place where? And does Mom know?" he asked, looking at me like I was crazy.

"No, Mom doesn't know, and I don't want you to say anything just yet. The place is in Rosedale, not too far from here, so it shouldn't be an issue."

"I don't know about it not being an issue, but you know Mom is not trying to hear about you moving out."

"I know that she doesn't want me to move, but, Ty, it's time for me to get my own place. You already know how Mom is. She's stuck in her own ways, and I've had just about enough of it. It feels like I'm living here as a child all over again, and I'm so ready to go," I explained, being honest.

"I feel you, and I'm not telling you not to do it, but I know she's going to feel some kind of way about it. Anyway, what's up with you and my nigga Qua?"

I just looked at him and shook my head. I didn't even know if I wanted to share what had happened with Qua. I had never kept anything from Ty before, but I was kind of embarrassed this time to tell him. But what the hell? He was probably going to find out from Keem or Qua, anyway.

"Tamia's sister, Tamara, is Qua's ex-girlfriend from North Carolina, and she came to visit. He put me out of his crib to accommodate her. So, the day after she showed up here and got her ass kicked, I get a video that night of Qua and her fucking, so you know my ass was pissed," I told him. "I let Yessenia see the video, and she and I both agree that he looks drugged in the video. He tried to tell me that he didn't send the video and that he didn't remember fucking her. I kind of just told him that I didn't believe him, and that it is what it is, because we weren't together."

"So, that bitch is living foul like that?"

"That's what I was trying to tell you. I know that Tamia's done pulled the wool over on every last one of you all, but trust when I say that the apple doesn't fall far from the tree. Both of those bitches are living foul."

Someone rang the doorbell just then, and Ty and I looked at each other. Neither one of us was in the mood for bullshit. I got up to get the door. If it was Tamia just dropping by, I was going to drop her ass right where she stood. I opened the door to find the two detectives from New Jersey who were investigating my sister's murder. I let them in. Ty went into the kitchen to let my mother know, and I ran up the steps to tell my father that they were here. Then we all gathered in the living room.

"I'm sorry to show up without calling, but I wanted to come by personally to give you an update on your daughter's case," one of the detectives said to my mother. He had spoken to her several times before.

"Not a problem, Detective James. Please have a seat," she told him and his partner.

They both took a seat.

"First, let me introduce you to my partner, Detective Brooks, who is also from the homicide unit. As I told you before, the gas station owner wasn't being cooperative with the release of the video from the night that your daughter was murdered, so we served him with a warrant and were able to retrieve the video footage from that night. On the night in question, the video does show her husband, Andris, being very aggressive, striking the driver's window of her car, and it also shows him pulling something out of his pocket. Unfortunately, we are unable to make out what it is on the tape."

Detectives James went on. "The gas station attendant comes out of the store and says something to Andris, who turns and runs to his car, and he leaves the scene. Minutes later, the video shows another car pulling up behind your daughter's car, and someone dressed in a black hoodie and black jeans walks over to her car and fires into the car before fleeing the scene. So, Andris didn't kill your daughter, Mrs. Smith. We are in the process of trying to get a make on the car from another video, one from the auto shop located next door. The angle of the camera doesn't give us much, but we have the best team on it, trying to get us something to work with."

So now we sat there, puzzled. If Andris didn't kill Cydney, then who the fuck killed her? And what was their reason to kill her? I still didn't feel any kind of way about Andris's ass being dead, since whether he killed her or not, he had still put his fucking hands on her. My brother didn't say much, and neither did my father. They both looked as if they were in deep thought. My mother thanked the detectives, who in return let her know that they were going to do everything possible to catch the person responsible for my sister's murder. Then the two detectives stood, and my mother showed them out.

Now that Andris had been cleared, if he were alive, he probably would have been of some assistance to the detectives: he might have offered them something that our family couldn't. For instance, he might have known if Cydney had any jealous friends or had a beef with someone who might have wanted to harm her. It could even have been that Andris was cheating, and the jealous female that he was dealing with had killed her. Now I felt as if we were right back at square one. I just hoped that the detectives were going to look into all of those possibilities that I had just thought of. Better yet, I was going to call Detective James tomorrow to let him know what I was thinking.

Right now I just wanted to lie down, so I left Ty sitting in the living room alone, talking on the phone to Chanel. I felt a headache coming on from doing too much thinking again, so I grabbed a bottled water before heading upstairs to take a couple of Tylenol.

Chapter Twenty

Jakiyah

I managed to make it through the next two weeks without pulling my hair out. I recruited Yessenia, Keem, and Ty to help me get my place move-in ready, so the work was done pretty quickly. With everything I had going on, I was lucky to have my friend April to take care of putting my things in storage for me and selling my car. My mother wasn't too happy about me moving, but she handled it better than I had thought she would. I thought her handling it so well might have had something to do with the fact that Tamia was visiting again. She had the wool pulled over all their eyes, but I knew something was mentally off with her ass. I couldn't for the life of me fathom what her attraction was to my mother, and it bothered me, but what could I do about it? My mother wasn't trying to hear anything I had to say about the psycho.

Yessenia told me that Qua had been asking about me, but given that I was in the process of getting my place together and getting back to work, I hadn't got the chance to reach out to him until today. We had agreed to meet up to talk. I felt good about that, because I really missed him. When I got to his house, I started to get nervous and was second-guessing if I really wanted to be there, if it made sense to give him another chance to hurt me. I was still feeling some kind of way about how he had handled the situation at his house and at the movie theater, so who was to say that his ass wouldn't play me again? I decided to get out of the car, at least give him a chance to say what he wanted to say to me, and then to proceed from there.

When he opened the door, he was wearing his signature basketball shorts and his college T-shirt, which was his norm, but it didn't stop me from getting that aroused feeling that I always got when I saw him. I had to tell myself to focus. It seemed that my mind was always on getting between the sheets whenever I was in his presence.

"Thanks for coming," he greeted, hugging me.

"No problem," I responded, keeping it short with him because I didn't want him to know just yet that all was forgiven.

I walked inside and headed over to sit on the sofa, and he came and sat beside me, his leg rubbing against mine, making me feel a tingling between my legs. I wished his ass would go and sit on the other side of the room. I crossed my legs, telling myself to focus again, but it was really hard with him sitting so close.

"Jakiyah, first, I want to apologize for the way I treated you the night Tamara came to visit. I had no idea that she had family in New York. If I'd known that, I would have never let her stay here."

"I'm not going to sit here and say that my feelings weren't hurt. They were, because I thought we were friends before anything. I never would have made you feel as if I was choosing someone over you. I felt you could have handled the situation differently, especially since you had me thinking that the two of you were more than just friends," I admitted to him.

"Again, I apologize if I made you feel that way. Trust me, it wasn't like that," he assured me.

"It wasn't just that incident, Qua. The whole movie theater scene was fucked up. You showed up with her, and instead of coming after me to explain, knowing what I was thinking, you just let me leave."

"Jakiyah, I didn't know how to handle that situation, and even though I knew that it was innocent, I knew it looked like something more, but it wasn't. I didn't come behind you, because at the time, it wouldn't have been right to just leave her standing there."

"Qua, you wouldn't have had to leave her standing there if you had just pulled me to the side and explained that what I was thinking wasn't the case," I said, getting agitated.

"You're right. I handled the situation ass backward, and I regret the shit," he replied. "I knew that she still had feelings for me, and that she wanted more than a friendship. I should have never allowed her to stay in my home, knowing that I was trying to be with you. I'm beating myself up about it now. All I was trying to do was be a friend, and she betrayed me in the worst way by putting something in my drink, forcing herself on me, and sending you the video. Yessenia told me that both of you watched the video, and now believe me, I just knew that you would never speak to me again." He put his head in his hands.

I could tell that he was really fucked up about what she had done. He had trusted her and had never thought that she would do something like that to him. She had violated him, and although we wouldn't expect a man to feel some kind of way about a female taking the dick, he was pissed and frustrated at the same time. His father had warned him early on, when he first started playing basketball and had a chance to be drafted into the NBA, that females would try to trap him. For that reason, he had always used protection—no matter what. He said that he had got tested since the incident and all was good, but he was still beating himself up about the situation because of what could have happened. I felt bad that this had happened to him, and I believed that he was sorry about how he had handled the situation with me. And so I was going to give him another chance to make it right.

"Qua, you good?" I asked him.

"I'm good. And again, I apologize. I hope that you'll give me another chance to make this right," he said, lifting his head and looking at me.

"Qua, I forgive you. I'm sorry that this happened to you, but I believe that all of this could have been avoided had you just kept it real with me. I'm not trying to make light of the situation, but I bet you'll take my advice next time I say to send that bitch to a hotel," I told him.

"Trust me when I say there will not be a next time. And I promise from this moment on that

I will keep it real with you," he said, then kissed me on my lips, causing an inferno between my legs again.

As much as I wanted to pick up from where we had started the last time I was at his place, I decided that I wasn't going to take it there. I knew that I had forgiven him, but I just wanted to take things slow, because he had to prove to me that he really wanted to have a relationship with me.

"So, are you chilling with a nigga tonight?" he asked, playing in my hair, causing me to smile.

"It depends on what you have in mind, because I have my own crib to chill in now."

"My bad. Congrats on the new place. Keem told me they helped you with getting the place ready to move in. I wish I'd been invited to help, but I know I fucked up my privilege to be in your personal space at that time."

"I should have invited you to punish you by having you clean some toilets, mop some floors, and maybe do some yard work."

We laughed.

"Anyway, I was thinking we could order in and watch some Netflix together," he suggested.

"Don't you have to be to work in the a.m.?" I asked him.

"I do, but so what? I want to chill with you tonight."

"Okay, as long as you don't be blaming me for keeping you up all night. And you have to order me some hot buffalo chicken and stuffed cheesy bread with spinach and feta from Domino's," I said to him.

"I will not be blaming you for keeping me up all night," he said, picking up his phone to place the order.

After the food was delivered, we sat and ate and watched *The Da Vinci Code*, enjoying each other's company. At some point we both fell asleep. I really enjoyed hanging out with him, and the next morning, when we awoke, I didn't want him to leave to go to work. He worked for sanitation, so it was, like, 6:00 a.m. when he had to get up. He told me that I didn't have to leave, and as much as I wanted to stay, I had an appointment later. I was finally going to get back to work, and to be honest, I couldn't wait. I was tired of just sitting at home, doing nothing, every day.

I had worked as a home health aide in Georgia, and I really missed my patient, Ms. Wilson. I was her aide for about a year, and she really grew on me. She was my first patient, and she used to give me hell because she was an old and cranky lady, but as time went on, she turned out to be a really nice lady. I called her prior to letting the agency know that I was leaving, and she was sad, but like I promised, I had been keeping in touch with her. She had a new aide now that she liked, but she said that no one would ever replace me. I got out of the bed to go into the bathroom to handle my morning hygiene. I didn't even remember what time we went up to bed. All I remembered was falling asleep on the couch last night.

"Jakiyah, you sure you don't want to stay?" he asked, walking up on me while I was brushing my teeth.

"No, I can't stay. I put going back to work off long enough," I answered after rinsing my mouth.

We walked out together. He escorted me to my car, hugged me, and thanked me for spending the night with him. His ass was wearing jeans, a hoodie, his orange and green sanitation jacket, and some black boots, but he still managed to look sexy to me. I was definitely taking a cold shower when I got home or pulling my vibrator out for a temporary fix, until I was ready for Qua to put it down in the bedroom. I kissed him on the lips and told him, "Anytime," before getting in my car and pulling out.

Chapter Twenty-One

Tyhiem

I was on my way to pick up Chanel from her crib. I had invited her to hang out with me tonight at the bowling alley. I was just hoping all went well tonight, being that German and Tamia were going to be there. Jakiyah had said that she was okay with this as long as Tamia didn't start no shit with her. Jakiyah had invited Yessenia and Keem out tonight, so that was another reason I didn't want nothing to pop off. Yessenia was a ticking time bomb with her crazy ass.

Chanel and I arrived at Whitestone Lanes at the same time that German and Tamia were heading toward the building. I noticed that they had Tamia's sister with them, or at least I assumed that was her sister. She was a pretty chick, a shade darker than Tamia, but she had the same build as her sister. I guess big asses and breasts ran in their family.

When Chanel and I caught up with them, I gave German dap, shaking my head. He already knew what I was thinking, but he didn't talk about it; he just hit me with the head nod. Tamia introduced her sister, who looked vaguely familiar, but I couldn't place where I had seen her before. Tamara was standing a little too close for comfort as she openly flirted with me, like she didn't see Chanel standing there. I had to take Chanel by the hand and walk off, because she was about to check Tamara. This chick was definitely trouble, just like Jakiyah had said she was.

When we walked in, I saw Qua's jaw tighten when he saw Tamara walk in with us. He walked toward her, but Jakiyah said something to him that stopped him. I had to say he was better than me: if I caught up with the bitch who did that foul shit to me, she would have been a dead bitch. I saw that they had already started a game, so Chanel and I walked over to get our shoes, order some food, and get me a drink. I knew I was going to need a few. I didn't know what was going on with German and Tamia, but it looked like they were having a disagreement about something. *His girl, his problem*, I thought as I kept it moving.

Chanel and I took a seat and waited to be called to pick up our food order. I could tell that she was still salty about what Tamia's sister had done earlier, but I told her that she needed to let that shit go, because I wasn't sweating that bitch.

"What's up with Tamia's sister just sitting there, staring at your sister like she's got a beef with her?" Chanel asked me after watching her.

"Jakiyah's dude is her ex-boyfriend," I told her.

"Well, she needs to get over it, sitting there like she's about to go postal," she joked.

"Nah, Jakiyah already had to tap that ass, so I doubt if she wants to go there again." I laughed.

"I just don't get the point of sitting there, being creepy, instead of enjoying herself. I would never let the next female know that I'm bothered," she said, rolling her eyes.

I knew that last statement was for me, because one of my jump-offs had called her the other night and told her crazy shit, and she had handled the call rather well. But when she got off the phone, she'd gone ham on my ass. So, she was already feeling some kind of way about that, and now this shit with ole girl flirting with me had her in her feelings again. I knew she was mad that I didn't let her check the bitch, but she needed to understand that she couldn't go at every female that flirted with me. If she did, she would be fighting every time we went out together.

I knew that I needed to stop playing games and make her wifey. She had proven that she loved me: even though she knew that we weren't exclusive and I still fucked with other bitches, she had remained loyal to me. She was still sitting with the mean mug, so I kissed her on her lips to let her know again to just let the shit go and enjoy herself. Before she got to answer, I heard a commotion. It just so happened to be Yessenia popping off, so I hurried back over, with Chanel following me, to see what was going on. All a nigga wanted to do was come out and have a good fucking time without all the extra bullshit.

"Bitch, flirt with my man again like you don't see me standing here," I heard Yessenia say to Tamara, trying to get at her.

"Bitch, I wasn't flirting with your man. He was flirting with me, so take that shit to him!" Tamara yelled.

I knew that Keem hadn't been flirting with her ass. She had just openly flirted with me, knowing that I was with Chanel, so the bitch must have done it again with Keem. Boy, was she being messy.

"Trust when I say that my man wouldn't touch your thirsty ass," Yessenia yelled.

"So why you mad?" Tamara asked, then stuck her tongue out, taunting her.

"Bitch, I'm mad because you're a disrespectful ho and a grimy ho, one who has to *take* the dick because a nigga didn't want to fuck with your stank pussy," Yessenia said, causing Jakiyah and Chanel to laugh.

Tamara didn't like that. She tried to lunge at Yessenia, but German pulled her back and led her away. Tamia walked behind them.

"I wish the fuck you would, because I promise you, I will be the last bitch you run up on," Yessenia yelled after her.

"Yo, Yessenia, chill, before we get kicked out of here," I said and laughed, shaking my head. She was so mad that she was shaking.

"Here, sis," Jakiyah said, handing her a drink, like she really needed another drink.

Chanel had to open her mouth about Tamara doing the same shit to her, causing Yessenia to get hyped all over again. I just looked at her, like, "Really?" We had just got Yessenia to calm down and agree that she was going to leave the shit alone, and now Chanel was riling her up again. Tamara, Tamia, and German walked back over, but no words were exchanged. Tamara and

Tamia both had drinks in their hands, and they were talking among themselves. I asked German if he was good, and he said that he was. That was all that mattered. I didn't give a fuck if Tamara and Tamia didn't want to hang with the rest of us.

We continued to bowl, drink, listen to music, and have a good time without anything else popping off. When it was time to go, I had to go take a leak. Everyone followed suit except for Tamia and Tamara, who waited until the other girls had come out of the restroom before they went in. Once we all left the building and were in the parking lot, out of nowhere Yessenia ran up on Tamara and punched her in the face. The shit happened so fast that nobody saw it coming.

The fighting grew intense, and Keem stepped in to try to break it up. I saw Tamia run over, and before she could even jump in the shit, Jakiyah ran up on her, grabbed her by her hair, and pulled her down on the ground. I couldn't even stop Jakiyah from fighting. I had to help Keem. He was having a hard time breaking up Yessenia and Tamara's fight. I was punched in the face, and I saw red as I pulled Tamara's ass and flung her, telling her to get in the fucking car. I saw Qua pushing Jakiyah and yelling at her to get in the car, so I told Chanel to get in the car too.

"You pussy bitch, you wait until my back's turned to pop off," Tamara yelled, trying to get around German to get at Yessenia.

"Fuck you!" Yessenia yelled, trying to get back out of the car.

Keem finally spoke up, because he was pissed. "Yessenia, get the fuck back in the car."

I waited a few minutes, just to make sure that my boys had shit under control, before pulling out. One of those women had scratched the shit out of my arm, and that shit was burning. I got pissed off all over again. I knew one thing. I wasn't hanging out with none of their asses again. I should have known Yessenia wasn't going to let that shit slide. I should have just told German to take them home and assured him that I would chill with him another time. I drove home, not even saying two fucking words to Chanel. I was kind of pissed with her for egging that shit on when it was already done.

"You okay?" Chanel asked me once we got home.

"I'm good now, but you didn't have to tell them that she did the same thing to you. All you did was hype Yessenia's crazy ass up again," I said to her.

"Well, I didn't know she was going to get hyped up again," she said, laughing.

"Don't think I didn't see your ass pull that girl's hair." I laughed at her ass.

"She's lucky that's all I did to her, with her disrespectful ass," she said.

"You damn females are too much. I got fucked up, and I wasn't even involved in the fight," I said, shaking my head.

I wasn't even mad anymore. After all, her ass did deserve that ass whupping, because that shit was disrespectful. I looked at Chanel's ass in them jeans and was ready to get it on in the bedroom. Yes, I had gone from being mad at her to wanting to bend her ass over and fuck the shit out of her until I had her screaming my name.

"Come take a shower with me," I said, hitting her on the ass.

I thought about all that I had been thinking lately about making her my girl and decided that tonight I wasn't going to just fuck her like I always did. After we got out of the shower, I wanted to explore her body as if I was touching her for the first time. I pushed her down lightly onto the bed, then laid my body on top of hers. Kissing her, I made my way down to her nipples and gave them some tongue action before putting my head between her legs. I was gentle with her as my tongue caressed her insides, causing her to moan as she released her juices into my mouth. Her legs shook lightly as I kissed the inside of her thigh, brushed my lips against her now sensitive clit before positioning myself behind her. I entered her and softly played with her pussy. I continued thrusting slowly in and out of her as she cried out in pleasure. I whispered in her ear, asking her if she was okay, but she didn't answer; she just ground her hips into me. I continued to make love to her until we came together. I didn't pull out. I just left my dick inside of her and put my face in the crook of her neck. As I fell asleep, I hoped that she realized that she had just officially become my girl.

Chapter Twenty-Two

Jakiyah

I was on my way to the Queens Center. I was starting my first case next week in the Bronx, so I needed to get a few uniforms at the mall. I really didn't want to travel all the way to the Bronx, but if I wanted a full-time position, that was all they had to offer right now. Though I accepted the position, I had been having second thoughts. I thought that maybe I should start off with a four-hour case daily, just to get the feel of being back at work again, after being home for so long. I was now used to taking naps during the day. I just hoped that I would be able to stay awake and take care of someone for eight hours every day.

I stopped to get me a pretzel roll and a strawberry lemonade before going to purchase my uniforms. When I used to live here, I never left the mall without getting a pretzel roll and that lemonade. It would be a crime to leave the mall today without getting my fix. I also needed to get a new pair of sneakers to go with my uniform. The only pair that I owned—pink and gray Nikes—couldn't be worn with my uniform. The agency had already told me that I was to wear either white or black footwear. Those pink and gray Nikes, which I'd brought with me to New York, just weren't going to work.

After leaving the mall, I stopped at the grocery store. Qua was coming over after work, and I wanted to cook something so that we didn't have to order out. Ordering out was becoming our norm, and it didn't have to be, being that I could cook, so I had decided to bless him with a meal tonight. He was kind of upset with me for telling him that he couldn't slap the fire out of Tamara's ass the other night. When he told me not to get involved in the fight between Yessenia and Tamara, I hadn't listened. I'd had to let him know that it wasn't the same thing. He was a man, and I understood how upset he was, but a man shouldn't be putting his hands on a female. But when it came to having my girl's back, no one was going to stop me. Shit, he should have just been happy that Tamara had got that ass whupping that she deserved after doing that shit to him.

You would think that she wouldn't have been trying to be messy after what she did, but just like I had been trying to tell them, those bitches weren't wrapped too tight in the head. I'd been kind of tight with my mother when she called and asked me about the incident, as I hadn't told her about it at all. I knew that Tamia must have said something, because my brother didn't gossip about bitch shit. She'd called me like I did something wrong, when it wasn't even my fight, so I was assuming that the little bitch hadn't told her the whole story. I didn't know what was happening with my relationship with my mother, but she was starting to treat me like a stepchild and that bitch like her daughter. The more I thought about it, the more it bothered me. Right then I decided the grocery store was going to have to wait. I drove to my mom's house instead.

When I got to my mom's house, she wasn't even home, and I was pissed that I hadn't called first. Ty and German were chilling in the living room with baby Andrea, who was sitting in her swing, sucking on her pacifier, and watching them play *Call of Duty*.

"Ty, where's Mommy?" I asked his ass, being that he hadn't acknowledged me, because he was playing that damn game.

"I don't know. Pops had the baby, and she was giving him a hard time, so I took her," he said, not even looking at me.

"This little girl is going to be the death of Daddy," I said and laughed, picking her up.

"Well, hello to you too," German said, trying to be funny.

"Don't even try it. You and Ty's ass were all up in that game, acting like I didn't walk in. So don't be all up in my ear now that you've lost the game," I said.

"You're the reason I lost the game, and I didn't need to see you walk in. I smelled you before you even made it to the living room," he smirked.

"What are you trying to say?" I asked, smelling myself.

"Nah, not like that. I only meant that I was distracted because I knew it was you before you even walked in the room," he said, causing me to smile.

"Don't even try it. You lost because my brother served that ass." I laughed. I walked into the kitchen with baby Andrea, and German followed behind me like a lost puppy.

"So, what's up with you and that dude?" he asked, causing me to give him the side eye.

"Why?" I answered his question with one of my own.

"A nigga can't ask?"

"No, a nigga can't ask, because a nigga lost that privilege when he was no longer my nigga."

"That's a lot of nigga in one sentence," he noted and laughed, causing me to smile at his ass.

"German, why are you in here, stunting me? Take your ass back out there and get that ass whupped again," I told him, laughing as I took out a jar of baby food and a baby spoon for Andrea.

"Nah, you're a distraction, so I might as well chill in here with you and the shorty."

"Look, I'm not in the business of tapping your girl's ass, so take your ass and chill with Ty," I told him. I sat down at the kitchen table and began feeding Andrea. German took the seat across from me.

"Nah, I'm good."

German's ass was trying to get me caught up, but it wasn't happening. I didn't care how sexy his ass was looking right now. But I couldn't front; his ass had me nervous as hell. I dropped the spoon I was using to feed baby Andrea, so he got up and picked it up off the floor. He rinsed it off and touched my hand when he handed it back to me, causing me to feel something I shouldn't have been feeling.

"Yeah, I still got it," he said, smirking as he walked out of the kitchen, singing "My Beyoncé." I just laughed at his stupid ass.

After I finished feeding baby Andrea, I gave her a bottle. I put her in the stroller in the living room, because her ass wasn't trying to go to sleep, and I had to go. I signaled to Ty that I was leaving and Andrea was again his responsibility.

"You out?" Ty asked me.

"Yeah, I got shit to do, bighead," I told him.

"Why you rushing off? Let me find out that nigga has you on a curfew," German said, staring at me.

"Never that, boo. I'm about to get my grown woman on," I joked. "Bighead, tell Mommy I came by to talk to her," I said as I walked toward the front door, with German following me again.

"I know I'm on celebrity status with my fine ass, but I don't need security," I said, flirting with him.

"No doubt," he said, then licked his lips as he got all up in my personal space.

"Ewww," I joked, then laughed and pushed him away from me.

When I got to my car, I looked back at the front door. He was still standing there, and he watched me as I got in my car, still laughing at his ass. I guessed tonight was going to be takeout, after all.

I wasn't trying to go to the grocery store now and trying to cook. I had stayed at my mom's house longer than I had expected to, so I would have to make it up to Qua another night. My phone alerted me that I had a text message. At the next light, I checked it. The text was from Qua.

I'm just getting off work, so I'm headed home to shower. I will see you in a few.

I just smiled at the message. I didn't have a chance to respond, because the light had already changed. He didn't usually work on Saturday, but he was picking up extra hours. That was why we had hung out at the bowling alley last night instead of tonight. I knew that once I started working, our time together was going to be limited, but he had told me not to sweat it and had assured me he was always going to make time for me.

When I got home, I went upstairs, stripped out of my clothes, and walked into the bathroom to shower. My mind drifted to German, but I shook that shit off quickly. *He has my ass tripping*, I thought as I got in the shower to handle my business for my night with my boo.

Chapter Twenty-Three

Tamia

I opened the door for Tamara, even though I felt like leaving her ass out there, knocking. I was still pissed at her ass for the stunt she had pulled last night, which had caused me to hear German's mouth about it all night. She was starting to be more trouble than help. I was really regretting having her here, and I was so ready for her to take her ass back down South. Sometimes, I wished that shit was different, but in her defense, I had to say that it wasn't her fault that she was a little off—and so was I—because our mother had been diagnosed with mental illness. It had never stopped her from raising us to the best of her ability, as long as she took her medication. She was good for a long time, but as I got a little older, I noticed a change in her behavior, as well as my dad's. I didn't know then if it had to do with what was going on with her and my dad or if she had stopped taking the medication.

One night, Tamara and I were in our bedroom, watching cartoons, when they started arguing. We shut them out, because them arguing was the norm at our house. He was always doing something to upset her. My mom could be heard yelling about how he had said he wasn't going to step out on her anymore and how she was sick and tired of him cheating on her. He tried to tell her that he wasn't cheating on her, and that if he wanted to cheat, he would have left her when he found out that I wasn't his child. I already knew that, but he was the only father I had known, so to me, he was my father.

I didn't know if his throwing in her face that I wasn't his child after he had acted like my father for seven years triggered something in her, but she started screaming even louder. He kept telling her to calm down. At one point I no longer heard my father's voice, and I started to get worried. I told Tamara to stay in the room, and I ran out to see what was going on. Tears formed in my eyes as I saw my father on the floor, with so much blood. I panicked because my mother was just standing there, with a crazed look on her face. I ran to the next-door neighbors' house to get help.

When all was said and done, my mother was taken into custody for attempted murder, but being that she had a mental disability, she was put in a mental institution, where she'd been for years. I ended up in foster care because when my father got out of the hospital, he took only his real daughter and moved down South, where his mother resided.

"Tamia, Tamia," Tamara called out, bringing me back to the present moment. I wiped the tears from my face. "Are you okay?" she asked me, with a concerned look on her face.

No one knew what I dealt with on a daily basis. I had been through so much while I was growing up that I had made a vow that I would cause just as much hurt to those who hurt me. Tamara was calling my name again, so I had to snap out of it. I hated to show weakness. I put a fake smile on my face and told her that I was okay. She looked at me like she didn't believe me, but I didn't care, because she didn't know half the things I had been through. She did know that I harbored some ill feelings toward her father. He was the only man I knew as Dad, so his leaving me behind really hurt me back then, and it still hurt. I knew it wasn't her fault, and she did find me on social media when she turned sixteen, but I still felt some kind of way toward her because she had got to go with him and I hadn't.

"Tamara, stop staring at me like I'm crazy. I said that I'm okay," I told her.

"I'm not staring. I'm just making sure that you're okay," she responded, rolling her eyes.

"Anyway, I'm going to need for you to chill out with the bullshit, or I'm going to have to send you back down South," I said to her, changing the subject, because she was starting to piss me off.

"Tamia, how many times do you want me to apologize? I told you it was harmless. She just took it the wrong way."

"Tamara, you had your ass all up on him, asking him to show you how to bowl, but it was in a sexual manner, and you know it."

She was looking at me with her hand on her chest, like I was making the shit up, when she knew that was exactly what she had done.

"I don't remember it like that, but, anyway, when are you going to let me come stay with you? I'm tired of being alone in that hotel," she whined, changing the subject, just as I had minutes ago.

"Tamara, you have to give me a few days, because German is tripping right now, and he's really not feeling you after what happened last night," I said, being honest with her.

"He shouldn't be your favorite person right now, with the way he sat drinking and watching his ex like he was in a trance," she blurted out, rolling her eyes.

I didn't even know that anyone had been paying attention, but I had been, and it had been clear that he was jealous as he watched Jakiyah and Qua—the same way he had at the club when he first saw them together.

"Well, I guess you and German were on some stalking shit last night, because you were staring at Qua's ass, drooling like he didn't play you to the left for that same bitch," I said to Tamara, but all she did was laugh, pissing me off.

I didn't find shit funny about it, but it was whatever. *It is time for her to take her crazy ass back to the hotel, before I forget we are sisters*, I thought, then wondered if she had taken her medication today.

Chapter Twenty-Four

Qua

It was finally Friday and quitting time. I couldn't clock out fast enough and get out of the office. I couldn't wait to get home. I didn't have to work tomorrow, so I would be spending the entire weekend with Jakiyah. We hadn't had much time together, being that she was now working. I didn't really see her during the week, but we spent as much time talking on the phone and texting as we could. I smiled at the thought of her, but that smile quickly turned into a frown when I saw that crazy ass Tamara standing near my truck. She had been calling my phone, leaving messages that she needed to talk to me, but I had ignored them all. I swear, she was lucky that I'd been taught never to put my hands on a female, since right now, all I wanted to do was connect my fist to her face. The nerve of her to show up at my job, like the shit was okay.

Her lying ass was supposed to have left and gone home by now.

"Tamara, what the hell are you doing, showing up at my job? I didn't take any of your calls, so that should have told you that I'm not fucking with you like that," I snapped when I reached my truck.

"Qua, I'm sorry for showing up at your job, but like you said, you wouldn't take my calls, and Jakiyah is always with you, except for when you're at work. So I had no other choice but to show up here," she replied.

"I have to say that you're a bold bitch to want to be anywhere near me after what you did to me," I said to her.

"I apologize for what I did. I wasn't trying to hurt you. It's not like we had never had sex before. I just wanted to make Jakiyah not want to be with you. That's why I sent the video," she sobbed. The fact that she had tried to justify what she did with that lame reason made me look at her like she was crazy.

"Tamara, you drugged me, forced me to have sex with you! I need for you to get it through your head that it was fucked up. Nothing you say will make me forgive you. I trusted you, and for you to do some foul shit like that, you're lucky to still be breathing. If I were you, I would get the fuck away from me. Now!" I yelled.

"Qua, please wait and just talk to me," she cried, grabbing my arm to prevent me from getting in my truck. "Qua, listen, I know what I did was wrong, but I need you right now. You see, my sister is threatening to send me back home, but I can't go home. I need to be here so that my baby can be near his or her father."

"Tamara, what does any of that have to do with me? I'm not going to ask you again to get the fuck on before I lose it on your ass," I snarled, pushing her away from my truck.

"Qua, please don't do this to me. I need you, and this baby is going to need you," she yelled. She started to beat on my truck like she was, in fact, crazy.

I tried to grab her, but it was like she was possessed. She started to chant some words that I didn't understand.

"Tamara, stop it," I growled at her, but she just continued.

"Yo, Q, you good?" I heard my coworker Vic yell from across the street.

Before I could answer him, Tamara looked at me with a crazed, glassy look in her eyes, then ran right into the traffic and was hit by an oncoming yellow taxi. I ran over to her in a panic, told her to hold on as I dialed 911. As she lay there, she tried to talk, so I put my ear to her mouth. All I could make out was that she was sorry and that it wasn't her fault, before her head slumped to the side, letting me know that she was gone.

The police arrived minutes later, and I was bugging out as they questioned me. I didn't know how to feel. The whole situation had me on edge, and I was thankful that my coworker had witnessed her running into traffic, without me pushing her, because those officers were acting as if they wanted to put the cuffs on me and convict me on the spot. I called Jakiyah to tell her what had happened so that she could call German and then he could break the news to Tamia. Although I hated Tamara's ass with everything in me, I felt bad for Tamia, and so did Jakiyah, because she was crying on the other end of the phone, with me trying to calm her down.

After about an hour of being questioned, I was finally allowed to leave. I went straight home, even though I was supposed to go to Jakiyah's place. I wasn't feeling up to it. I had so much on my mind right now. I was now thinking that if Tamara really was pregnant with my seed and I had just talked to her there in the parking lot, I could have saved her life. So many thoughts were going through my head; I just needed a few drinks right now to take my mind off what had happened.

I had been home for only about twenty minutes, and I was already on my fifth drink, but I still couldn't get the image of the cab slamming into Tamara's body out of my head. I heard a knock at my door. I knew it was Jakiyah, so I got up to let her in. She had already told me that she was on her way. She'd said that she was worried about me. When we'd talked over the phone earlier, I had started blaming myself for what had happened. I believed that this was my fault and that I could have prevented it if I had tried harder to calm Tamara down, instead of continuing to push her away.

As soon as Jakiyah stepped through the door, she continued to try to convince me that I wasn't responsible for Tamara's actions, but I still felt like there was something I could have done.

"Bae, she said she was pregnant," I slurred.

"She may have or may not have been, but you can't beat yourself up about it. It's unfortunate that she had to lose her life, but this is not your fault. Remember, you're a victim in all of this. You didn't owe her anything," she stressed.

"She was trying to tell me something before she died, but all I could make out was her saying this wasn't her fault."

"Well, we will never know, and you have to stop this. It's over, and there's nothing you could have done," she offered before she kissed me on my lips.

I went upstairs to shower after Jakiyah offered to make us something to eat. Even though I told her that I didn't feel like eating, she insisted. I called my pops to tell him what had happened, before he saw it on the news tonight. My father no longer lived in New York, but I knew he still watched the news, and anytime he saw a shooting in New York on television, he would call to make sure I wasn't the victim. My mother had left my father when I went to college, which didn't surprise me, because they had always had a rocky relationship. He had always been cheating with the kind of women he always told me to steer clear of. My mother now lived in Vermont with her new husband, Donovan. She wanted me to move there with them, but I wouldn't feel comfortable living with either of my parents if they weren't together. I visited them both from time to time, but I would never consider an offer to stay.

After I got out of the shower, I went back downstairs to have dinner with Jakiyah. I thanked her for being here for me and for cooking. She asked me if I had told the officers about what Tamara did to me, and I told her the truth, that I hadn't.

Tamara was already dead, so I hadn't felt that it needed to be mentioned. I'd just told them that she was an ex-girlfriend who had snapped because I didn't want to be with her anymore. I changed the subject. I didn't want to talk about what had happened today anymore. After dinner, we watched television, until she went up to shower. Then we got in bed, and I held her until we both drifted off to sleep.

Chapter Twenty-Five

Tamia

I was so hurt and confused right now. I couldn't, for the life of me, understand why Tamara would take her own life. I knew she cared for Qua, but I didn't know she was that far gone over him to end her life. Had I known, I would not have asked her to come back here to do this for me, and it was eating me up inside. I was hurting because her father had had her body flown down South and had told me that I wasn't welcome at her funeral, so I didn't get to say good-bye to my sister. How could he blame me for her taking her own life? I'd had no idea that she stopped taking her medication. I'd had my suspicions, but I didn't know for sure. I swear, he made me hate him that much more than I already did, and I wished he had died when my mother stabbed his ass.

The only good thing that came out of my sister's death was the fact that German was back to being attentive to my every need. I thought about when my sister had said that I fell in love with German the same way she had fallen for Qua, and it made me think that had I kept it strictly business with German, maybe she would have done the same with Qua and thus would still be here. I was starting to think that maybe it was my fault that she killed herself, because when I sensed that she wasn't taking her medication, I should have said something to her. Tamara and I both had been diagnosed with borderline personality disorder, and for the most part, I did take my medication. I knew that when I didn't, it would always cause problems in my relationship with German. I would always become unstable, and that would have him questioning my sanity.

"Tamia, can I get you anything?" German called from outside the bathroom door.

I was sitting in the bathroom because I needed a breather from him. I wished that he would just leave and hang out with Ty, like he did after work sometimes. I needed some space to think, and he was smothering me right now. I hadn't even had time to sit and mourn my sister in peace. It was really starting to irk me. Although it had felt

good in the beginning to have him back to have
him showing me that he cared, I had had enough
of him not letting me do anything for myself.
For instance, he had offered to call my job to ask
for bereavement leave on my behalf when he
noticed that I hadn't made the call. He'd picked
up my phone to get the number, causing me to
panic and grab the phone and tell him that I
would call myself. He'd looked at me strangely,
but he hadn't say anything.

So I decided that soon I was going to tell him
that I had lost the job when I did not return to
work after the four bereavement days that they
had given me. I was tired of pretending to go
to work every day, anyway, and the manager
at Starbucks was starting to get suspicious of
me; I'd been going there every single day, and
I would just sit there, looking crazy, with no
laptop, book, or even a notebook.

"I'm fine, German. I'll be out in a minute," I
huffed, annoyed.

I got up from sitting at the vanity and got in
the shower to try to take my mind off my sister,
because I felt myself getting depressed. I was
feeling that same feeling I had experienced
when I lost my child all those years ago. After
getting out of the shower, I dragged my feet to
the bedroom with a heavy heart, just wanting

to turn all the lights out, crawl in my bed, and sleep. I heard the doorbell ring and wondered who was visiting at this hour. It wasn't late, but it was going on 9:00 p.m., too late for anyone to be visiting.

"Tamia, someone is at the door for you," German called from downstairs.

I slipped on my cotton pajamas pants that I wore whenever I was on my time of the month. Those were the ones that let German know that sex was off and not even to try to get any. I put on my tank, slipped my feet into my slippers, and headed downstairs to see Mama Smith standing in my living room. As soon as she hugged me, the tears fell from my eyes.

"It's okay, sweetie," she said, gently rubbing my back, walking me over to the sofa.

"I'm sorry. I just miss her so much, and it hurts that my last words to her were me threatening to send her home," I cried, wiping at my tears.

"Sweetie, trust me, she knew that you loved her, so even if the two of you were bickering and fighting, that doesn't outweigh how you felt about her," she soothed.

"Her father didn't even allow me to fly out to say good-bye to her. He knows how much she meant to me, but it didn't stop him from blaming me," I sobbed.

"Tamia, honey, I'm so sorry that you're going through this. I would love to tell you that it gets better, but that would be far from the truth," she said sadly. "I just want you to know that if you need me, call or come by the house. I don't want you walking around feeling like you have no one. I'm here for you, just as you have always been here for me when my daughters haven't, and I want you to know that I really appreciate you," she said.

I really felt better now that she was here. I really needed someone to talk to other than German, because he couldn't really understand. He hadn't lost anyone. She gave me some good advice, told me that I didn't need Tamara's father's permission to visit my sister's grave to say good-bye. She even explained that whatever I felt I needed to say that I didn't get to say to her before, I could say now, and she stated that she talked to her daughter all the time when she visited her grave.

After she left, I went upstairs to the bedroom. German was fresh out of the shower and was in bed, with just his boxers and no shirt. I kind of got distracted and abandoned my earlier thoughts as I lusted over his muscular body and the dick print that was on display.

"Hey, how you feeling?" he asked, looking up from his cell phone and acknowledging me.

"I'm feeling better. And thanks, because I know you called her." I smiled, something I hadn't done in weeks.

"I had to. I didn't know what else to do or say to make you feel better," he admitted.

"I appreciate you, and I understand you did what you felt you needed to do for me, so I'm not mad."

I removed my pajama pants and tank—I had thrown them on only to go downstairs—so I now stood naked. I attempted to put on my nightie, but German stopped me.

"Come here," he said, pulling me into him, kissing me, and causing my nipples to get aroused.

He laid me down on the bed, kissed my neck, and moved down to suck on my now erect nipples, causing me to moan his name. He made his way between my thighs, and I wrapped my legs around the back of his head as he sucked on my pussy, causing me to moan again. My body started convulsing as I pumped uncontrollably, fucking his face until I released my juices. With my legs still on his shoulders, he entered me with full force, causing me some pain, until he slowly pumped in and out of me. I lifted my hips up and down as I rode his dick, meeting him stroke for stroke, screaming out for him to fuck me harder. He obliged by banging my pussy out until we both came together.

"I love you," I said as he collapsed beside me.

"I love you too," he responded, pulling me to him and placing his face in the crook of my neck.

Minutes later, he was lightly snoring, so I closed my eyes and fell asleep too, thankful for this temporary weight off my mind.

Chapter Twenty-Six

Jakiyah

"I'm really starting to believe that you don't have your own place, because you're always here, bighead. What's up, Chanel? German?" I said, rolling my eyes playfully at him.

"Hey, Jakiyah. You know your brother is a mama's boy," Chanel joked.

"So what's German's excuse?" I asked, laughing.

"My excuse is that I be checking for you," German declared, getting all up in my space again.

"Boy, how many times do I have to tell you to fall back?" I asked, punching him in his chest.

"We're about to go out to get something to eat. Do you want to go?" Ty asked me.

"Please?" Chanel whined.

"I guess I can, being that I don't have anything else to do."

"Cool. You can ride with me, shorty," German said, grabbing my hand.

"Release me, punk," I joked, then walked away to go and say hello to my parents and to give baby Andrea a kiss.

I knew I kept putting off talking to my mother, but since I had had time to think about it, I didn't want to come off as a spoiled brat, so I left the notion of a conversation alone for now. We ended up at Outback Steakhouse, where we ordered the Bloomin' Onion, the Aussie Cheese Fries, the wings, and the chicken quesadillas from the starters menu. Chanel and I both ordered a drink called a Naturally Skinny 'Rita, and the shit was so strong that it had my ass feeling tipsy almost immediately, but Chanel seemed to be handling hers like a champ. We were having a good time, too good of a time, if you ask me, because German and I had become flirty friendly right there at the table. Ty kept telling him that Qua was going to fuck him up, and he kept telling Ty that he wasn't worried.

I needed to get control of the situation, but it felt like old times hanging out with German. I didn't know if it had something to do with Tamia being down South for the past week. She was there visiting her sister's grave site and hadn't come back yet. He wasn't uptight, which was how he acted whenever she was around. He was the German that I used to sit up all night talking on the phone with, the one who made me laugh, and would not want to hang up. A lot of those nights I would fall asleep on the phone, because neither of us wanted to be the first to hang up.

When it was time to leave, Ty told German to take me straight home since I had already had two drinks, and I was bound to be down for whatever. I knew that I didn't need that second drink, but I wasn't about to let Chanel outdrink me. I should have told German to drop me off at my man's place, so Qua and I could fuck, because I was tipsy and horny as hell. I looked at German with misplaced lust in my eyes, thinking about doing things to him that shouldn't have even been in my mind, since I knew I was with Qua.

Don't ask me how we ended up at a hotel, with me riding his dick like it belonged to me, because I couldn't remember anything as I threw my head back and bounced up and down on his dick, crying out in pleasure. He kissed me passionately as he grabbed my ass, pumped in and out of me. Feeling his dick pulsating, I knew he was close to releasing, so I tightened my pussy muscles, putting his dick in a vise grip, as I cried out at the explosive orgasm I was having.

He was minutes behind me and let out a loud growl, thrusting hard into me, making sure he released every one of his kids up in me.

My body was spent, but he wasn't finished. He put his face between my legs, softly kissed and sucked on my pussy until I reached another orgasm. Soon my body started to relax, and my legs stopped shaking from having two orgasms back-to-back. By then he was lying on his back, trying to return his breathing to normal. I knew at this point that I had fucked up by giving my body to him, but the way he had me feeling, it was well worth it. We lay in each other's arms, with no words spoken, and both drifted off to sleep.

When I woke up the next morning, I was unsure of where I was, until last night hit me like a Mack truck as I remembered what had taken place between German and me.

"Shorty, I already see it in your eyes. Don't even do it to yourself. I told you you're my Beyoncé, G and J," he said, then kissed my lips.

"German, now is not the time to be joking," I said, feeling like I was on the verge of tears at the many calls that I had missed from Qua last night.

German joking about me being his Beyoncé from the song, "My Beyoncé," by Lil Durk, was cute, but I wasn't his Beyoncé. I belonged to someone else. I didn't want to blame what I did solely on the alcohol. I was still very much attracted to German, and my subconscious knew what I was doing when I was doing it. I wanted to call Qua, but I didn't know if I should call while I was still at the hotel with German, so I opted out and decided to wait until I got home.

The ride to my house was a quiet one. I was lost in my own thoughts, trying to figure out what I was going to tell Qua when he asked me why I didn't answer or return his calls. When I opened the car door to exit, German pulled me over to him and kissed me on my lips, but I pulled away and got out of the car. I wasn't even in the house but for a few minutes when my phone alerted me that I had a text message. It was from German.

G & J.

Ugh, I thought, but at the same time, I couldn't help but smile, because his ass was always playing, knowing I was feeling some kind of way. He didn't have to explain his whereabouts; I did. So I went and sat on the couch, put my head back, and closed my eyes, trying to think of something that Qua would believe.

Chapter Twenty-Seven

Jakiyah

It had been days since I went to the hotel with German, and it was eating me up inside. Qua already felt betrayed by what Tamara had done to him, and he had started to have trust issues. I didn't want to hurt him, but I needed to tell him. Did I want to lose what we had started? No, but like I said, the shit was weighing heavily on my mind. I had never cheated on any man before. German hadn't texted me anymore since that morning, and that was a good thing. Hopefully, he was looking at it the same way as I was: two adults who had loved each other at one time, who were still sexually attracted to each other, and had a moment together, and that was it.

After work, I was meeting Qua downtown, at the Spanish restaurant near his job, so that we could talk. I needed to tell him in public so he'd avoid making a scene. I wasn't going to lie.

When I got to the restaurant, my ass was scared.
I wanted to turn around after I saw him sitting
there, wearing that mad scowl on his face,
which didn't make my panties wet this time. My
stomach was in knots as I got closer to the table
he was sitting at, because his facial expression
never changed. He had on his sanitation jacket,
and I was wearing my scrubs. Both of us had
just got off of work. He had probably had a
stressful day, and now I was about to add to it.

I took the seat across from him. "Hey," I said,
feeling uneasy about the conversation we were
about to have.

"What's up?" he responded with no emotion.

I already knew he was on edge. Men get nervous when a female says, "We need to talk,"
because they're already thinking the worst.

"Something has been bothering me, and I need
to get it off my chest, is all," I said, avoiding eye
contact.

"Speak," he said, his jaw tightening.

"I was hanging out with my brother, his girl,
and German the other night, and I had too much
to drink, clouding my judgment, and I slept with
German," I confessed.

He just sat there looking at me, chewing on
the toothpick that he now had in his mouth. His
stare was intense, causing me to lower my head
in shame.

"So, let me ask you a question. You're sitting here, telling me that the liquor clouded your judgment, causing you to fuck that nigga, right?" he asked, raising his voice, and now I wasn't so sure he wasn't going to cause a scene.

"Yes," I answered meekly.

"Well, why the fuck, when that nigga dropped you off, did you kiss him before getting out of the car? I was missing you, so being that I had to work OT Friday night, I called in the next day to spend some time with you. So you can imagine how fucked up I felt seeing you pull up in his car, and to add insult to injury, you kissed that nigga," he barked.

"Qua, I'm sorry."

"You females always claim you want something real, but when it's right in your face for the taking, you backpedal. Does that shit make any fucking sense?" he asked. "Look, this hooking back up shit is cool, but this isn't what you want, shorty. What we used to have was real, so I didn't mind hooking back up. I fucked up, not realizing that people change. So check this. I'm not going to keep you clearly where you don't want to be."

"Qua, it's not like that. Yes, I messed up, but that's not what I want. I want you. That's why I'm telling you the truth . . . so we can move on," I stressed.

"So, it's that cut and dry, huh? I'm feeling you, but I'm not about to be in no competition with no nigga. I don't have to be."

"I'm not asking you to compete with him. It was a mistake, one that I promise will never happen again," I said, being honest.

"How can you be so sure?" he questioned. "He's your brother's best friend, so he's going to always be around."

"I know because I can admit that I messed up, and I'm sitting here, telling you. If I had any intentions on fucking him again, I would have just kept it on the low," I said.

He didn't respond. He just sat there like he was seriously thinking about whether he should forgive me or not. I started nervously shaking my leg, wondering if this was the end before it even started. I didn't want to lose him but would respect his decision without any hard feelings. I was also wondering whether, if he didn't forgive me, I would lash out at him or just get up and walk away, defeated. My emotions were starting to get the best of me as I waited for him to respond, because I hated not knowing, and his staring at me wasn't helping at all. It was like he was trying to ascertain if I was telling the truth or not about sleeping with German again.

"Yo, what are you eating?" he asked, breaking his silence.

So he was going to make me stress about whether we were going to be together or not. Well, I had to say that he wouldn't be Qua if he didn't, so I decided to just go with the flow. Anyway, what other choice did I have?

"Just get me the guava-glazed *pollo*, but instead of the coconut rice, get me black beans with rice please," I replied. Anybody who knew me knew that my greedy ass wasn't about to turn down a meal.

When he got back to the table with the food, I wasted no time digging in. Rather than eating, he sat there and watched me. I wanted to ask why he was staring at me as I ate, but I too was afraid, I thought. He finally started eating his own food, so we just sat and ate in silence. But inside, I was dying. I was thinking that we were having our last meal together. After we finished eating, he cleared the table and then sat back down, with a real serious look on his face.

"Listen, we all make mistakes. I made the mistake of trusting Tamara, just for her to do that foul shit. And then I trusted you, and you turned around and did this foul shit to me. I don't know if I'm going to regret this, but I'm not ready to lose what I know we had and what we can continue to have. Call me a sucker for love, but I'm all in. But just know that I won't be a fool for love. A mistake is just that, but trust, don't let that shit happen again. Because I will not forgive you again."

"Thank you," I said and bawled. I tried to stop the tears from falling, but to no avail.

"I said I forgive you," he joked, wiping my tears. And then he kissed me on my lips.

When I say the tears were falling, they were *falling*. His very first words after we finished our meal had had me convinced that he was going to kick me to the curb. So, these tears were shocked, happy tears, and I didn't care how I looked to anyone right now. The onlt thing that mattered was that I didn't lose him, and it felt like hitting the lottery or some shit. He told me he would call me when he got home, and I was a bit disappointed. I had expected him to tell me to follow him back to his place. He had forgiven me, but I understood that I was still in the doghouse, and I didn't like it.

When I got home, I was in a funk, so I went upstairs to shower and then got in the bed and turned on the TV, feeling some kind of way, because Qua still hadn't called. Did he really forgive me? I thought as I flicked through the TV channels, really not caring what was on the damn television. Just as I was about to say fuck it and just go to sleep, my phone alerted me that I had a text message. I hoped it wasn't German. He was part of the reason I was spending the night alone, instead of with Qua. I grabbed my phone. He had picked the wrong time to text, and his ass was going to get some choice words. But when I opened the text message, the biggest smile formed on my face. I read the text from Qua. In it he told me to open the front door. I ran to the front door, and when I opened it, he was standing there with roses in his hands. My tears fell again.

"Are you going to let me in?" he asked, smiling.

I nodded.

He came in, grabbed me in a bear hug, and held me tight.

"I'm sorry," I whispered in his ear.

"I know," he responded, releasing me and handing me the roses.

"Thank you," I said. Then I took the roses into the kitchen to put them in a vase.

We didn't sleep together that night, but I was happy that he stayed the night, and he held me in his arms as we slept. That might mean nothing to some, but it meant a lot to me, and I really was thankful that he was so forgiving.

The next morning, Qua and I awoke early. I wanted to visit my mom today but feared that I would run into German, because he and Ty didn't know how to chill somewhere other than at my mother's house. I was in no mood to have the morning-after conversation with him, and it wasn't necessary, because sleeping together would never happen again.

My mother had told me that Tamia was back and had been acting strange, and she thought it had to do with her not knowing how to channel her feelings about losing her sister. I knew exactly how it felt to lose a sister, so I'd be the first to say that there wasn't a day that went by when I didn't think of Cydney. So I could image what Tamia was going through. Some days I just wanted to sit in a dark room and just cry, so I honestly could understand why she seemed stranger than usual. She probably had a million emotions running through her right now, and she had no idea how to turn them off.

Qua walked back into the bedroom just then, interrupting my thoughts. He was fully dressed. "I'm about to head out. I'll be back around eight p.m. to pick you up for the movies," he said.

I didn't want him to leave, but he said that he needed to handle some business. I wanted to ask him, "What business?" but I didn't. I just kissed him, told him okay, and followed him downstairs to lock the door behind him. After he left, I heard my phone ringing, so I ran upstairs to get it. I didn't recognize the number, but I still answered the call.

"Hello," I answered.

"Hello. Can I speak with Jakiyah Smith?" the caller said.

"This is she. Who's calling?"

"Hello, Jakiyah. This is Detective James. I got your message, so I did some digging into Andris's background. Also, we were able to get a partial plate number off the second car, so we are working on that. Hopefully, we should know who the car is registered to by tomorrow. What I want to do is come out tomorrow, at about two p.m., to your parents' home to see if any of these names from Andris's past are familiar to any of you."

"Thank you so much for not giving up on my sister's case."

"Just doing my job. And I promised your parents that I would find whoever is responsible for your sister's death. I plan on keeping that promise," he stated.

"Thanks again, and I will see you tomorrow," I said, then ended the call.

As soon as I hung up, I called my mother to let her know what the detective had said. I asked her to call Ty and tell him to stop by tomorrow at 2:00 p.m. I prayed that he would leave his sidekick, German, at home.

Chapter Twenty-Eight

Tyhiem

A nigga was tired after being up all night, fucking with Chanel. It seemed that ever since I told her that we were exclusive and I was leaving all those other chicks alone, she had been riding my dick every night. Trust, I wasn't complaining, but she was draining my ass and had me not wanting to do anything else. She had been staying at the crib every night and leaving in the mornings to go home to get ready for work.

"What's up, Mom?" I asked as I walked into the living room, where her and my pops were sitting, watching TV. "Hey, Pops. You good?"

"I'm good, son. Just waiting on this detective, praying for some good news," he said.

"No, he didn't kick my ass. Well, I'm here, so I'll call you later, sis." Jakiyah could be heard saying as she walked into the living room.

She said hello to everybody, but I was giving her ass the side eye, because I knew she and German's ass didn't go home that night. Her car was still parked when I came to my mom's house the next morning to drop something off.

"Boy, I'm grown," she said, giving me the side eye, because she knew exactly why I was giving her that look.

She had better be glad that damn detective knocked on the door right then, because I was going to blow her up right in front of Mom and Pops. I let him in, and we all greeted him as he took a seat on the sofa.

He got right down to business. "Okay, so like I explained to your daughter, Jakiyah, I did some digging into Andris's background. It seems that last year he started a relationship with a female named Tori Kelly, and according to her, they were still together at his time of death. She also stated that she didn't know that he was married. I spoke with Andris's mother, and she confirmed the relationship and the fact that Ms. Kelly knew nothing about Andris being married. She also stated to me that Andris was involved with a woman in his past who was kind of off mentally. She said that when Andris tried to break it off with this woman, she tried to stop him from leaving by attacking him, and she slipped and fell down the stairs, losing her unborn child."

He went on. "The reason I mention this woman is that your son, Tyhiem, has an ongoing case for the murder of Andris, so maybe he can give this information to his lawyer to look into this woman. She was stalking and harassing his mother about his whereabouts for a month before his death. I don't have reason to believe that she was involved with my case, but she can very well be questioned in the murder of Andris." he said. He had been addressing my parents the whole time, but he handed me a piece of paper with information on it after he ripped it out of his notepad.

I looked at the information on the paper. I was shocked and confused at the same time. I clenched my fist, crushing the paper in the process. I could hear my mom, dad, and sister asking me what was wrong, but I ignored them, just as I ignored the detective, who had asked if I knew the woman. The wheels started spinning in my head. Now it was all coming back to me. When I saw her the day that I was arrested at my club, I had just come downstairs from my office to go announce the start of the showcase. It was Tamara, Tamia's sister, and she was standing by the bathroom. There was no line, but she was just standing there, and at the time, I thought nothing of it. That was why, when I saw her at the bowling alley, I thought she looked familiar, but I hadn't been able to place her until now. That bitch had probably started flirting with me because she knew I was trying to figure out where I remembered her from.

"Tyhiem!" my mother yelled. She got my attention.

"Mom, I'm good," I said. I wasn't going to tell them anything in front of the detective. I tried to sit as calmly as possible as I listened to him finish up.

"So, we don't have confirmation on the plate number as of yet, but we do have a few leads. I will be in contact with you in a few days," he stated, causing a look of disappointment to appear on Jakiyah's and my parents' faces.

We had thought he was going to at least have the name of the person to whom the car belonged, but he didn't, and I was ready for him to go so that I could talk to my family. After Jakiyah let him out, she came back and sat down, looking defeated.

"Look at this shit," I said, handing her the paper. She took a look and gasped.

"What is it?" my mom and pops asked at the same time.

Jakiyah handed the paper to them. They gave it a glance. My mother had a confused look on her face, but my father had the same reaction that I had. Anger.

"The night at the bowling alley, when Tamia introduced me to her sister, she looked familiar to me, but I couldn't place her. When I saw that slip of paper with Tamia's name on it, it clicked almost instantly where I had seen Tamara before. The night I was arrested at the club, Tamara was there, standing near the bathroom. I think those bitches set me up."

"What reason would that chile have to set you up?" my mom asked, pissing Jakiyah off.

"Well, that's what we're going to find out," Jakiyah snapped.

"Well, she's not going to come out and admit it," my pops added.

"We have to trap her. So you need to call German. We're going to need him on this," Jakiyah said.

My mother still didn't believe Tamia would do something like murder Andris and set me up. And to be honest, I didn't know whether it was true, either, but I needed to find out. This case didn't look to be going in my favor, so if I could clear my name, I was willing to do whatever. Although I hadn't had any gunpowder on my hands when I was arrested at the club, the district attorney could argue that I had gloves on. The gun was registered in my name, and I had a motive at the time of the murder. Since all the evidence pointed at me, proving my innocence was an uphill climb. Therefore, I was willing to do anything. We all agreed not to talk to anyone about this. As much as my mother cared for Tamia, she cared for me more, so she was on board.

Chapter Twenty-Nine

German

"Are you sure?" I asked Ty as my jaw tightened. I couldn't believe what he was telling me. I wasn't upset with him—he was my best friend, and I was riding with him regardless—but I still wanted to be sure.

"G, man, I don't know. All I know for a fact is what the detective said about her history with dude, how she's been stalking his mother and quizzing her about his whereabouts, and the fact that her sister was in the club that night. Why she would frame me, I have no idea, but I need you on this," he stressed.

"What do you need me to do, bro?" I asked him.

"Well, we all know that I don't have any cameras in my office, but you can have a conversation with her and let on that I put one there months ago and forgot. You could state

that the police officers didn't even notice. On
Saturday you can bring her out to the club,
after planting the bug in her head that I'm
going to look at the camera in the office that
I forgot was even there. I will handle it from
there," Ty said, convinced that she was going
to take the bait.

I rubbed my temples. This was a lot to take
in, but I was rocking with my boy. I was somewhat stressed out. Who the hell was I living
with for all these years? She'd lied about having a sister, and she had never told me about
Andris being her ex-boyfriend or even about
being pregnant before. Her ass had come back
acting all crazy and shit, and I didn't know if
it had to do with missing her sister or with the
fact that she had lost her job, but this shit was
beginning to be too much. I gave Ty dap and
left up out of his mom's crib to go to the bar.
I wanted to get a drink before heading home
and putting this plan in motion. I was hoping
it worked, because I needed to know the truth.

When I got home, Tamia was sitting on the
sofa, watching *Mob Wives*, so I went and took
a seat next to her, looking stressed out. I was
getting into acting mode.

"What's wrong?" she asked, never taking her
eyes off the television.

"I'm good. I was just thinking about something," I said.

"And what is that?" she asked, now giving me her attention because a commercial was showing.

"It's no big deal, just something that Ty mentioned about his case that has me hoping it works in his favor," I said.

"Did his lawyer say something that might get him off?" she asked, no longer caring about her show.

"Nah, he just remembered that he installed one of those mini cameras above the inside of his office door and that the police didn't even notice. He said that after the club closes on Saturday, he was going to take a look at it to see if anything on the tape can prove that he's innocent, before handing it over to his lawyer," I told her.

"So why is he just remembering now?" she asked.

"He said Chanel was telling him about her cousin using a nanny cam, and that's when he remembered the Minicam that he installed behind the I'M THE BOSS sign above the inside door to make sure that none of the employees entered his office when he wasn't around," I lied, making up shit off the top of my head.

"I hope it clears him. I like Ty and would hate to see him go down for something he didn't do," she said, making me think that maybe she was innocent . . . until she spoke again. "So, are we going to the club on Saturday?"

"Do you want to go? Because I think that Jakiyah and Qua are going to be there, and I don't want no problems at the club," I said, trying to convince her to change her mind.

"I want to go, and I'm not thinking about them. I just want to go out and have a good time," she responded. I hoped she didn't see the disappointment on my face.

"Okay. So I guess we're going," I said, getting up.

I went into the bedroom, pulled my shirt over my head, and removed my jeans and boots before stepping into the bathroom to take a shower. I swear, I didn't want to believe that she would do this, and if she did, I was confused as to why she would set him up. It just wasn't making sense to me. After my shower, I called Ty and let him know that we would be at the club on Saturday. Then I got in bed and called it a night because my head was banging behind this shit. Tamia had been sleeping downstairs for the past few days, so I didn't expect her to be joining me, which was a good thing. I didn't feel like sleeping with the enemy, if, in fact, she was.

When I got up for work the next morning, my head was still banging. I really hadn't got any sleep, because the shit was weighing on my mind heavily. I took two Advil before getting ready for work, as that was the only way I was going to be able to get through the day. Tamia was still sleeping peacefully on the couch, hugging her pillow, so I just grabbed my keys and headed out without waking her to let her know I was leaving.

I couldn't seem to focus at work today, but I made it through half the day. When I was on lunch, sitting in my truck, really not feeling like going to get something to eat, I decided to give Jakiyah a call. I didn't think that she was going to answer, but she did.

"Hey, German," she answered dryly.

"Did I catch you at a bad time?" I asked her.

"Nope. Just running some errands for my patient. What's up?"

"I forgot you started working. How's it going?"

"It's going," she offered.

I could tell that she didn't really want to be having a conversation with me, but it didn't stop me from engaging her in conversation until she said she had to go.

"You know we never got to talk about what happened between us," I put out there.

"German, aren't you at work?" she asked, letting out an annoyed sigh.

"Yeah. I'm on break, sitting in my truck, so I'm good to talk," I told her.

"Well, there really isn't anything to talk about. It happened, and it's over," she stated.

"I agree, but I don't want our friendship ruined because of what happened."

"German, I don't think that we can be friends after what happened, because I didn't feel right not telling Qua what happened. He knows, and I don't think he is going to be comfortable with us having a friendship, being that we crossed the friendship line already," she admitted.

"Wow. Are you serious right now? We've always been friends before anything," I said, a little disappointed in her.

"German, we can still be cordial. I just don't think that he's going to feel comfortable with us hanging out again."

I understood that she and Qua had a history, but they hadn't been back together long enough for him to be telling her who she could kick it with. I was a little bothered that she was going along with it, but what could I say?

"Jakiyah, I'm not going to say that I'm not bothered by what you just said, but trust that I will respect it. Enjoy the rest of your day," I told her, then ended the call. My damn headache had returned.

Chapter Thirty

Tamia

I was upstairs, trying to find something to wear to the club, when German walked into the room. He wanted to know if I really wanted to go out tonight, because he was tired. I told him that I was sure that I wanted to go out, and he had me starting to wonder why the hell he really didn't want to go out. He never missed hanging out at the club with Ty, so he had me thinking something had happened between the two of them.

"Did something happen between you and Ty?" I asked him. I needed to know.

"Ty and I are cool. I just worked all week, and I'm kind of tired," he answered.

"Well, we don't have to stay long. I just want to get out of the house," I told him, because I wasn't about to stay home.

I needed to be at the club tonight, and I needed to find a way to get to this mini camera that Ty's ass just so happened to remember that he installed. German was dragging his feet, so I went into the bathroom to take a shower. We were going to the club whether he wanted to or not. After I showered, I didn't get all dressed up in my normal club attire, because I was on a mission. I wore some black leggings, a black tank with a scooped neckline, and some pumps. Simple but still cute.

We had been at the club for about forty-five minutes now, and I'd been waiting for German to come back from the bathroom for about ten of those minutes. I saw Jakiyah when I first got to the club, but she had disappeared too, so I was guessing she'd gone out on the dance floor. I didn't know if I should attempt what I had come to do without knowing everyone's whereabouts, but I was anxious, and the more I just sat here, the more anxious I got. I honestly doubted if anyone would be up in the office, so I gulped down the rest of my drink and got up to handle my business. German had stressed that he wasn't feeling well, so the quicker I took care of this, the quicker we could go home.

I headed up to the office. I stood in front of the office door, looking around to make sure no one was watching me, before I turned the knob and entered the office. *Ty wouldn't need a damn mini camera if he stopped leaving his door unlocked*, I thought to myself as I felt around for an office chair, which I intended to stand on. I didn't want to turn the light on, because I was sure that Ty would notice the light if he happened to look in the direction of his office. Just as I put my hand on one of the office chairs, the door opened and the light came on, causing me to panic slightly.

"Tamia, what are you doing up here?" German asked me.

"I—I just came up here to use the phone," I stuttered, caught off guard.

"You need to use the phone to call who?" he asked, walking farther into the office, looking at me like he didn't believe me.

"Why is that important? You're acting like I came up here to rob the place or some shit," I responded, getting defensive.

"Tamia, I'm going to give you one last chance to tell me why you came up here to Ty's office," he said in a tone that let me know that he was serious.

"German, I don't know what the big deal is. I just wanted to use the fucking phone," I spat, walking around him to leave the office. My heart started beating fast when I opened the door and found Jakiyah and Ty standing there. I took a step back into the office.

"Ty, what's going on?" I asked him.

"Why don't you tell me what's going on, starting with why you're up here in my office?" he barked, which caused me to walk closer to German.

"Ty, just like I told German, I didn't think it was a big deal to come into your office to use the phone."

"Stop lying, bitch!" Jakiyah yelled, trying to get to me, but Ty stopped her.

"I thought you would be woman enough to tell the truth, but I guess that would be asking too much of you. If you were searching for the video, I already looked at it, and I saw what you did. So again, are you going to be honest and tell German what you did?" Ty said, holding up the mini camera that I had come to take.

I started to shake my head. My nervousness was now turning into anger, and I started to lash out at him, because he had just pissed me off.

"So, what you want to hear me say is that I killed Andris. You're damn right I killed his ass.

He deserved it, and if I could do it all over again, he would still be dead!" I shouted.

"Tamia, what the hell do you mean, you killed Andris? What reason did you have to kill Cydney's husband?" German asked me, in disbelief.

"He wasn't always Cydney's husband. He used to love me, and he's the reason I lost my baby," I cried out.

"Tamia, what the hell are you talking about?" German asked, getting impatient.

"Andris was my boyfriend, until he met Cydney. He told me he was leaving me, and I begged him to stay for his child and me. He told me he would take care of the baby, but he was in love with her, and that's who he wanted to be with," I revealed. "I tried to stop him from leaving, and I lost my balance, fell down the stairs, and lost my unborn child. He didn't even stay at the hospital long enough to know that I had lost the baby."

I went on. "So, yes, when I saw him show up at the bitch's burial—when he didn't even show up for me when I lost our child—I made sure to make him pay. Once I tracked him down, I followed him to the house we used to share together and shot him multiple times, until he took his last breath."

"So what reason did you have to frame Ty?" German asked, grabbing me like he wanted to hurt me.

"Get your fucking hands off of me," I snarled. "You have always been so fucking gullible that you never knew that I was sleeping with your best friend. Don't look so surprised. Why do you think I was always over his mother's house so much? After I found out that I was pregnant with his baby, I wanted to be a family—just me, him, and the baby. But he said he wasn't ready and promised me that if I got the abortion, we could tell you that we were going to be together."

I continued. "Once I got the abortion, he told me that we could no longer see each other, and that if I told you, you wouldn't take my word over his. I was so upset that I befriended his mother. I decided that once she trusted me, I was going to take her life to let him know how it felt to lose someone you love. But I couldn't do it, because I had really started to love her as my own mom. So, when I heard that Andris had killed Cydney . . . What better revenge than to kill Andris and frame the grieving brother?"

When I finished speaking, Jakiyah attacked me. Ty pulled her off me, but German just stood there, looking like he wanted to cry, being the punk that I knew he was.

"You dirty bitch. I hope you rot in prison!" she yelled, trying to get out of Ty's grasp.

"Jakiyah, I'll be a dirty bitch, but you should ask your perfect boyfriend about me. He's walking around like he doesn't remember me, but trust, he used to love me too. He's just another fucking man who needs to be removed from this world, and had my sister not fallen in love with him, he would be dead too," I spat at her.

"You're a crazy bitch, but you're a stupid bitch too, because we set your ass up and you fell for it. There was never a tape, but we've got one now. So thank you, dumb ass," she said, smirking at me and pointing to the camera that has been set up in a corner of the room.

I couldn't believe that they had set me up, and that German had helped them do it, with his weak ass. Now I didn't feel sorry for sleeping with his best friend for almost the entire relationship. *Fuck him*, I thought as I was being taken away in cuffs.

Chapter Thirty-One

Jakiyah

Tamia's ass had turned out to be crazy, just like I had said her ass was. I wasn't going to lie. I was thankful that my mother's life had been spared, because this bitch had said that she was going to kill her. I couldn't believe that Ty had been fucking with her behind German's back, and I had no idea what was going to happen between them. I wanted to reach out to German, but after I told him that we could no longer be friends, I didn't know if he would even speak to me at this point.

I didn't even get a chance to ask Qua what in the hell the psycho was talking about, because after Ty closed the club, I followed him to my parents' house, where we'd been ever since. My mother was really hurt behind what Tamia did. She had really cared for Tamia and had had no idea she was just a pawn in her sick game. We were scared to leave her since we didn't know if Tamia was going to get bail or not. Thus both Ty and I would be staying at my parents' house until it was all figured out.

I went into the living room, where Ty was sitting up, playing a game that I was about to interrupt, because I needed some answers from him. He looked up from the game with his "I'm not in the mood" face on, but I didn't care.

"So, do you want to tell me why you were sleeping with German's girl behind his back?" I asked him.

"The same reason you slept with him behind your dude's back," he responded, being sarcastic.

"Well, I doubt if it's the same reason, because I can admit that I was intoxicated, and it happened only once," I said to him.

"Well, she lied. I wasn't sleeping with her like that, and it happened only, like, three times before she pulled that 'I'm pregnant' bullshit. I told her that it wasn't mine. She was still sleeping with G, and I wasn't about to let her blame that shit on me. Yes, I told her what she wanted to hear until she got rid of it, and then I stopped fucking with her, like she said."

"So, what are you going to do about your friendship with German?"

"I'm not going to do him like you did. We're boys and will always be boys," he said, making me feel some kind of way.

"You can't be serious. Again, not the same thing. I can't continue to be friends with him like that after fucking up and sleeping with him. Qua is not going to go with that 'We are just friends' bullshit after what happened."

"Whatever. Grab the other controller so I can kick your ass in some boxing. I need to let off some steam," he said, trying to hand me the controller, which I kindly declined.

"I'll pass. I'm going to take a shower and talk to my boo until I pass out, bighead. If you're bored or need to release some stress, you better call Chanel and have her come over or go to her house. Mom and Dad are good, and if I need you, I will call you."

"Nah, I'm good," he said, dismissing me.

I went upstairs to my old bedroom, pulled out something to sleep in before going to the linen closet to get a washcloth and towel. I headed into the bathroom and took a shower. After I got out of the shower, I couldn't help but wonder if German was good, so I dried off and called him. I knew I should have just left that shit up to Ty to fix, but both of them were stubborn and would not reach out to the other. I waited for him to answer, but the voice mail picked up instead. I decided to send him a text message, to see if he would respond.

Hey, German. I was just texting you to see if you were okay.

I was going to call Qua while I waited for German to respond, but he texted right back.

I'm good. It's just fucked up that Ty would do some sucker shit like that and not say shit to me. He didn't even call me to offer me an apology.

My fingers flew on my phone, and then I hit SEND.

Well, we're at my mom's house. Why don't you come by tomorrow, so we can all sit down and talk?

I don't know right now, but if I decide to come through, I will let you know, German texted back.

I shrugged. Okay, I texted.

I knew he was hurt behind this. Ty was my brother, but he was wrong when it came to this shit. It was kind of late, almost two in the morning, and I knew Qua had worked yesterday, so he was probably sleeping by now. I still decided to call. I wasn't going to be able to sleep without getting some answers about Tamia's accusations. As big as New York was, you would think it was a small town with limited hookups, the way our small circle was sharing.

In my defense, both men were familiar territory, but Ty's ass didn't have to go behind German's back and hook up with Tamia After all, Ty already had plenty of chicks, including Chanel. My boo didn't answer, so our conversation would have to wait until tomorrow. I called it a night and lay down on my bed, then turned on the television. At some point, I dozed off during *Martin* reruns.

When I woke up the next morning, I handled my hygiene, then went downstairs to join my mother and baby Andrea in the kitchen. My mother was making Sunday breakfast before heading out to church with my dad and li'l mama. She invited me to go to church, but nope, I had enough of her dragging me to church when I was younger. I believed in God, and that was enough for me.

"How are you feeling this morning?" I asked her as I took a seat at the table.

"I'm feeling okay. I'm going to pray for Tamia today in church," she responded, catching me off guard.

We all needed prayer, but I didn't know if I'd be praying for the person who had attempted my child's downfall. She looked at me, expecting me to argue with what she had just said, but I didn't even bother to say anything, other than that she should pray for me too. I heard someone moving about in the living room, so I went in to see who it was. It was Ty. He had never made it upstairs to his bedroom last night.

"Good morning, bighead. Mom cooked breakfast, so go take care of your stinky breath and wash your face," I told him, laughing.

I could hear my phone ringing from the kitchen, so I rushed back there to answer the call, already knowing it was my boo because of the ringtone.

"Hello," I answered.

"Good morning. I see I missed a call from you. What's up?" he asked me.

"I needed to talk to you about something last night. Do you want to come to my mom's house for breakfast, and we can talk after?" I asked him.

"As long as it's not one of those talks where you're breaking a nigga's heart again," he joked.

"No, I won't be breaking any hearts this morning. It's Sunday."

We both laughed.

"I'll see you in a few," he said. He ended the call after I told him okay.

"Mom, Qua is coming by for breakfast. Is that okay?" I said, knowing it wasn't a problem.

"No problem, honey," she responded, taking the biscuits out of the oven.

She had a nice little spread going, and I couldn't wait to dig in. She had made eggs, grits with cheese, pancakes, hash browns, bacon, sausage, salmon cakes, and biscuits, and there were fresh strawberries. If I missed anything about being home, Sunday breakfast was one of those things.

Qua arrived twenty minutes later. I refreshed Mom's and Dad's memory of him before setting the table. Ty was in the kitchen, feeding baby Andrea eggs and apple sauce, while he waited for the food to be placed on the table so that we could say grace and get our eat on. After breakfast, Mom, Dad, and baby Andrea left for church, Ty went upstairs, and Qua helped me clear the table while I washed the dishes.

"Jakiyah, I'm out. Later, Qua," Ty said, walking into the kitchen.

"Okay. I'm going to call you later. I need to talk to you," I told him.

I locked the door after Ty left and went back into the kitchen.

Qua grabbed me from behind. "What do you need to talk to me about?" he asked.

"So, you knew what went down at the club last night. So, anyway, Tamia admitted to being the one who killed Andris and to setting Ty up. After she admitted all of that, she made a few more accusations."

"Like what?" he asked, pulling me into the living room. We both sat down.

"Well, she told German that she's been sleeping with Ty for their entire relationship," I told him.

"Are you serious?" he asked.

"Well, that's not all she said. She also said that you used to be in love with her too, and you're walking around, acting like you don't remember her."

"What? I don't know that chick," he said with a disgusted look on his face.

"I have no idea where she says she knows you from and how it came about that you were in love with her, because she never said. She got upset with how things went down, so she blew up Ty's spot by telling German, and then she lashed out at me, like, 'Ask your man, Qua, about me, because he used to love me. And had Tamara not fallen in love with him, his ass would be dead too.'"

"I have no idea who she is, and maybe the reason she didn't say where she knew me from is that she was bullshitting you," he said, making sense.

I wasn't about to dwell on what Tamia had said, and to be honest, I believed Qua. Her crazy ass had probably just been trying to get under my skin.

Chapter Thirty-Two

Qua

Jakiyah was staying with her parents until they found out what was going on with Tamia as far as whether she would receive bail or not. So, what that meant for me was that I had to take my ass home, even though I didn't want to leave. It was getting late, and it didn't help that her mother kept coming downstairs to make sure Jakiyah didn't try to sneak me in her room. We both had to work tomorrow, so I wouldn't have spent the night even if her mom said it was okay. But what I would say was that if Mom Dukes wasn't walking back and forth, I would have taken Jakiyah upstairs for a quickie.

"I wish you didn't have to leave," Jakiyah whined as she walked me to the door.

"Even if I didn't have to leave, your security detail was going to make sure that I did," I said, referring to her mother.

"Yeah, my mom doesn't play no staying over." She laughed.

I held on to her, just taking in her scent, really not ready to leave, but I had to get up early for work.

"Let me get out of here before I end up kidnapping your ass," I told her. I kissed her neck before releasing her.

"I'm going to try to stop by your place after work tomorrow," she said, then kissed my lips.

"Cool. Just call and let me know if you're coming through or not, because, tired and all, I might hook something up in the kitchen for you," I called over my shoulder as I headed to my car.

"I'm coming," she yelled, laughing, before closing the door.

Once I got home, I ended up talking to Jakiyah until, like, 1:00 a.m., which caused me to be late for work the next morning, so I had to meet the truck en route. My supervisor was pissed, but I didn't give a fuck, because my reason for being late was well worth it. He should have appreciated the fact that I hadn't left him hanging by taking days off after that shit happened with Tamara. My mental state had been fucked up then and was still fucked up behind that shit, but I still came to work faithfully. I had to work an hour longer than I normally would have, so

I was getting off at 3:00 p.m., instead of my normal quitting time of 2:00 p.m.

After work, I headed to pick up a few things so that I could make dinner, as promised, for Jakiyah. I thought about what Jakiyah had said about Tamia insisting that I used to love her. I was bugging out about it, because I really didn't know that chick. I knew that people might not believe me, but I could honestly say that I didn't know her ass from a can of paint, and I was wondering why she would even put me in that mess. Also, her saying that if her sister hadn't loved me, I would be dead was fucking with me. So, did that mean that Tamara could have killed my ass that night, had she not had feelings for me? That was the way I was taking it.

Jakiyah hit me up to tell me that Tamia was being held without bail. That was a good thing, because that chick had turned out to be fucking crazy and didn't need to be on nobody's streets. I was now leaving the grocery store, so I was about to head home and get my chef on. I was going to make steak and potatoes over some yellow rice.

When Jakiyah got to my crib, she had to take over because my ass trying to get my chef on had left. I didn't know what had happened. I had pulled up a recipe for the steak on Google, but for some reason, the steak wasn't tender. In fact, it had a rubbery taste to it.

"Go on and clown a nigga, because it's written all over your face." I laughed at her trying to hold her laughter in.

"I'm not going to kick my man when he's down." She laughed. "But how the hell do you jack up making steak, after talking like you were a master chef?" she asked, still laughing.

"Well, I have to admit that I exaggerated just a little on the chef thing, but don't a nigga get points for trying? I should have kept it real and just made my specialty," I told her.

"And what would that specialty be?" She laughed.

"I can make the hell out of some Oodles of Noodles with cut-up hot dogs and my special seasoning," I said, causing her to really have a laughing fit.

"I need for you to promise that you will never make me your specialty," she said, shaking her head.

"Don't knock it until you've tried it."

"Nah, I'm good on that, boo," she said, then walked away to finish what I had started.

Jakiyah slayed dinner, so I did the dishes while she picked a movie that we were going to watch. I had promised her that I would give her a foot massage for saving my dinner, so she was getting a movie and a massage for her services.

I had just finished drying the dishes and putting them away when I heard my phone ringing, but before I made it out of the kitchen, Jakiyah was bringing me my ringing phone. I checked the screen. If it was one of my boys, I was going to let the call go to voice mail and get up with him later. I didn't recognize the number, so I let the shit go to voice mail, but my phone rang again and displayed the same unknown number. I answered because Jakiyah was giving me the side eye.

"Speak," I said into the phone, annoyed that I was being interrupted.

"Hello. This is Savannah. Can I please speak with Quameek?"

"This is Quameek speaking," I responded, even more annoyed, since I did not know who this chick was who was calling my phone.

"Quameek, I'm Donovan's niece, and I'm calling you to inform you that my uncle and your mother were both involved in a car accident this afternoon. Your mother is in surgery right now, as well as my uncle," she said calmly, but I could tell she was trying not to cry.

"What hospital?" I asked in a panicked voice, alarming Jakiyah, who was now standing by my side.

"They are both here at Springfield Hospital. I know that you live out of town, so I'm going to be here for both of them, along with other family members. So if you can't make it, I will keep you updated on their condition," she said, no longer able to hold in her tears. I could hear it in her voice that she was crying.

"Nah, I'm only five hours away, so I will be there. And thank you," I said. I ended the call, feeling like I was about to lose it.

"What happened?" Jakiyah asked, with a worried look on her face.

"My mom and her dude were in a car accident, so I have to get to Vermont," I told her as I walked out of the kitchen and up the stairs to pack a few things.

"I'm going with you," I heard her say, not even realizing that she had followed me upstairs.

I told her that she didn't have to go with me, being that she had just started working, but she shut me down, telling me she was good, as I wiped at the tears that fell quickly. My mother was my heart, and if anything happened to her, I didn't know what I would do. So to hear Jakiyah say that she would drop everything to be there with me pulled at a nigga's heartstrings. Jakiyah drove the five hours to Vermont. I was happy to have her in my life, because I wouldn't have been able to make the drive alone.

When we got to the hospital, my mother had just gotten out of surgery and was now in recovery. We were allowed to see her. She was heavily sedated, so she was still sleeping. I thanked God that he had spared their lives. My mother had suffered a broken leg, and the surgeon had had to insert rods, and she also had two broken ribs. Her husband had suffered rib and sternum fractures from when the air bag deployed, and he also had a broken arm.

"Babe, the doctor said it will be about an hour before your mom is put in a room. It's already eleven p.m., so he suggested that we come back tomorrow. He said that she should be more alert, and we can visit her in her own room tomorrow," Jakiyah said.

I really didn't want to leave my mom, but it made sense, so I kissed my mom on her cheek, told her that I would be back tomorrow. I didn't know if she heard me or not, but just in case, I wanted her to know that I was there. On our way out, Donovan's niece approached me and said she recognized me from the picture at my mom's house. She was a redbone chick who stood about five-six, weighed around one hundred forty pounds, and had a nice-looking body, which had me off my game for a minute.

"Thank you for calling me and making sure to be here for my mother," I said, not knowing what else to say after getting stuck with Jakiyah looking at me like she wanted to slap me.

"I'm Jakiyah, his girlfriend, and we both thank you," she said, letting her presence be known.

"Nice to meet the both of you. It was no problem at all. I'm about to go, but I'll be back up here tomorrow. My uncle just got to recovery, so not much is needed from me right now," she said and smiled.

"Same here, so I guess I will see you tomorrow—" I said before being rudely interrupted by Jakiyah.

"*We* will see you tomorrow," she said, then pulled me away from Savannah.

"Yo, what was that about?" I asked her once we got to my truck.

"Which part? Do you mean the part where you were drooling all up in her face, like I wasn't standing there, or the part when you told her ass you would see her tomorrow, like you two were hooking up and not coming to check on your mother and her uncle?" she asked with an attitude.

"Jakiyah, she's kin to my mother's husband, which makes her family, so trust, I wasn't drooling over her," I lied, because shorty was fine.

But I hadn't been drooling; I'd just been stuck for a minute.

"Well, I couldn't tell from the way you were looking at her," she said, rolling her eyes.

"I only have eyes for you, Jakiyah. Now, stop being petty, and let's not forget why we are here," I told her, not wanting to talk about it anymore.

We checked into a hotel, and she went and got in the shower. She still had an attitude, but her ass would get over it. It was late, but I called my dad to let him know that I had made it here and to give him an update. He was going to come, but his wife was tripping, so he said for me to just continue to keep him updated on my mom. I didn't understand women these damn days. They got jealous over the stupidest things.

Chapter Thirty-Three

Jakiyah

As soon as we got checked into the hotel and entered the room, I went to take a shower to calm down, because Qua was going to make me fuck him up. I really didn't want to act this way, knowing that we were here for his mother, but he was not about to disrespect me by acting like he didn't see me standing there. I wasn't going to lie; she was a bad bitch, and that could be the reason why I was in my feelings, but I didn't care. And that kicking "She's family" shit . . . He could miss me with that bullshit. She was a female and not his blood family.

When I got out of the shower, I was exhausted, so I got in the bed, and he went to shower. Neither of us said anything to the other. I didn't even realize how tired I was until I got up the next morning and saw that it was going on 9:00 a.m. I slid out from under the hold Qua had on me and tapped him. Visiting hours started at 10:00 a.m., and I knew that he wanted to be there as soon as they started.

"Qua, wake up." I tried tapping him again because he hadn't budged after my first taps.

"I'm up. What time is it?" he said, stretching and getting out of bed. My eyes got lost staring at his morning hard-on as he adjusted his underwear.

Damn, this man was fine, and if we weren't pressed for time, mad or not, I would have had my mouth wrapped around that hard-on of his. He caught me looking and glanced at me with a smirk on his face. We didn't have time for foreplay, but we had time for a quickie. So yes, I joined his ass in the shower and let him bless me with all his morning thickness.

Qua's mother was awake when we got to the hospital. I could tell that she was in a lot of pain, but that didn't stop the smile that graced her face when she caught sight of Qua.

"Mom, how are you feeling?" he asked her.

"God is good, and I'm thankful to have my life. Besides me having some pain, baby, your mama is good. Thank you, Jesus," she responded, giving praise to the Lord.

I remember his mother was always preaching the Word when I used to visit, and I saw that much hadn't changed. Yes, she had a lot to be thankful for, because, like she'd said, she could be dead right now, so I welcomed her praise. But visiting her house back then had annoyed the hell out of me. My mother had had our asses in church three evenings out of the week, and then, when I'd visited his house, it was like being back at church all over again.

"Mom, do you remember Jakiyah?" he asked her.

"Chile, how could I forget Jakiyah? She was always so pleasant to be around," she said, smiling.

I walked over to her bed to give her a hug, without putting too much of my weight on her, being that her ribs were broken. She was trying to be strong for Qua, because I could see the pain etched on her face. We were there for a good forty-five minutes before that Savannah chick came in with an older gentleman, whom she introduced as her father, Roy. I watched as they all talked among themselves after Savannah let Qua's mother know that her husband was okay but in a lot of pain, same as her. I sat watching Qua as he laughed with Savannah, and it was making me hotter than the sun on a summer day.

I didn't know if his mother saw the look on my face or just picked up on my vibe, but whatever her reason was, she pulled me into the conversation by asking me how her son and I had hooked up again. I really didn't want to talk about what had brought me back to New York, because that meant talking about my sister. Qua, knowing me, changed the topic of the conversation by asking his mom what had caused the accident. That was when I excused myself and went to call Ty to see if everything was good.

"What's up, Ty?" I asked him when he answered the call.

"Not a damn thing, but how's Qua's mom doing?" he asked me.

"She suffered a broken leg and a few broken ribs, but she's okay."

"What's wrong with you?" he asked, noticing I wasn't my normal bubbly self.

"I'm good. I was just calling to make sure all was good."

"We're good. And you could have given me the heads-up that German was coming through."

"Did you two make up?" I asked, hoping they did.

"Yeah, we're good," he said. He said no more about it.

"Okay. I'm about to head back, so I'll give you a call later," I told him before ending the call.

When I walked back into the room, Roy was the only one there with Qua's mother, leaving me to wonder where the hell Qua and the Savannah chick had gone. I wasn't going to ask, and I hoped that Roy or Qua's mother would offer the information, but they didn't, so you know what I did.

"Where's Qua?" I asked, feeling annoyed for some reason.

"He and Savannah went to get us some soup. He said to tell you that he would be right back," Roy said, annoying me more. If Qua told you to tell me, why did I have to ask? I thought.

"Okay. Thank you," I responded.

I was pissed off, and not because he went to get them some soup, but because he didn't take me with him. Yes, I remembered his mother, but it had been years, and I didn't know Roy's ass, so what made him think that I wanted to be left in the room with them? *I should take the car and go back to the hotel*, I thought as I sent him a text message.

WHERE ARE YOU?

Up the street, getting Mom some soup. Do you want anything? And what's up with all the caps? he texted back.

NO, I DON'T.

LOL. I will see you in a minute, he texted me.

Oh, so he thought this shit was funny. I swear, I would have left his ass at the hospital, but I knew that if I did that, Ms. Savannah wouldn't have a problem giving him a ride. When they walked back into the room, I put my game face on. I wasn't about to let no female know that I was bothered. As innocent as their inter-action might have been, I knew females, and this Savannah person's body language spoke volumes when she was around my man, and it wasn't screaming, "We're family."

The ride back to the hotel was a quiet one. I didn't have two words for his ass right now, and he caught it, because he didn't say anything to me, either. I didn't want to seem childish and petty. I was neither of the two, but sometimes when you were loving on a man the way I was loving on his ass, it brought out all those traits that were living inside of you, and they came out full force without warning. Jealousy was rearing its ugly head, and I couldn't for the life of me turn it off—no matter how hard I tried.

"You mad?" he asked once we got back to the hotel.

"Who said I was mad?" I asked him.

"If you're not mad, what's up with the silent treatment?"

I swear, I wanted to choke his ass to sleep sometimes, but his fine ass was now wearing that face that I loved so much, making it hard for me to stay mad.

"I'm not mad, Qua," I told him, trying to keep the mad face going, but a smile deceived me as it slipped onto my lips.

"Give me a kiss, and stop playing with a nigga."

I was really smiling now that his lips touched mine, sending a tingling sensation to Ms. Kitty. He had her purring for his touch. His hands went to my waist, made their way up my blouse, and caressed my breasts. A small moan escaped my lips once he made contact with my mouth again. He slipped his tongue inside my mouth, and I sucked on his tongue. I wrapped my legs around his waist, and I wiggled my butt to help him get me out of my jeans. My panties followed, and then he dove in, with me riding his tongue.

Soon my juices flowed from the orgasm I was having, and my body jerked. I had to bite down on my bottom lip to stop from screaming out from the way he was assaulting my insides. Any pent-up stress that I was feeling about the earlier situation was gone as he thrust in and out of me. No longer able to hold in what I was feeling, I screamed out in pleasure. I could tell the pressure was building up in him, as he let out a growl and began aggressively hitting me with deep, long strokes. I responded by digging my nails in his back. We both came together, then collapsed. We were both trying to catch our breath when I looked at him, ready for round two.

"You good?" he asked, pulling me into his arms.

"I'm better than good," I said. I turned to face him, then kissed his lips.

"I need to talk to you about something," he said, causing me to sigh.

I didn't know what he needed to talk to me about, but I did know that I just wanted to relax and savor the ride he had just taken me on. Hearing the tone of his voice, I just knew I wasn't going to like the words that were about to come out of his mouth.

"Can it wait until tomorrow?" I whined, not wanting to ruin the moment if I didn't like what he was going to say.

"I'd rather get it over with now," he responded, rubbing my thigh.

"Okay. What is it?"

"My mother's doctor said that it's going to be about six to eight weeks before she has healed."

"And?" I asked, already knowing what was coming next. I had got defensive before he even finished.

"I'm going to have to take a leave from my job to be with her until she's able to do it on her own again. Had her husband not been involved in the accident with her, he could have taken care of her, and I wouldn't have to," he explained.

"Well, who's going to take care of him?" I asked, again already knowing the answer.

"His niece, Savannah, will be staying with him to care for him. She'll be taking a leave from her job as well," he said.

"So, when was this decision made?" I wanted to know.

"Well, when we went to the store, she told me that she took a leave to care for them both, but I don't want to burden her further with the care of both of them. My mother has me, so I told her that I would care for my mom."

"Really? So that means the two of you will be under the same roof for six to eight weeks. Is that what you're telling me?" I asked, getting upset.

"Jakiyah, we're family. You have nothing to worry about," he said, getting upset too.

It was easy for him to say that I had nothing to worry about when he was going to be away from me for almost two months. It felt the same way it had when he left for college, after telling me that I had nothing to worry about, because the long distance wasn't going to change the love we had for one another. Those words were proven wrong when he'd been gone for only a year and a half before he called to say that the relationship wasn't going to work. No, I didn't want a replay of that, but what could I say? I couldn't stay with him here for almost two months, and I couldn't ask him not to stay and take care of his mother. I put my game face on again, trying to hide how I really felt about the situation.

"Qua, I guess you have to do what you have to do. I have no choice but to trust you when you say I have nothing to worry about. But I do have a question."

"What is it?" he asked.

"We drove here together, so how will I get home?"

"I'm going to get you a rental to drive back, and you can drop it off to a New York location."

"So, you've got it all figured out, huh?" I asked. Then I got up to take a shower, not even waiting on a response.

Chapter Thirty-Four

Jakiyah

I had been back home for about a week now and was missing Qua something awful. Even though work and Yessenia had been keeping me from hitting the highway to go and stay with him, they didn't stop me from thinking of him. He called and texted me often, but it wasn't satisfying this appetite, this need to feel him inside of me.

Ty had invited Yessenia and me to the club tonight, but we had decided just to chill at her house. He was having open mic on a Wednesday night, and if I didn't have to work tomorrow, I would have gone to hang out. I shouldn't even be at Yessenia's house right now. I knew I wasn't going to want to get up and go to work tomorrow after the two glasses of wine that I had already had.

"So, what's up with Qua?" she asked me as we sat on the couch.

"Girl, I'm missing his ass something awful," I responded, making the sad face.

"So, you're good on ole girl staying with him at his mom's house?" she asked, knowing damn well I didn't need a reminder.

I had a little time to dwell on my answer to her question, because someone was knocking on her door just then.

"Are you Yessenia DeCruz?" a male voice said through the door. It sounded like the voice of Detective James, so I got up to go to the door.

When I got to the door and looked through the peephole, sure enough, it was Detective James and his partner. I opened the door, and my eyes met Detective James's. Mine were filled with confusion. Then he took his attention off me and told Yessenia that they had a warrant for her arrest for the murder of Cydney Wilks. It didn't register with me at this point that she was being arrested for my sister's murder. All I saw was my friend being put in handcuffs. I yelled out for Keem, who came running downstairs, in his boxers and nothing else.

"What the fuck is going on?" he asked, rushing toward the officer who had Yessenia in cuffs.

"Sir, I'm going to need you to step back," Detective James informed him, with his hand now resting on his weapon.

I heard a loud noise outside and glanced out the window. When I noticed the tow truck taking Yessenia's car into custody, I felt light-headed and unsteady. Realizing I needed to sit, I made my way to the couch and plopped down on it. Detective James walked over to where I was sitting on the couch, then told me that Yessenia's car was the car in question the night of my sister's murder, and that was why she was being arrested. My eyes pleaded with him to tell me that this was all some misunderstanding and they had the wrong car, but he just gave me a sympathetic touch on my shoulder. A moment later, he informed me that he would be in touch, and then he and his partner led Yessenia out of the house, leaving me broken as tears flowed from my eyes.

Keem touched my shoulder, causing me to flinch. I knew that he was only offering me comfort, but I didn't want him to touch me. At this point, I didn't know who to trust anymore. Did he know that she did this? I thought as I looked up at him with questioning eyes.

"Jakiyah, I don't know what's going on." He spoke as if he had read what my eyes were asking.

I didn't know what to believe anymore, and I was giving myself a headache, trying to figure out why Yessenia would be accused of murdering my sister. They had been wrong about Andris being a suspect, so maybe they were wrong about her too. My sister and Yessenia had never been friends and probably had no interactions that didn't include me, as they had never hung out together or anything. I had always had to force them to be in each other's company. Since Yessenia was my best friend and Cydney was my sister, I had wanted them to get along.

Cydney never liked Yessenia and only tolerated her because of me, I thought as I looked up. Lost in thought, I had forgotten that Keem was standing in front of me. My eyes noticed that he was still in his boxers, and the view gave me a better understanding of why Yessenia always wanted to be home, under his ass. I averted my gaze as I stood and told him that I was leaving. He told me that he was headed to Jersey as soon as he put some clothes on and that he would keep me updated.

When I got to my parents' house, I summarized what had happened for my parents and Ty. By then I had one of those pulsating headaches. What was so bothersome to me was the fact that someone whom I would give my life for and whom I considered family would commit this type of betrayal. My heart hurt, but at the same time, my heart was betraying me, as I felt the need to know if Yessenia was okay. I called Qua. I needed to hear his voice. I felt that, besides my family, he was the only one I had left. His voice mail picked up, so I just left a message, telling him to call me as soon as possible. My mother handed me two Tylenol and a bottled water and told me to go lie down. I gratefully accepted the Tylenol and the advice, because my head was really hurting.

When I woke up, it was six the next morning. I hadn't even realized how tired I was. I knew my mother was up because I could hear the church music that she was playing downstairs. I reached for my phone and checked for any missed calls, but I didn't have any. This made me wonder why Qua hadn't returned my call, especially after hearing the urgency in my voice. I didn't know why I expected a call from Yessenia from the police station, one in which she told me that this was all a mistake, but I didn't receive that call, either. I thought about calling Keem but quickly dismissed that idea. Instead, I showered and got ready for work. I wasn't about to sit at home and drive myself crazy with my thoughts. At least if I was at work, I could keep busy, the time would seem to go faster, and maybe I would get some answers by the time I got off work.

Once I was dressed, I headed downstairs.

"Good morning, baby. I didn't think you would go in today," my mother said, seeing me in my scrubs.

"I thought about it, but I've missed too many days already. And if I sit home, all I'm going to do is drive myself crazy," I told her.

"I didn't wake you up last night to go home, because I knew that you were tired and needed to rest."

"You did right, as I wasn't going home last night, anyway. Did Ty spend the night too?" I asked her.

"No, he didn't spend the night. He left about ten minutes after you went upstairs. He got so angry with me because he wanted me to be angry, and I refuse, since I put it in God's hands. I wouldn't be a child of God if I didn't believe in forgiveness," she said, giving me the same feeling my brother must have felt. I told her I had to go.

I was all for forgiveness, but it was just hard when it was someone that you'd trusted, someone who you'd believed would never do anything to hurt you or anyone you loved.

After a long day at work, all I wanted to do was go home, get in the fetal position, and cry, as once again, I felt alone. Qua not reaching out didn't make it any better. I decided not to go home and instead went back to my parents' home. When I got there, Detective James was exiting his car.

"How are you?" he asked me as I let him in the house.

"I could be better," I said to him.

I walked him into the living room, where my parents were sitting, watching the news. I walked over and picked up the remote to turn the television off. I offered Detective James a seat, but he remained standing.

"Okay, so it wasn't easy, but we did get a written confession from Yessenia DeCruz," Detective James announced. "She states that your sister, Cydney, was having a relationship with her boyfriend, Keem—"

"What the fuck does she mean, Cydney was having a relationship with Keem?" I asked, interrupting him.

"Again, she states that they were having a relationship, which he broke off. She insists that your sister kept calling and texting him for months, stating that she needed to talk to him, but he ignored her. She said that on the night in question, Cydney texted her boyfriend's phone, telling him that she had been trying to get in touch with him, and that she understood that the relationship was over, but she and his daughter needed him."

"His daughter?" my mother questioned.

"Yes, his daughter, according to her. Ms. DeCruz said that she was hurt and was not thinking straight when she texted the phone back, pretending to be Keem, and asked Cydney where she was. Cydney supposedly texted the phone again on the night of her murder, stating that she was going to leave Andris that night. Ms. DeCruz, still pretending to be Keem, asked for the address to where she was staying, and when she received the address, she left work and headed to Jersey.

The detective went on. "She admits that when she got to the home, she sat in the car, not knowing what her next move was going to be, until she saw your sister pull out. Ms. DeCruz followed slowly behind her. She said that all she wanted to do was tell Cydney that her boyfriend, Keem, wasn't the father of her child and to just leave them alone. Before she got the chance to approach her, another car pulled into the gas station, with a man behind the wheel. We now know this was Mr. Wilks."

Detective James took a deep breath and then continued. "After the gas station attendant scared him off, threatening to call the police,

Ms. DeCruz said she pulled up, just to see if Cydney was okay. She admits your daughter started going off on her, telling her that her boyfriend was going to leave her once he saw his daughter. She said this caused her to snap, and she pulled out the weapon and shot her."

I tell you, I was numb and had no words as tears fell from my eyes. I didn't understand how you could kill my sister over a fucking man who she clearly knew wasn't shit because he was having a relationship with her. If Yessenia knew that Keem had broken it off with my sister, and thus wanted nothing more to do with her, that meant Cydney was no longer a threat to Yessenia. I didn't believe the part about my sister saying that her daughter was his, and if she did, she probably said it just to get under Yessenia's skin.

"So, what now?" I heard my father ask the detective.

"She will be formally advised of the charges against her and will be asked to enter a plea to the charges. The court will decide if she will be released pending her trial. She wanted me to let you know that her boyfriend, Keem, knew nothing about any of the text messages or what she did," Detective James replied. He then told us he would keep us informed once the trial started.

After he bid farewell to my parents, I let the detective out. I continued to my car, having decided in that moment that I needed to get away. I was headed to Vermont to see my man. I needed him.

When I got to Vermont and pulled up in front of Qua's mother's house, I grabbed my bag and got out of the car. I had tried to reach Qua while en route but received no answer. It was kind of pissing me off because I didn't know what the hell was going on with him that he couldn't answer or return any of my calls. I rang the doorbell, and some female answered the door, wearing nothing but a T-shirt. Just as I was about to tell her that I was there for Qua, I saw him come from the kitchen, wearing just his boxers.

I ran down the front steps to my car, climbed in, and pulled off as the tears fell. My judgment clouded, I decided to make the drive back home. I didn't understand what the hell I had done in my life to be getting hit after hit of betrayal. By the time I had driven for three hours and had made one stop to fill up my tank, the whole sordid affair had started to take a toll on me. I thought that Qua would have at least been blowing up my phone by now, but he wasn't—and he had not even sent a text message—which hurt me more.

I felt much better when I saw that I had a little less than two miles to go before my exit, but before I made it to my exit, I fell asleep at the wheel. When I opened my eyes and realized what had happened, it was too late. I tried to regain control of my car as it swerved across the road and hit the gravel shoulder. A moment later another car hit mine, and my car jerked right before I blacked out.

Chapter Thirty-Five

Qua

I had just got the call from Ty, telling me that Jakiyah was in a car accident. And to think I wasn't even going to answer the call, but something had told me to. I was en route to New York, and I swear, I had had no idea that she was even coming to Vermont. I had been dealing with my own shit and had blocked her out, but now I felt fucked up. I felt like it was my fault that she was in an accident. Ty had told me what happened with Yessenia and what she was dealing with, and that made me feel even more fucked up. We both were going through some shit, and instead of me reaching out to her for comfort, like she was reaching out to me, I decided to deal with my shit on my own. Ty didn't give me any details on her condition. He just said that I needed to get there, and he instructed me to drive safely. I drove safely, but I drove fast as hell and got to

North Shore Hospital in three hours. I pulled up, found parking, and headed to the emergency entrance, where I saw Ty and Jakiyah's parents.

"What's up, Qua? What did you do? Fly here, nigga?" Ty asked me, giving me dap.

"Nah. I just drove the hell out of that truck, and there wasn't much traffic on the road. How is she doing?" I replied after saying hello to her parents.

"We haven't heard anything about her condition as of yet. We were told by the officer on the scene that she may have fallen asleep at the wheel," Ty said.

By around 6:00 a.m., which was about an hour after I arrived at the hospital, we still hadn't heard anything about Jakiyah's condition. Jakiyah's parents were starting to worry, but I told them that no news was good news. Well, at least that was what my mother had always told me. I had almost forgotten that I wasn't traveling alone, until I saw him walk in the door. I had left his ass in the dust. When he walked up on me, Ty and his parents looked at me with questioning eyes, but before I could say anything, we heard the doctor call for the family of Jakiyah Smith. Her mom and dad rushed over to the doctor.

"I'm Dr. Evans," he informed them. "Ms. Smith has a concussion, as well as a couple of bruised ribs. I'm sorry for the wait. What took so long was we had some x-rays done to check for potential skull fractures and the stability of her spine. Those came back negative. We are going to admit her into the hospital because we need to run a few more tests before we feel comfortable releasing her. She's awake and alert, so I will allow you to visit. but no long stays. You can return tomorrow, during visiting hours."

The doctor then escorted Ty and his parents to her room. I decided to wait for them to come out before I went in. Prayer worked. I had prayed during my entire ride for her to be okay. I was kind of nervous about seeing her, being that I hadn't been there when she needed me most. I stood when I saw her parents approaching. Her mother looked as if she was crying, making me think the worst.

"I'm going to get my parents home, but we will be back up here tomorrow. I'll holla at you then," Ty told me before leaving with his parents.

I took a deep breath, and then I and the guy who was with me headed to Jakiyah's room and stood outside her open door. Her head turned toward the open door, and upon seeing me, she rolled her eyes and turned her head toward the wall. I stepped inside the room and walked over to the bed, but she refused to give me eye contact.

"Jakiyah, how are you feeling?" I asked her, hoping she would look at me, but she didn't.

I walked over to the other side of the bed so that she wouldn't have any choice but to look at me.

"Qua, I just want you to leave," she said, just above a whisper.

"Jakiyah, let me explain. I—"

"I don't want you to explain what I saw with my own eyes," she said as tears left her eyes.

I knew that she wasn't going to let me explain, and I didn't know how much longer I had before they told me that I needed to go. So I went to the door and signaled to the person I had waiting to enter the room. Jakiyah's eyes bucked wildly as she looked from me to him with questioning eyes.

"Jakiyah, when you came to my mother's house, this is who you saw with his girlfriend. It wasn't me," I told her.

"B-but how could that be?" she asked, stuttering, her voice still just above a whisper.

"Jakiyah, this is my twin brother, Quinton, who I didn't know existed until a few days ago. I wasn't staying at the house, nor was I speaking to my mother. I wasn't responding to any of your messages, because of what I had going on, and for that, I'm sorry. I really can't explain what I don't know, so we will have to have that conversation another day," I said, being honest, because I didn't know the details.

"I'm sorry we had to meet under these circumstances, but I'm glad that you're okay. I would have tried to stop you at the house, but I had no idea who you were. Savannah saw you from the window when you first pulled up and was coming to say hello, but you had already left," Quinton said to her, but she didn't respond.

"Jakiyah, I have to go. They said we couldn't stay long, but I will be back tomorrow, during visiting hours," I told her, then kissed her on her lips. As Quinton and I were leaving, a nurse walked in the door.

I knew Jakiyah was trying to digest it all, as she still looked confused as I was walking out, my identical twin following me.

Quinton and I left the hospital together.

"I'm going to get a room and drive back in a few hours," he said, as we walked to his car.

"You don't have to do that. You can follow me to my crib. I have a guest room," I offered, since he had agreed to come to the hospital.

I didn't know what Jakiyah's condition was before I got here, but I knew I was going to need him, because had I told her it wasn't me that she'd seen, without offering any proof, she wouldn't have believed me. Honestly, I wouldn't have believed me, either, if I hadn't seen Quinton, whose face was exactly like mine.

"Okay. I'll take you up on your offer," Quinton said.

Once we got to my place, I showed him the room he would be staying in. Then I went into the kitchen to get a Corona from the fridge. I really needed it. Corona in hand, I stepped into the living room and sat on the couch. Quinton came to join me in the living room, and I offered him a Corona, but he declined.

"Can I ask you a question?" he asked me.

"What's up?"

"I'm just curious about why you're so upset with your mother, when you didn't even give her a chance to explain."

"What's there to explain? She lied to me all these years, so of course I'm going to feel some kind of way, regardless of her reason," I told him.

"True, she lied to you all these years about you having a brother, but I was the one given up at birth. If that wasn't a hard enough pill to swallow, imagine how I felt when I found out that not only was I given up, but I was a twin, but not the twin that was chosen to have a mother and father."

After pausing for a moment, he continued. "The first time the agency reached out to her, I was seventeen years old, and when the agency told me that she told them she wanted to remain anonymous, I was crushed. She reached out to the agency a few years later to set up a meeting, and I told the agency that I no longer wanted to know, because I was still hurt. The agency talked me into going to the initial meeting. They knew how badly I wanted this, so I agreed. She told me that she didn't have a choice, because at the time, she wasn't able to care for us both. Was her excuse bullshit to me? Yes, it was, because you don't just give up a kid that you carried inside of you for nine months.

"Was I angry? Again, yes, I was, but I forgave her. It's been five years, and I love her as if I've known her all my life. She had her reason as to why she didn't want to share with you that I was in her life, and I respected her decision. She said she wasn't ready to tell you. I'm going to tell you the same thing I told your girl. I'm sorry we had to meet this way, but I'm glad we finally got to meet," he said, all in one breath, giving me something to think about.

"It really feels crazy to be sitting across from you. I feel like I'm looking in the mirror right now. I'm just so tight that they would keep something like this from me, and I swear, I wouldn't have been upset had they just told me," I admitted.

"Well, according to our mom, I'm the oldest by three minutes, so as your older brother, I think you should at least hear her out," he said.

He was better than I was, because I didn't think I would have been able to forgive my mom if she had let me go. And he was the firstborn, so how did she choose?

"How was your life growing up, man?" I asked, ignoring the fact that he had told me that I should talk to my mother.

"I had a pretty decent life, but I was never adopted. But I was placed with a nice family. Sharon and Mike, an older couple who had no children of their own, cared for me up until the age of five. They both got sick and were no longer able to care for me, so I was back and forth between foster parents until the age of fifteen. My last foster parents had two other foster children, an eight-year-old boy and a fifteen-year-old girl. They treated us like shit, and that was when I first started thinking about my birth parents, making a promise to myself that

I was going to find them. I swear, if it weren't for their foster daughter, Tamia, I would have killed myself. We developed a bond that turned into a relationship, until our foster parents got wind of it and sent her away."

I sat there for a minute, shaking my head, because it was a small fucking world. There was no doubt in my mind that he was talking about the same Tamia that I had encountered. So, that was what she'd meant when she said I used to love her crazy ass. He was looking at me like I was crazy. He must have thought that I was shaking my head and laughing at his situation, but I wasn't. The shit just had me bugging for a minute. I decided to share with him what had me looking crazy right now, before he got up to punch me or some shit.

"Are you serious?" he asked me, with a shocked look on his face, after I told him about Tamia.

"Very serious. I swear, I wouldn't even play about nothing like that," I said seriously.

"Damn, I really dodged a bullet, because I was really feeling shorty at the time," he said and smiled.

We talked until, like, three in the morning, and I had to admit he was a cool dude, and we had a lot in common. He'd played high school and college basketball. He hadn't got drafted, but he had finished college, and he was now a coach at the same college he'd attended. He lived in Virginia, but he promised that he would keep in touch with me, if that was okay with me, which it was. He made me agree to speak with my mother, who had probably already called my father, because he had been calling me, and I had been sending his ass to voice mail. They were my parents, so eventually, I was going to have to forgive them, but I wanted them to know that what they had done was wrong. Once I was of age, they should have told me.

I also found out that Quinton's girlfriend back at the house wasn't his girlfriend but his wife. He had been married for a year now. My parents had attended the wedding. That news pissed me off all over again. I took my ass upstairs to take a shower and call it a night. I had digested a lot, and I now had a damn headache.

Chapter Thirty-Six

Jakiyah

I swear, you couldn't tell me that I didn't have more than a concussion when Qua's twin brother walked into my hospital room. I had really felt like I was losing my mind. I couldn't imagine his parents keeping something like this from him. I didn't know the backstory, but no matter what that backstory was, they should have told him. I was happy that he wasn't cheating on me, but he might as well have, because his ass had shut me out when I needed him most, so I still felt some kind of way about it. I was also upset with myself. There was no way I should have driven all the way to Vermont and then tried to make it back home on no sleep. That was a suicide mission, and I was thankful to be alive. I promised myself not to let anything cloud my judgment and cause me to be stupid again.

My head was killing me, so I hit the call button for the nurse so that she could give me something for the pain. It felt like my head was about to explode. I wanted to sleep, but I was waiting on the doctor to make his rounds to let me know if I would be released or not. Visiting hours were about to start, and I didn't want my parents visiting if my doctor was going to let me go home. Thirty minutes after I took the medication, I dozed off. When I heard the door to my room open again, I stirred. I looked up and did a double take, the same as when Qua's twin had walked up in my room last night. Keem had just walked into my room. He seemed hesitant, and he had every right to be, because I really didn't want to see his ass.

"I know I shouldn't be here, but I heard that you were involved in a car accident, and I wanted to make sure that you were okay, because Yessenia was stressing from not knowing. I tried to reach Qua, but he hasn't been answering my calls," he said.

The mention of Yessenia's name made me angry, and I was minutes from telling him that Yessenia could kiss my natural-born ass. But I thought twice about it, because I needed some answers from him. I tried to refrain from taking a deep breath like I wanted to, as it would only add to the pain I was already feeling from my ribs. The ice packs that had been given to me last night, along with the pain medication, had really helped. The doctor had told me not to avoid taking deep breaths, but I wasn't going to lie. I was trying my hardest not to. He had warned me that if I avoided taking deep breaths and coughing, it could put me at risk for a chest infection. The nurse had added that I should take ten slow breaths every hour and let my lungs inflate fully each time to help keep my lungs clear, but I hadn't been doing that, either.

"Keem, I'm fine, but I have to be honest with you when I say that you shouldn't have come. Your being here confirms that you don't understand how I feel right now. Yessenia was like a sister to me, and I would have laid down my life for her. She took someone who I also loved dearly over something that could have been replaced. No disrespect, but I need to keep it real with you. If she needed to take someone's life, it should have been yours, because my sister didn't owe her shit," I said, getting emotional.

"Jakiyah, no, I don't understand how you feel, but I know how I feel, because your sister's blood is on my hands. If it weren't for me, she would still be here. I thought by breaking off the relationship and admitting it to Yessenia, I was doing the right thing. I never knew that Cydney was trying to contact me. When I broke it off, she said that she understood and was going to focus on her marriage. For what it's worth, I'm sorry. And I mean that shit with all sincerity," he said, pounding his right hand on his chest.

I knew if I started crying, my ribs were going to be inflamed by the time I stopped. I bit down on my bottom lip, trying to hold my tears in, but it was hard, and a few escaped. I studied his face, trying to read his eyes, and the sincerity in them matched the sincerity in his voice.

"It hurts so bad, and I just feel like if she just snapped the way she said she did, no matter how painful the truth would have been to hear, she should have been honest with me. Instead, she chose to be a coward and hide behind the lies and deceit, and she still remained in my presence, knowing what she did," I cried out, no longer able to hold back my tears. They streamed down my face.

"Jakiyah, are you okay?" he asked, concern written on his face.

"Keem, I'm not okay, and the fucked-up part of this whole situation is that I was betrayed, not by an enemy, but by a friend who I considered my sister. I doubt if I can ever forgive her or feel bad about her possibly spending the rest of her life in prison," I told him, being honest.

"I miss her," he whispered as tears fell from his eyes.

I wasn't expecting that at all. Even though I knew he was talking about Cydney, I wanted to hear him say exactly who he missed. After all, he could have been speaking about Yessenia. Even though she wasn't dead, she was gone.

"Keem, you miss *who*?" I asked, wiping at my tears.

"I miss Cydney, and I know it was wrong of me to get involved with her, but I loved her, and she loved me too. We both belonged to someone else. That was the only reason we weren't together, and if her daughter is mine, I need to know. If she's a part of me, I want to be in her life," he declared.

"That's a conversation you have to have with my parents," I told him.

"No doubt. I'm glad you're okay, sis, and I'm going to go and get up out of here," he said before leaving.

I wanted to be mad at him, but it was hard. I cared for him too, and I considered him family as well. I had been away for years, and when I came back, it was like I had never left, as we all picked up where we had left off. I had kind of always known that Cydney had a crush on Keem, but

I had never known that he would take it there with her. He and Yessenia had been together forever, and he had always acted like he didn't even like Cydney. I guessed they had both been fronting, and that was probably the reason why Cydney had never cared for Yessenia. I started to wonder if Qua knew about the relationship that Keem had had with my sister, being that they were best friends, but I decided to just leave well enough alone.

Chapter Thirty-Seven

Qua

Jakiyah had been home for a few days now, and she had been staying at her mother's house, because she needed to be cared for. I did as much as I could until it was time for the warden to put me out every night. My brother had left the morning after our talk, but he was heading back to my mom's place, where I told him I would be in a few days.

That day had come. I was heading back today to have a sit-down with both of my parents and Quinton. I was ready to get it over with. Jakiyah didn't get upset this time; she knew this was something that I needed to do. She didn't want me to stay mad at my mother any longer than I had to. I got up at five that morning to make the drive. I didn't plan on staying overnight and was hoping to make it back sometime tonight.

When I got to my mother's house, my brother, his wife, and my father were sitting in the living room, watching television.

"Hey, son," my father greeted me.

"Hey," I responded dryly.

"Boy, get your ass over here and give your pops some love," he said in a tone that let me know he wasn't really asking.

I went over to him and gave him a man hug, which was how I always greeted him when visiting him, but I wasn't feeling the love this time, because I was still tight. It wasn't going to be easy to express how I felt with him being here. I was certain that all he was going to do was explain the situation, and I would have no choice but to accept it.

"I'm going to let your mother speak, but what's not going to happen is you being disrespectful to her. You may not like what she has to say, but you will respect it," he said, causing my jaw to tighten, but I knew not to try him.

Quinton just sat quietly and watched the interaction. He didn't say anything, but he did offer me a smirk when my dad gave me that look that said he was going to knock me on my ass if I got out of line. My mother must have told him how I slammed the door after telling her I didn't want to hear shit she had to say. I was wrong for doing that, and I had intended to apologize after

I calmed down, but I had never got the chance to, because of what happened with Jakiyah.

All of us except my brother's wife headed upstairs to my mother's bedroom to have the meeting. I watched as my mom tried to get comfortable on her bed, looking like she still wasn't ready to have this conversation. I could have made it easier on her—Quinton had already told me what she had told him, so she didn't have to repeat it for my sake—but I still wanted to hear it from her.

"Son, first, let me apologize to you for the way you found out about your brother, Quinton," she said. She paused for a moment, as she was already getting emotional. "You shouldn't have had to find out this way. After I reconnected with him, I promised myself that I was going to sit you down and tell you. Each and every time I came close to telling you, I lost my nerve. You see, I wasn't ready for you to hate me."

She gave a long sigh, then went on. "Your father begged me to tell you, but I kept telling him I wasn't ready. So don't blame him for you not knowing sooner. Your father and I made a selfish decision, though it didn't seem selfish at the time. We have lived with that guilt every day, and it destroyed our marriage. I turned to the church for support, and he sought comfort in other women."

She took a deep breath before continuing. "Qua, I need you to believe me when I say that giving up Quinton was one of the hardest decisions that I have ever had to make. The second hardest thing was looking in his eyes and explaining how I had selfishly given him up, when, in reality, I should have sought help. I could have got government assistance or family support, and I sought neither. And for that, I'm sorry." She began crying.

"Anita, I've been telling you for years to stop beating yourself up. We were young, and your family, as well as mine, turned their backs on our relationship, and no one stepped in to offer us any assistance. We now have to focus on forgiveness and make up for all the years we lost at being a family. We have a blended family now, and we could start with getting together during holidays," my dad offered, but he knew good and well his wife wasn't going to blend into the shit we had going on.

I got up to give my mom a hug and to let her know that I was sorry for the way I had disrespected her and that I had forgiven her. I also told her that I would have never looked at her differently if she had just told me the truth, because I loved her unconditionally. This made her cry harder. After she thanked me, kissed me all over my face, and thanked Jesus, like, five times. We sat around talking until it was time for my dad to fly out. Quinton and his wife were going to stay with my mom, and I was driving home to be with Jakiyah. Before I left, I promised my mom that Jakiyah and I would come visit when Jakiyah was feeling better, And Quinton and I exchanged numbers and promised each other we would keep in touch.

Chapter Thirty-Eight

Jakiyah

I had been back at work for about a week, and my patient's wife was so happy to have me back. She said that the replacement aide had been lazy, and when she'd gone on errands, she wouldn't return in a timely manner, the way I always had. I couldn't for the life of me understand why some of these aides took this kind of job if they could care less about the patients. I would never mistreat or take advantage of any patient. And, God forbid, if my parents needed an aide, and one of them mistreated my mom or dad.

I had been off work for a good hour now and had stopped by the nail salon. When I was leaving, I ran into Keem. I didn't stop to have a conversation, but I was polite and spoke to him but kept it moving. I didn't care to hear him tell me how he was doing, nor did I care about Yessenia and how she was doing, so there really was no need to stop and attempt a conversation with him.

I already knew that she had pleaded out to fifteen to life, with the possibility of parole after she served the fifteen years. I didn't agree with her sentence, because she had a possibility of living her life again, and my sister didn't. The only thing that I was pleased about was that she had taken the plea and saved my family from the stress of a trial. My sister could rest in peace now that her killer was behind bars. She killed my sister, and baby Andrea didn't even belong to Keem.

I was happy today was Friday, because I was having a get-together at my house tomorrow. I hadn't done anything since the accident, and I was ready to unwind. It was just going to be me, Qua, Ty, Chanel, German, and some chick Chanel had hooked German up with. Yes, German was invited, and I know what you were thinking. I could admit that I had had a slipup when it came to him, but I had promised it would never happen again, and I meant it. German was a part of Ty's life, as well as mine. He and I had always been friends before anything. My man trusted me and my word, so he wasn't threatened anymore by German's presence.

I had to say that Ty and I always used to get upset when my mother spoke about forgiveness, because we just didn't understand. However, recently, she had preached that forgiveness didn't excuse a person's bad behavior, but it did stop that behavior from preventing us from trusting again. She had also said that once you let go and let God, the healing process began. As a result of her explanation, Ty and I had started attending church with her every other Sunday. But she made no demands on us, acknowledging that this was a start.

Baby Andrea was starting to walk and was saying a lot of words, but every time she called my mother or me Mama, it broke my heart. One thing was for sure, though: she had a lot of love surrounding her. And we made sure she knew who her mother was by talking about her and showing her pictures. Even if she didn't understand right now, she would when she was older, and her mother's spirit would always live through us.

I almost forgot. . . . If anyone cared about what happened to Tamia, she would be spending the rest of her days in a state mental hospital. I had always known something was wrong with her, but I had never known she had a documented mental illness. I still thought she had got off too easy for taking someone's life, even if it was Andris's life that she took. I decided to live by the words of the famous physicist Albert Einstein: "Life is like riding a bicycle. To keep your balance, you must keep moving."

complain to the agency that my life was to keep and, while working at her home, I was paying that by the time I got back from this thing vacation, I would have a new case. I refused to go back to that situation.

Qua asked me, rubbing my protruding belly. "Just making sure I'm going to eat before we head out." I told him, thinking it was too good earning. "Aw, my babe really out love me," he teased. "You have to know that I love everything." "I didn't. I wouldn't be carrying all this extra weight around," I said seriously as I went back to fixing him and that good proportions.

Chapter Thirty-Nine

Jakiyah

One year later . . .

I was in a good mood today. I was excited about the road trip that we were taking this weekend with our friends to the house of Qua's mom and her husband in Vermont. They were having a big barbecue celebration for the Fourth of July, and I couldn't wait to get away, because work had been stressful. I hated to complain about work, but the family of this new patient that I had had for the past six months had been taking my ass through the ringer. Her grown-ass children still lived at home and did absolutely nothing for her but cause her stress with their dysfunctional relationships and lack of paying their way. There was always something going on, and as much as I felt sorry for her, I had had to complain to the agency that my life was in jeopardy while working at her home. I was praying that by the time I got back from this mini vacation, I would have a new case. I refused to go back to that situation.

"Hey, babe, what are you doing up so early?" Qua asked me, rubbing my protruding belly.

"Just making something to eat before we head out," I told him, then kissed him good morning.

"Aw, my babe really does love me?" he teased.

"You have to know that I love you, because if I didn't, I would not be carrying all this extra weight around," I said seriously as I went back to finishing up my breakfast preparations.

It had been a year since all the craziness in my life began, and Qua and I had been living together for about six months, ever since the night he proposed to me. The night he proposed to me, I was already pregnant, but he didn't know it. He surprised me with the proposal in front of all our family and friends at what I thought was baby Andrea's birthday party. So I got him back by revealing that I was pregnant. When he heard that, he was crazy like a damn baby, because he was so happy. Ty and German would not let him live it down, and they clowned him the entire night. He wanted us to get married before the baby was born, which meant we had only a month or two to make it happen.

It really could be done, but I just didn't know if I wanted to get married while I was pregnant. So I had told him I would rather the baby take his name first, and then I'd take his name after the baby was born.

"Babe, you don't hear me talking to you?" he asked me, snapping me out of my daze.

"No. I'm sorry. I didn't hear you. I was thinking about the night you proposed to me and you crying like a baby when I told you that I was pregnant." I laughed.

"Ha-ha. Not funny. I remember that you were crying too," he said, grabbing me around my waist, as much as my belly would allow, and kissing me on my neck.

"Yeah, yeah. Let's eat," I told him. I moved out of his grip, then brushed past him to fix our plates. He gave me a helping hand.

After we finished eating breakfast, I headed upstairs to finish packing before taking a shower and getting ready to go. We were picking up the others from my parents' house because I wanted to see baby Andrea and my parents before I left for the weekend. Qua and I were both ready about an hour later, so I wobbled my behind to the rental, while Qua stayed back to get the bags and lock up. I called Ty to let him know that we were on our way and to find out if German and his girlfriend, Desirae, had gotten to the house yet. Ty said they had just got finished arguing, but they were there. I had to shake my head, as they had been together for, like, eight months now and that was all they did. Their quarreling made me hate to hang out with them most times.

"Everybody ready?" Qua asked me once he was in the car.

"Yeah. Ty said that they were. And he said that German and Desi was on that arguing shit again." I laughed.

"I'm telling you, if they start that shit, I'm putting both of their asses on the side of the road, and I'm not playing," he said seriously.

I laughed as I laid my head back against the headrest. I enjoyed the ride to my parents' house in silence, rubbing my baby bump. When we pulled up in front of the house, German and Desi were out front, having a heated argument. I jumped out of the SUV and told both of them that they needed to cut that shit out in front of my parents' house.

"Nah, we not having that shit, because we all about to be traveling together, and I'm not trying to hear no damn arguing all the way," Qua told them.

"Whatever the argument is about, you two can squash it or catch us on the next trip," I added as I walked inside, with Qua behind me.

"Why you got German and Desi out front, disrespecting the house with that bullshit?" I asked Ty, slapping him on the back of the head.

"Yo, chill. I just kicked both of them out of here, with that bullshit," he said.

"Boy, you better watch your mouth," my mom said to him as she walked into the living room with my li'l stinka.

"Hey, auntie baby," I said. I picked her up and kissed her all over her face, causing her to laugh.

"Babe, I told you about bending down and lifting her up like that," Qua fussed.

I paid him no mind, because if it hurt me to pick her up, I wouldn't be picking her up, but I wasn't going to say anything. I didn't want to be arguing with him after I had just told German and his girl that we weren't going to be having no arguing.

"Mom, we're about to head out. Are you going to be good with baby Andrea for the whole weekend?" I asked her.

"Girl, please. I have her every day during the week, so what's the difference because it's the weekend? Get your brother, Chanel, Qua, and the fighting duo, and get out of my darn house," she said, laughing. But she was serious, so we headed out.

Chapter Forty

Qua

The barbecue wasn't until tomorrow, so before going to the hotel, we decided to stop by my mother's house, just to let her know that we had made it and to say hello. I also wanted to know if she needed any help with anything or needed me to run errands for her before I went and got comfortable at the hotel. As soon as my mother's door opened and I saw that it was Savannah who had answered it, wearing a pair of booty shorts and a tank top, I regretted stopping by.

Jakiyah already felt that Savannah wanted me; she'd stated that she could tell when a female wanted her man. I'd been constantly telling her that we were family. I grabbed her hand to calm her, because I could tell that she wanted to say something. It didn't help that Desi had just popped German in the back of the head for staring. I couldn't even say that what

Savannah had on was inappropriate. After all, it was summer and today was a hot day. And in her defense, she didn't know that we would be stopping by today, so it was not like she had dressed this way because she knew that we were coming.

"Hey, Mom." After I greeted her, I introduced her to everyone, being that she didn't know Ty, Chanel, German, and Desi as she hadn't been at the engagement party.

"Hi, everyone. I'm Savannah," Savannah said sarcastically when I didn't introduce her.

"My bad," I responded, getting a roll of the eyes from Jakiyah.

"Mom, we just stopped by to see if you need help with anything before we head to the hotel," I said, ignoring Jakiyah and her little attitude.

"You guys don't have to stay at the hotel. We have plenty of room here. And, Jakiyah, are you sure you're going to be comfortable sleeping in those hotel beds?"

"Yes, ma'am. I'll be fine. And next time we'll stay with you," she promised.

"Qua, I don't need any help here at the house. Savannah has been a big help, and Donavon is out picking up some things for tomorrow," my mom said.

"Okay. So I guess we will see Donovan tomorrow, because we're about to head out. It was a long drive, so we're going to go to the hotel and chill," I told her, hugging her.

"Okay. I wish you guys could stay longer, but I guess I'll see you all tomorrow," she said, walking us to the door.

After we had got to the hotel and everyone had separated and gone to their rooms, I noticed that Jakiyah still had an attitude.

"What's wrong, babe?" I asked as soon as we got inside the room.

"You didn't tell me that *she* would be here," she said with attitude.

"Come on, babe. Don't go stressing yourself with bullshit," I told her.

"And it's bullshit because . . . ?" she sassed.

"Jakiyah, this is a family barbecue for the Fourth of July. And being that she's family, why wouldn't she be here?" I said, getting upset. She was acting like I had some control over my mother and her husband's guest list.

"Whatever," she said, grabbing her bag. She went into the bathroom and slammed the door behind her.

I swear, I wasn't in the mood to go through this Savannah bullshit with her again. I was tired of stressing to her that Savannah was family and that was how I looked at her. I might have been caught off guard when I first met her, and

I might have stared a little longer than Jakiyah had liked, but since then I had given Jakiyah no reason to think that I would even go there.

I hit Ty up to let him know his sister was tripping, and he thought the shit was funny, talked about how, as soon as he saw the chick, he put his eyes to the floor. This caused me to burst out laughing. I let him know that we would meet them downstairs, by the pool area, before I ended the call.

"Jakiyah, do you still want to go down to the pool?" I asked her through the bathroom door.

No response, so I moved away from the door and waited for her to exit the bathroom so that I could take a quick shower. She came wobbling out of the bathroom, like, twenty minutes later, wearing a sexy two-piece bathing suit with a sheer cover-up. She was looking sexy as fuck with her big belly and all, but I was going to play her game. I discreetly looked out the corner of my eye, not letting her know my ass was turned on. I walked by her like I hadn't noticed all the sexiness she had going on, and she didn't like it. I watched as she rolled her eyes and sucked her teeth before I closed the bathroom door. I came back out of the bathroom, wearing only my trunks and my Adidas slides, with no shirt on. I showed off my toned body as I strolled around the room like I was modeling, all the while smirking at her. This caused her to smile, and I walked over to her.

"You play too much move," she said, pushing me.

"Nah, I'm not playing, babe. I need you to know that all of this belongs to you, so you should have no worries. I love you. That's why I asked you to marry me and planted my seed," I said, rubbing her belly.

"I love you too, and I'm sorry, but I just don't like that girl," she admitted.

"Trust that you don't have to worry about her, or any other female, for that matter," I told her before kissing her.

Fifteen minutes later, everyone but Jakiyah was in the pool, clowning. Jakiyah sat on a chair, with her feet up, looking cute and causing me to lose my focus from time to time on the water volleyball game we were playing.

"Come on, man! You playing or what?" German barked after I missed a hit, letting the ball fall in the water.

We fooled around in the pool for another hour, before deciding to go change and go out to get something to eat. Jakiyah was tired, so she didn't want to go and was going to take a nap, but she told me to bring her something back. I kissed her on the lips before heading out the door.

Chapter Forty-One

Jakiyah

When I woke up this morning, I was not feeling well, but I wasn't about to let Qua be around Savannah's ass without me being there. I knew she was up to no good. Qua could act as if he didn't see it, but trust me when I say, "A woman knows." And I knew she was feeling him and was not looking at him like he was family.

"Babe, Mom needs help setting up the backyard, so me, Ty, and German is going to head over there to give her a hand," Qua said. He'd just come out of the hotel bathroom and was fully dressed.

I didn't answer him right away, because this was the bullshit I'd been talking about. And don't get me wrong, because I didn't have a problem with him helping his mom. He had clearly asked her yesterday if she needed help with anything, and she had stated that she didn't. Therefore,

I could bet money that bitch had sent for my man. I promise you, six months pregnant and all that, bitch didn't want to take me there by pushing up on my man, because it was going to be her ass.

"What does she need done today that she didn't need done yesterday?" I asked, and it came off as me being sarcastic, but I didn't mean it that way. I was just asking.

"She needs help setting up the grill, tables, and chairs, and someone has to clean the pool," he responded. I was pissed because that shit could have been done when he asked her yesterday.

"Did your brother and his wife get in yet?" I asked. I was wondering if his brother had got the call to come and help too.

"Yeah, they got in last night. He's on his way to help us, and his wife is going to help Mom in the kitchen," he said.

Someone knocked on the door, so he went to answer it. It was the guys and both Chanel and Desi. The women didn't look too happy about the guys leaving, and again, I could bet money on what the reason was.

"Hey, Jakiyah. We came to stay here and keep you company and order breakfast, if that's okay with you, Ms. Thang," Chanel said.

"That's fine, because I didn't know I would be eating alone this morning," I said, still salty.

Qua ignored my comment. He kissed me on the cheek and said he would see me later.

After they left, Chanel, Desi, and I decided to go down for breakfast, instead of sitting in the room, waiting on room service.

"You know that bitch is the one that probably told his mother to call Qua and ask for help," Chanel barked, clearly upset, just as I was. This let me know that I wasn't crazy for thinking Savannah was up to no damn good.

"Girl, I was thinking the same thing, because he asked his mother yesterday if she needed help, and she said no," I said.

"Well, if that bitch even looks at German the wrong way, it's going to be a problem," Desi chimed in.

"I know she didn't know that we were stopping by yesterday, or maybe she hoped we would. But did you notice how she put in an extra swish of her hips as she walked away, with those small-ass shorts on?" I said.

"I noticed, and so did German. His eyes followed, looking like his ass was about to drool from the mouth. That's why his ass got popped in the back of his damn head," Desi said, causing us all to laugh.

"I just hope no bullshit pop off, because I came to have a good time and to meet the rest of his family before the wedding actually takes place," I mused.

"Speaking of the wedding, did you guys set a date yet?" Chanel asked.

"The baby is due in November, so I'm not sure if I want a winter or a fall wedding. Or maybe we'll just wait for the summer to roll back in again. My baby shower is going to be in September—that I do know—so I might just choose a June date for the wedding."

"I don't know why you stuck on giving yourself a baby shower, when April and I wanted to do it," Chanel whined.

"What's so bad about us all doing it together?" I asked her.

"Your ass supposed to be chilling and letting us handle it, but your stubborn ass isn't going to let the happen," she responded.

"I just want to be involved with my first child's everything," I told her honestly.

Before stuffing a sausage link in her mouth, she said, "Yeah, whatever," letting the conversation go, because she knew I wasn't budging.

We sat in silence as we ate. But I was thinking that even though Chanel and Desi both agreed with me that Savannah looked as if she was up to no good, I needed to stop blaming Qua. I didn't know if she did or she didn't have anything up her sleeve, but it was not his fault that she pranced around like she wanted his ass. I trusted him—I really did—but these tricks make it hard for a dude to stay on track when they were enticing them with a big butt and a smile.

After we finished eating, we went to our separate rooms. I didn't know what they were going to do, but I knew I was taking a nap. The barbecue didn't start until 4:00 p.m., so I had time for a few hours of sleep before getting in the shower and getting dressed to head out.

Chapter Forty-Two

Qua

After introducing Jakiyah to just about all my family, I went to hang with the men, stopping along the way to get a Corona from the cooler. I joined them just as they were about to start a spades game, so I decided to partner with Ty, and my brother, Quinton, teamed up with Donavon's brother, Roy. This was, like, my third time seeing my brother since I first met him, and it still felt bizarre, considering that his face looked exactly like my own.

At one point during the game, I looked over at Jakiyah and couldn't read her facial expression. She was talking with Chanel and Desi. I just hoped that they weren't hyping her ass up about Savannah, who was walking around in a two-piece bathing suit but hadn't once got her ass in the water. I guessed she rubbed all women the wrong way, because Quinton's wife wasn't feeling her ass, either, and had no problem expressing it. Savannah had been extra touchy earlier in the day, but I had brushed that shit off, because I got that she was normally flirtatious. After Roy and Quinton whupped our asses at spades, they were clowning us, so I took my ass over to see if Jakiyah was ready to eat, since she hadn't eaten anything since breakfast. She was ready to eat, so I went to fix her and myself a plate. Then I headed inside to get her some of the strawberry lemonade punch that my mom had made especially for Jakiyah, because she had mentioned that it was her favorite. When I walked inside, Savannah was leaning against the refrigerator, and German's ass was a little too close. He was smiling up in her face as they talked. He was being a dumb ass right now, as he knew that Desi popped off at the drop of a dime.

"Yo, German. Let me holla at you real quick," I told him.

"I already know what you're going to say, man, but I was only talking," he said.

"Listen, you already know how your girl is, and I don't want no bullshit at my mom's crib. So you need to take your ass back outside with your girl," I told his ass.

I watched to make sure he took his ass outside. Trust me, if we were anywhere else, I would have minded my business, but him disrespecting his girl in my mom's crib wasn't going down.

"Let me find out you cock blocking," Savannah whispered in my ear after walking up on me.

"Baby girl, trust when I say that what that man does with his cock is his business, but if he wants to step out on his girl and be disrespectful when she's right outside, well, that is on him. But he's not going to do it in my mom's crib," I told her.

Now I could have told her to have some damn respect for herself and stop acting thirsty for other women's men, especially when she knew that man came here with his girl, but I didn't. I was starting to see exactly what Jakiyah was seeing, and I didn't think it had anything to do with the men. I just thought she had a thing for pissing off other females.

"So, you saying I'm being disrespectful when he came in here, talking to me?" she said, touching my arm. This caused me to move away from her ass.

"Now, you know those words didn't come out of my mouth, but if I was you, I would steer clear of the men that are taken, shorty," I told her ass.

"Whatever," she said, with a roll of her eyes, as she put an extra swish in her walk, then turned back to look at me. I guessed she wanted to see if I was looking at her ass.

I knew what I just said to her had gone in one ear and right out the other, but that shit was going to catch up with her ass soon enough if she kept playing this game she got going on.

When I got back outside with Jakiyah, a glass of lemonade punch in my hand, she was wearing that face again, and I swore, I couldn't wait until she had our baby, because ever since she'd got pregnant, everything had annoyed her ass.

"What took you so long to get me something to drink?" she said nastily, and I knew it had to do with me coming outside right behind Savannah.

"I had to break up the little flirt session that Savannah and German was having in my mother's crib," I whispered to her.

"What was they doing?" she asked me as she looked around for Desi, as if she was going to say something about it to her. So I knew I couldn't say the wrong thing.

"They were just talking, but I let them both know that the shit was disrespectful. Also, I told them to leave out of the house and go back outside," I said, hoping that was enough to keep her mouth shut and prevent her from saying anything to Desi.

I started eating my food, and the shit was banging. I had some barbecued ribs, macaroni and cheese, baked beans, and two burgers on my plate, acting like I hadn't eaten in months. I just wished the plates were bigger, as I wanted some of my mom's lasagna and chopped barbecue, but I didn't even have room for it. But trust, my ass was taking me a pan of food home when it was time to go. No way would I come all the way to Vermont and not eat all my mom's favorites.

"That girl is a damn hot mess . . . and her stank-ass friends," I heard Jakiyah say, causing me to look up from my plate. I watched as Savannah and her friends threw those asses in a circle as they danced.

To be honest, I was surprised that my mom and Donavon even allowed that type of music and dancing, being that they were always playing gospel music, but if they were cool, I was cool.

As quick as my head went up, it went back down, because I didn't want to be accused of staring too damn hard. But shit, it was a sight to see, and I bet I wasn't the only man whose shit was hard right now.

"Babe, eat your food and let that girl be," I told her, but all she did was roll her eyes.

"Do you want to get in the pool later?" I asked her, hoping she said she did, because she probably wasn't going to want my ass to get in if she wasn't getting in.

"Nah, I'm good, but you can get in if you want," she responded, knowing damn well if any other female besides Desi and Chanel got in the pool, she was going to have a problem with it.

My mom walked over to check on Jakiyah, and that was when I excused myself to dump my plate. Jakiyah was still eating, as she was picking over her food. Just as I was about to hop my ass in the pool with the rest of my dudes, I heard Desi's ass going off on Savannah. This let me know that Jakiyah had opened her big-ass mouth. I saw Savannah's friends getting hyped, so I hurried to the other side of the backyard, where they had gathered. Chanel had already made it over there, and Jakiyah was wobbling her ass across the yard like she was about to fight. She had done lost her damn mind for even getting up out of her seat. I didn't give a fuck who was going to swing first at this point. I just needed to stop Jakiyah's ass from making it over there before all hell broke loose and she ended up getting hurt. Ty and German were out of the pool by the time I made it over to Jakiyah, so hopefully they, along with my uncle Terrance, could get that shit under control.

"Yo, what are you doing?" I barked at her ass.

"Qua, if you think I'm about to let them jump Desi, you done lost your mind," she said, trying to get around me, pissing me off even more.

"So, you really about to put our baby at risk over some bullshit right now? You can't be serious. I'm going to need you to fall back now," I said, my voice raised, letting her ass know I wasn't playing.

She sucked her teeth and rolled her eyes, but she backed her ass up. Then I walked over to see if they had the situation under control. This was exactly what I had been trying to prevent, and if Jakiyah was going to say anything to Desi about Savannah and German flirting, she should have waited until we had left my mother's crib. All day I had been saying the same bullshit about having no drama here. I had German take Desi inside to calm down, and within minutes Savannah was acting as if nothing had happened. I swear I wanted to ring her damn neck too.

"I'm ready to go now," Jakiyah said as she stood with her arms folded against her chest and her lips poked out, daring me to say that I wasn't ready. Little did she know, I was ready to go.

"Fine. We can go. Let me just go let my family know that I'm leaving," I told her.

"Whatever. I'll be out front," she sassed before walking off.

I knew Jakiyah was probably pissed right now, but my mother wanted to give us some food to take with us, so I waited on her to fix the plates.

I told Chanel and Desi, who were also ready to leave, that they could go out front and wait with Jakiyah, and I asked them to let her know that I would be coming out in a few minutes. I knew it wouldn't matter, because she still was going to be pissed regardless.

I just wanted her to understand that she was pregnant now, and she needed to be mindful of that. She had been acting like she hadn't been putting our baby in harm's way. Same shit with her job. She had come home several times and had told me her patient's son and his girlfriend had been up in there fighting. Still, when I told her that she needed to stop working there, she got upset. The only reason she had finally called the agency and asked for another case was that I had told her ass that I was going to that house to fuck that nigga up for putting her and my child in harm's way.

When I finally made it to the car, Jakiyah was in her feelings, which I deduced from the shaking of her leg. For that reason, I didn't say shit to her, and when I dropped her, Desi, and Chanel off at the hotel, I handed her the room key, but I didn't go upstairs with them. I needed to clear my head before I said some things that I wasn't going to be able to take back.

I parked the car and took my ass to the bar in the hotel and had me a few drinks, as I was stressing right about now. I hated to argue with Jakiyah, and it seemed like ever since she'd got pregnant, her mood swings were always on ten and I had to tell her all the time that I was not the enemy. If I said anything to her out of anger, it was because I loved her and didn't want anything to happen to her or the baby. It was my job to protect them. I didn't even know if I wanted a wedding, surrounded by family and friends, because shit was always popping off. Given that my son or daughter would be in attendance, I was really reconsidering it. Jakiyah had never wanted a big wedding, anyway, so maybe we would do something really intimate. *Something with just a few family members and friends who are drama free*, I thought as I downed another shot.

Chapter Forty-Three

Jakiyah

When Qua didn't come up to the room when I got back to the hotel, I decided to call his mother to apologize for not saying good-bye to her. I explained that I'd been upset but that I still should have been polite about it. She said that she understood and that she hoped that she could see me again before we left to go back home. I told her that she would, though I really did not know if that was true.

I was just so pissed, because Qua had jumped to conclusions and had accused me of saying something to Desi. I had nothing to do with Desi flying off the handle. It was Savannah who had said some slick shit out of her mouth that had set Desi off. He had every right to be upset about me trying to fight in my condition, but it was a normal reaction when you saw some bitches trying to all come for your friend. Yes, I considered her a friend. Desi, Chanel, and I had become really close, so any one of us would have had the same reaction. To be honest, I had forgotten all about being pregnant. All I'd focused on was them surrounding Desi, and I'd been ready to get it popping, just as my girls would have done for me. But Qua didn't see it that way.

I was done with this mini vacation, and I was now ready to go home. Coming here to meet his family had turned out to be the opposite of what I had thought it would be. There was a knock at the door just then, and it brought me out of my little vent about today's events, which was a good thing, because all I was doing was hyping myself up.

"Hey, bighead. What do you want?" I asked Ty after I opened the door and found him standing there.

"I just came to ask you why you got my dude stressing the hell out," he said, walking in.

"He stressing himself out," I said, rolling my eyes before going to sit back on the bed.

"You know damn well your ass had no business trying to go nowhere near the area they were about to fight in," he said, chastising me.

"That might be true, Ty, but I wasn't thinking clearly at the time. But his ass going off the way he did wasn't called for," I retorted, defending myself.

"It *was* called for. That's his seed you carrying, in case you forgot."

"No, I didn't forget, but like I said, he just overreacted when speaking to me. I'm his fiancée, not his child," I said, getting heated.

"Calm your ass down and make that shit right with your man. You were wrong, and you know that shit. I'm out," he said, then left.

So, I was at fault, it seemed, according to Ty and Qua. So I guessed I was going to have to be the one to apologize, I thought as I got up to go to the refrigerator. A smile spread on my face when I saw that Qua's mother had sent me the rest of the strawberry lemonade punch. I grabbed me a glass to pour me some. My greedy ass warmed up some macaroni and cheese with chopped barbecue to go with my punch. Just as I sat down to eat, Qua walked in.

I could tell he'd been drinking, because I smelled it on his breath as he kissed me on my neck after whispering in my ear that he was sorry. I tried to eat, pretending to still be mad at him, but he was making it hard as he started massaging my breasts. My kitty tingled from his touch. I let out a small moan, not caring about the food sitting in front of me, as I allowed him to pull me into his arms. He kissed my lips, forced his tongue into my mouth, and I tasted the Hennessy that he'd consumed. It still lingered on his tongue, giving me a little taste of what I couldn't have, since I was pregnant. His hands caressed my body until they reached between my legs, teased my clit through the shorts I was wearing. I couldn't take it anymore, as my legs got weak.

"Fuck me, Qua," I moaned as he undressed me. He pushed me down lightly on the bed, and then he dived between my legs.

I put one of my legs up on his shoulder and tried to find the perfect position, one where I wouldn't be uncomfortable with my big-ass belly.

"Oh, shit, Qua." I cried out just as I came in his mouth.

He stood there, with that cocky-ass grin he was known for, then removed his shorts and underwear as I anxiously waited on him to enter me. Qua wasted no time positioning me on my side and entering me slowly. In that moment I forgot about any stress I was feeling earlier. Qua switched positions: he pulled me to the edge of the bed, and then he pounded in and out of me, causing me to rock my hips and my big belly as I received every stroke of pleasure he was giving me. I felt his dick swell inside of me, which meant he was on the verge of cumming, and so was I. He let out a deep groan as he pumped with deep, long strokes until we both came together.

"I'm sorry, babe," he said as he helped me up off the bed so that we could take a shower together.

"I'm sorry too. And I'm going to try to keep in mind that I'm pregnant," I said, then kissed him on his lips.

After we got out of the shower, he oiled my body and helped me into my nightshirt. Then we both headed to the kitchen for some more of his mom's food. Once we'd fixed our plates, we didn't bother to sit at the table. We both went and sat on the bed and ate there while we watched a movie on the TV. After I finished eating, the movie was watching me as my ass dozed off.

When we got back home, I was the first to say that I was happy to be home—so happy that I was on my way to my parents' house. I had missed my parents, but I had missed baby Andrea more. She was my li'l stinka butt, and I had hated not seeing her. Baby Andrea was fussy today, and my mom said she wasn't feeling well, so I went upstairs to my mom's bedroom to get the Children's Motrin. Some things I saw on my mom's dresser pissed me off. I grabbed them, and I took two steps at a time as I dashed back to the kitchen, where she was.

"Mom, what the hell is this?" I yelled, throwing the envelopes down on the kitchen table.

"Jakiyah, you need to lower your voice. And remember who the hell you're talking to," she said.

"Mom, what reason would you have to be accepting mail from Tamia?" I asked, lowering my voice this time, but the anger I felt was still evident.

"Jakiyah, what did I tell you about forgiveness? She wrote me, apologizing, so I sort of been mentoring her," she said.

I looked at her, trying to figure out if my mom was losing her mind, because why would you want to mentor someone who had taken another person's life? Tamia was someone who probably would have no problem murdering again, so why would my mom want to associate with that kind of person? Tamia was mentally unstable, and my mom needed to know how dangerous it was to continue communicating with her.

"Mom, you don't need to be communicating with her. She's unstable, and she's a smart unstable. She's manipulating you, and soon she's going to play you into telling her whatever she needs to know to try to hurt us again," I told her.

"Jakiyah, I'm not a fool, and I would never give her any information concerning any of us. And I doubt that she wishes to harm us. She just wants our forgiveness, and I believe that she deserves that," she said, sounding like her normal crazy self.

"Mom, it's okay to forgive, but accepting mail and corresponding with her is not acceptable," I told her.

"Not acceptable to who, Jakiyah? Because at the end of the day, I'm grown and I make my own decisions."

I was going to need my father and Ty on this one, because she really had done lost her damn mind, and I didn't know what to do to help her find it. After giving baby Andrea some medicine and putting her to sleep, I went out front to call Ty. I needed him over here like yesterday. While I waited on Ty, I sat reading through the letters. I had a problem with how my mom couldn't read between the lines. Tamia was playing my mother like a fucking game, and my mom was feeding into it. But what alarmed me most was the last letter. In it Tamia told my mom that they were considering her for outpatient treatment. Who the hell in their right mind would let her murdering ass out for outpatient services, when she had killed someone?

I didn't know if there was any truth in what she had written, but I knew that I needed to contact someone, even if that meant pleading with Andris's parents to team up with me to keep Tamia's ass in there. She mentioned in the letter that her being off her medication was what had triggered her aggressive behavior toward Andris, as had remembering the traumatic event of losing her child, which she blamed him for. I swear, that was bullshit, and whoever her doctor or psychologist was needed to be locked in a damn institution.

Chapter Forty-Four

Ty

Jakiyah called me, upset about my mother corresponding with Tamia's crazy ass, and I didn't blame her, because my mom should have known better. I didn't know what was going on, but my mom was losing her mind, and now this had convinced me even more that maybe her ass was unstable too. I didn't understand what would possess her to want to have any kind of relationship with the girl after what she did to me. I wasn't interested in arguing with my mom, but I had to go to my mom's place because Jakiyah needed me. I was well aware that trying to get through to my mom was going to be like pulling teeth.

"Hey, Mom. What's going on?" I asked her after walking into the kitchen, her favorite place.

"If you're here to give me the third degree, like your sister did, don't bother. You two are going to stop acting like you don't know who's the parent," she said.

"Honey, you know you have no business talking to that girl after what she done to Ty," my father said as he walked into the kitchen. He greeted her with a kiss.

"Who didn't Jakiyah call! And I'm not going to allow you all to gang up on me," my mother fussed.

"Mom, we are not ganging up on you. We just want you to realize that this girl is dangerous," I told her.

"She's no longer dangerous. She admits that what she done was wrong, and all she wants now is to right her wrongs and ask for forgiveness," she said.

I got up and walked into the living room, where Jakiyah was stationed. I just couldn't remain in that kitchen without saying something that I knew that I would regret later.

"Jakiyah, I really think that Mom is really losing it. Some of the shit that comes out of her mouth just don't make no damn sense," I mused.

"Now you see what I be talking about. Now, something is up with Mom, like she bumped her damn head or something. She really had me thinking that I need to take baby Andrea home with me, because if she wants to put her life in danger, I be damned if I sit back and let the baby be in harm's way."

"How are you going to take care of the baby and your six months pregnant?" I asked her.

"Well, unless she cut out this foolishness, I'm going to have to do what I have to do, because Mom still looking at Tamia as her damn friend. I'm going to see if I could contact someone, because I'm sure that Tamia shouldn't be contacting her after what she did to you. She's the mom of a victim, so that alone is a reason for her to not write mom," she said, pissed off.

I stayed at the house for about another hour. After Jakiyah threatened to take baby Andrea, my mother finally agreed that she wasn't going to accept any more letters from Tamia. I didn't know if I believed that she would stop all contact, but I was praying she did, because Tamia's ass wasn't dealing with a full deck. I didn't bother to stay for dinner. Chanel was cooking dinner, so I bounced after saying my good-byes.

As soon as I walked through the door, the smell of some good cooking hit me and my mouth began to water.

"Smells good, bae. What you cooking?" I asked Chanel before grabbing her from behind and kissing her on the lips.

"I did something different. I was tired of fried chicken, and I know you are too, so I made oxtails, cabbage, rice and beans, and some plantains," she said. "Oh, and for dessert, I made banana bread to go with some vanilla-bean ice cream."

"Damn. What did I do to deserve all of this?" I asked, then kissed her on the neck.

"Do I need a reason to get in the kitchen and cook for my man?" she asked, getting defensive.

"Yo, what's up with you? You just took that shit all the way left," I said, looking at her ass sideways.

"I'm sorry. It just came out the wrong way. I didn't mean anything by it. Let's just eat," she said, turning back to the stove.

We sat at the table and ate in silence, and that never happened. Chanel always had some story to tell about her workday. I kept watching her, and I could tell that something was bothering her, because this was not my Chanel. My Chanel had always been the chatty type, so I needed to know what was going on with her.

"Chanel, what the hell is going on with you?" I asked her.

"Nothing is going on with me, Ty. I'm fine," she lied. But it was written all over her face.

"So, if nothing is wrong with you, why the hell you cook all this food, just to pick over it? Stop playing and tell me what's going on with you," I said, getting frustrated.

"I'm pregnant," she said just above a whisper as she looked at me with a nervous expression on her face.

I didn't know what to say about her being pregnant. We weren't trying, and she'd been on birth control, since we'd been sleeping together without a condom, so I was a little shocked. I didn't want to take too long to respond. I didn't want her to think that I was upset about it because I wasn't just a little curious as to how we got caught up.

"I know what you thinking, and I don't know, so that will be a question for the doctor when we go to see him," she said, knowing me all too well.

"It's a legitimate thought because you have been on the pill since we stopped using condoms. So yeah, the doc is going to have to explain some things," I told her.

"Well, he's going to tell you that birth control is ninety-one percent to ninety-nine percent effective in preventing pregnancy. However, that still means there is a very small risk of pregnancy, and it just so happened that we are that small risk," she said, sounding like she had read that shit straight from Google.

"Yes, I googled it," she said, again showing me that she knew me so well.

"Well, I guess my baby is having my baby, and since you're so good at reading my thoughts, you should know that I'm happy. Now can we go back to eating this good food, before it gets cold?" I said, then dug right back in.

I didn't know how I felt about having a baby right now, and I knew that I had said that I was happy, but I just didn't feel we were ready to have a child right now. I knew how Chanel was, so I knew that she was going to want my last name for herself and the child. That meant she was going to expect a marriage proposal. I had settled down and had stopped creeping in these streets, but I wasn't ready to get married. I was still young, but I knew that excuse wasn't going to work with her, especially since she knew that Jakiyah had got a proposal. After we finished eating dinner, she heated up the banana bread and put the ice cream on top. After dessert, we were both in relax mode and chilled on the couch, with the television on. The TV watched us, as we both were lost in our own thoughts.

Chapter Forty-Five

Jakiyah

Qua and I had been getting along so well lately, and I was enjoying not being my normal hormonal self, which caused us to argue just about everything. I'd been spending a lot of time at my mom's house since I hadn't been back to work. I was seven months pregnant now, and this new patient that they had assigned me to had only wanted a damn maid. The work had taken a toll on my back, so I was now officially on maternity leave. Qua couldn't be happier. He'd been trying to get me to stop working since he found out I was pregnant.

My mom felt that I was there to babysit her, but I really wasn't, and I tried to explain to her that I was just there to offer a hand with baby Andrea and my father since I had more time on my hands. My father's health has been failing for the past few weeks, and I had just honestly been helping her out. I'd also been checking the mail on the low, but she didn't need to know that.

I wanted to have a conversation with her today about Andris's mom, because when I'd reached out to her about Tamia, we had got to talking, and she had expressed how much she missed her son and not spending time with her granddaughter. I'd had to take a minute to think about how I felt when I lost my sister. My first thought had been to hold on to the one thing that I had left of my sister. I had told Andris's mom that I would talk to my mother about bringing baby Andrea to visit. Hopefully, my mother, who was always talking about forgiveness, would have no problem forgiving and would let the baby spend time with her father's side of the family. Just as baby Andrea had offered us comfort after Cydney passed, I believed she would do the same for them, so I just hoped my mom would allow that to happen.

I went upstairs to check on my father after noticing he wasn't in the living room, sitting in his favorite chair in front of the television. He was in his bed, sleeping, but something seemed off about his position on the bed. It looked like he had fallen on the bed instead of getting in the bed. I nervously walked over to the bed, my hands shaking. I checked for a pulse, being that I didn't see his body moving from breathing. He didn't have a pulse, and he didn't respond when I called out to him, so I screamed for my mother, and she came rushing up the stairs.

"Jakiyah, what's going on?" she asked, out of breath. Then she grabbed her chest when she realized that I was standing over my father's lifeless body.

"Mom, call nine-one-one," I said as the tears fell, because I already knew that he was gone.

We were all in the living room now, still waiting on the coroner to arrive. We'd been waiting for over an hour now, and all the while my father's body had remained upstairs, making the situation that much worse. My mom had been given a sedative, and she was now upstairs, in my old bedroom, sleeping. That was a good thing, because she was losing it. I had never got the chance to speak to her about the baby and her visiting Andris's mother, but I called Andris's mother and asked her if she could pick the baby up and look after her for a few days, because no one was stable enough at my mom's house to care for her right now.

Ty was upstairs with my dad and was just sitting there. He refused to leave him, and it broke my heart to see him so broken, as he was usually the strong one. I called German and asked him to come over, because I knew that when it was time to remove my dad's body, Ty was going to lose it, and I was in no condition to stop him. We had to wait until my dad had an autopsy before we could bury him, but they believed that he had had a heart attack. I was beating myself up, wondering whether I could have saved him if I had checked on him sooner.

The coroner arrived about forty-five minutes later, shortly after Qua showed up. Just as I had thought, when they tried to remove my dad, Ty flipped out. I thanked God that Qua had arrived when he did, because German would not have been able to handle Ty on his own. Chanel couldn't even get him to calm down, and I was holding on by a thin thread, trying not to lose it myself, because I felt like dropping to the floor and kicking and screaming for my father to just wake up.

"Are you okay?" Qua asked me.

I just shook my head no, because I wasn't okay.

"Babe, I'm so sorry for your loss. I wish I could take your pain away," he stated.

I buried my face in Qua's chest as they carried my father's body down the stairs and out of the house to the awaiting van. Qua held on to me as my body shook uncontrollably. I couldn't get it to stop as I wailed loudly for my father. Later, Qua rocked me in his arms up in my old bedroom, and I eventually fell asleep. I did not wake up until the next morning. Qua had to be to work at 6:00 a.m., but he didn't want to leave me. I told him to go ahead and assured him that I would be okay. After I expended a little more effort at convincing him that I was good, he left. His boss was a pain in the ass when the workers had last-minute call-ins, and even though Qua didn't care, I didn't want him to get in trouble.

Chapter Forty-Six

Jakiyah

Ty and I arrived at Browne Funeral Home. I knew I had to be the strong one, because he was already freaking out. I was numb to everything that was being said, as I was having a déjà vu moment, reliving when I was here, in the same position, when my sister passed. After we took care of business there, we went back to the house to deal with my mother. My mom looked like she had aged overnight, and I felt so bad for her because I couldn't take away the pain she was feeling right now.

When we got to the house, she was sitting in my dad's chair, trying to feel that closeness that she was missing. This broke my heart too, and I knew she wasn't going to be the same without him. He could calm her craziness when she went overboard with it or when she needed to be told that she was wrong, but we no longer had him to balance us out as a family. She kept asking me about baby Andrea's whereabouts, so I called Andris's mother and she said that she would come right over with the baby and that she understood. I assured her that this wouldn't be the last time that she saw baby Andrea, and she couldn't stop thanking me. She said just having her for that one day had caused her to smile, and she hadn't smiled since the day her son died.

By the time I finished making my mom some tea and getting her two aspirins for her headache, baby Andrea was home. She lifted my mother's spirits. I went upstairs to go through my dad's closet to find him something to be buried in for the funeral next week. I tried to prepare myself mentally for this task, but it didn't work, as the waterworks started. I could smell the cigar smoke mixed with Old Spice on some of his things, and all the memories of Ty and me teasing him about still wearing Old Spice caused me to smile. I missed him so much, I wished that I had spent more time with him. Whenever I'd visited, I stayed in the kitchen with my mother and never went in the living room to sit and watch one of his favorite programs with him.

I wiped my tears as I carried his things downstairs and to my car. When I went back inside, I let my mom know about all the arrangements and what I had decided to bury him in, to see if she agreed or wanted to make any changes. Ty had been quiet the whole time and was just watching television and messing with his phone, but I could tell that he was hurting and didn't know what to do with himself. He told me that Chanel was pregnant but that he hadn't got a chance really to digest how he felt about it, because of dad's sudden passing. I was happy for him, but I was sad that dad wasn't going to get to know our children and that our children would not get to know their grandfather.

I stayed with Mom until about 6:00 p.m. I needed to stop by the funeral home to drop off my dad's things before 7:00 p.m. Ty said that he was going to stay with her tonight, so I didn't feel too guilty about going home after. I needed to get some rest and to try to get my mental state on point, because I didn't know if I was coming or going with all that was going on. When I finally got home, Qua was making dinner. I greeted him with a kiss and a thank-you before heading upstairs to take a shower. Before I stepped in the bathroom, I called Ty to check on my mother and make sure that she was okay. He said that she was sleeping and that Chanel was giving the baby a bath and was going to put her to bed.

I knew that I was going to have to have a conversation with my mother when the funeral was over. I didn't want her staying in the house alone with the baby, and given that I wouldn't be moving back home, she was going to have to come and live with me and Qua. I knew that she probably wasn't going to want to leave her home to come live with me or Ty, but I really hoped that she would consider it.

I wasn't feeling well the next morning, but I knew I needed to get myself together, as I needed to go to my mom's house and get the place ready for my uncle Tony and his wife, who were arriving today. Qua had already gone to work, but he had said that he was going to meet me at my mother's house when he got off work. I went into the kitchen to make myself some toast and tea before leaving.

I knew that my mother and Ty had plenty to eat at the house. My mother's neighbors had been more than generous with all the food and bottled water that they had dropped off at the house. My father was loved by everyone. Before he got sick, he was the neighborhood mechanic and fixed everybody's car for free. He was a generous man and did what he could to help anyone in need, so it was only right for them to return the favor and be there for his wife.

When I got back to my mother's house, my uncle and his wife were already there and had everything covered, so I didn't have to do anything. I could sit down and relax. And once Qua got there, he made sure that I didn't lift a finger to do anything, that I ate, and that I stayed off my feet, which had swelled up from being on them so much. For the rest of the day, we all sat around and shared memories of my dad. It felt good to see my mom feeling somewhat better.

Chapter Forty-Seven

Qua

It had been a few weeks since Jakiyah's dad's home-going service, and Jakiyah had been kind of depressed. Since today was my day off, I decided to get her out of the house. She fussed about not wanting to go anywhere, because the swelling in her feet had just gotten better, but I assured her that we wouldn't be doing much walking, and she agreed to go. When we got in the car, her phone rang. She answered the call with a worried look on her face and told whoever it was on the phone that she was on her way.

"What happened, babe? Is everything okay?" I asked her.

"I'm not sure. Ty said that my mother hasn't been feeling good and hasn't been out of her room since this afternoon. I just want to stop by there to make sure that everything is okay," she said.

When we pulled up to her mother's house, I got out to help her out of the car, followed behind her, then waited for her to open the front door. As soon as she opened the door, everyone yelled, "Surprise!" and I made sure to be right behind her, in case she was so startled, she tripped or something. She jumped and screamed so loud, and although I felt bad that they had scared her, I was laughing my ass off.

"Ty, I'm going to kill you. Do you know how worried I was all the way over here?" she told him.

"It's not my fault. It was all Qua's idea to set you up. He knew if he tried it any other way, you weren't going to go for it," he replied, snitching.

"OMG! April, you were in on this too," Jakiyah said, hugging April.

"I'm sorry, but, girl, you know how you are, so this was the only way," April told her.

Chanel and Desi had done a great job decorating the house, and I loved the color scheme that they had used. We didn't know what we were having yet, so the green and yellow were perfect. Jakiyah walked around thanking everyone for coming out. She was surprised to see my mother, Donavon, Quinton, and his wife. I sat around talking shit and drinking beer with Ty, German, and my brother until it was time for Jakiyah to open her gifts. She looked happy, but I knew it was a bittersweet moment for her. But she did her best to enjoy herself, and I was glad that we were all able to get her out of her funk, even if it was only for a day. We had so many gifts that I didn't think we had to buy anything for the baby until he or she was, like, six months old. These mofos had overdone it.

"How you feeling?" I asked Jakiyah, being as she hadn't been feeling well earlier.

"I'm good now, and before I forget, thank you for doing this," she said.

"Nah. This was all your homegirls' doing," I told her, because all I did was help set her up.

"Well, thanks for getting me out of the house," she said, then reached over to give me a kiss.

After we all cut the cake and enjoyed it, I got help getting as much of the stuff into my car as we could fit, which wasn't much, so I had to recruit Ty, German, and April to get all the other gifts back to the house. After we got to the house, unloaded everything into the living room, and said our good-byes to Ty, German, and April, I grabbed Jakiyah's hand and led her upstairs. I told her to open the door to the room the baby would be sleeping in. When she did, she gasped, before tears fell.

"Qua, this is beautiful! But when did you have the time to do all of this?" she cried as she walked around the room, in awe.

"Babe, I'm a man of many talents, but trying to get anything past you is a hard task. So I had the decorators come as soon as we left today, and they did all of this within a matter of hours," I told her.

I had opted out of having the baby room painted, because of the smell, so I'd picked a wallpaper with a teddy bear design that matched the curtains, the lamp, and the bedding for the crib.

"Thank you so much for doing this, bae." She smiled.

"Anything for my boo," I said, slapping her on the ass.

After Jakiyah admired the nursery, I called my mom to see if they had made it back to the hotel and to let her know that I wanted to treat them to lunch before their flight tomorrow. I wished that she hadn't moved so far away. I really missed her being only a borough away.

When I got off the phone, I found Jakiyah sitting on the edge of the bed. She looked worn out from today's event, so I went into the bathroom and turned the shower on. I had been running her baths, but my mother had said that she shouldn't be taking baths this far along in her pregnancy. I didn't know how true that was, but since I had no idea, I just went with what my mother had said.

"Babe, I left the water running for you, and I'm going to leave your nightclothes on the bed for you. I'm going to start putting some of the stuff away. I be back when I'm done," I told her.

"Okay. Thanks. And could you check the mail? I haven't checked it all week," she said.

I told her okay as I left the room.

My phone alerted me that I had a text message, and when I looked down at the message, an instant frown graced my face, because I had told this chick to stop calling and texting my phone. Jakiyah and I were arguing one morning, before I left for work, and I was in a funk the whole day. When I went to clock out that afternoon, my coworker Kim approached me, being flirtatious as usual, but on this day, I took the bait. Honestly, I was interested in nothing other than going out to get a few drinks with her, but one thing led to another, and I fucked up. But it was only that one time, and I let her know that I loved my girl, and she fronted like she understood.

She had basically been on some bullshit, to the point where it was starting to piss me off. I didn't want to report her ass for sexual harassment, because without a doubt, she would lose her job, pending an investigation. I was willing to take the punk way out of this shit if she didn't back off, because I wasn't about to let anything or anybody come in between Jakiyah and me walking down the aisle. I had yet to tell Jakiyah that I still saw Keem from time to time. I didn't know how she was going to feel about it. I just couldn't cut him off. He was my best friend, so anytime that I hooked up with him, I would have to make up some shit, like telling her that I was hanging out with my dude Vince from the job. I knew that I couldn't go into this marriage with secrets, so I was going to eventually tell her. I just hoped that she understood, because I refused to hold him responsible for something his girl did.

After I finished putting all the things in the baby's room, I went out front to get the mail from out of the box. Then I went back upstairs and placed it on the dresser. I hopped in the shower, and after I got out, Jakiyah was already sleeping, so I decided to respond to Kim's text message and plead with her to leave me the hell alone. If she didn't bite, I was going to threaten to report her for sexual harassment. I would show every text message she had sent and would reveal the phone call that she had made. About twenty minutes passed after I texted Kim, and she still hadn't responded, so I turned my phone off and put it on the charger. Then I got into the bed and cuddled behind Jakiyah and went my ass to sleep.

Jakiyah wasn't feeling well again the next morning, and her feet were swollen again. I was starting to worry, but she said that she had a doctor's appointment next week. I was going to make sure that I was at that appointment: I needed to be there to speak to the doctor myself.

"Babe, are you sure that you're going to be okay? Because I could cancel lunch with my mom and my brother and stay home with you," I told her.

"Qua, I'm going to be fine. I'm just feeling a little nauseous, and my feet big as shit, but I'm good. So go and have lunch, like you promised. Tell everyone that I'm sorry, and thank them for everything," she said, basically dismissing me.

I made her something to eat and left her a bottled water and a few snacks to hold her over until I got back home.

Lunch went well, but I couldn't lie and say that I wasn't distracted, because I was worried about Jakiyah. I texted her so many times that she texted back and told me that if I sent one more text, she was going to turn her phone off. This caused me to crack up. It felt good spending time with my mom and brother, and I hated to see them leave, as I knew it was going to be a while before I saw them again. Over lunch my mom said that she was going to try to come a week before Jakiyah's delivery and would stay at the house so that she could be here for the delivery. I didn't know how that was going to work, because my dad had said that he wanted to be here also, and I was really looking forward to his visit. I hadn't seen him in, like, forever.

On my way home, I stopped at the store to get Jakiyah her ice cream and party mix, because once I was in the house, I was not going back out to get it for her, like she had had me do one night, like, at two o'clock in the morning. Had my ass out in the streets, looking for a twenty-four-hour bodega. That shit wasn't happening again, so I made sure to try to stay on point.

Chapter Forty-Eight

Jakiyah

"Jakiyah, just try to calm down," April said, coaching me over the phone, but I was tight right now.

"April, how am I supposed to calm down? I'm so pissed right now at him. I'm supposed to be marrying this man and having his baby, and he keeping shit from me," I whined.

"Are you sure the letter said Keem got the address from Qua? I mean, think about it. . . . Wouldn't Keem know the address, being that he's Qua best friend?" she said, making sense, but I didn't care.

"We're best friends," I shouted, not meaning to.

"Jakiyah, you need to calm down, seriously. I can't have you stressing my godchild the hell out!" she shouted, getting my attention.

"It just bothers me, because Qua knows how I feel about being lied to, and it makes me think that if he lied about this, then what else is he lying about?" I began crying from frustration.

"Jakiyah, honey, don't cry. I'm sure he was going to tell you. And I'm going to need you to remember that Keem might have known the address and given it to her, and she just assumed that he got it from Qua," she said, trying to convince me. "What did she say in the letter? To be honest, I'm surprised she waited this long to reach out to you."

"She didn't say much in the letter . . . just that she would like to speak to me face-to-face. She feels that words on paper are just that, and that she needs for me to see that she's being sincere. Honestly speaking, I could care less what she has to say, because it's not going to bring my sister back," I said, getting emotional.

"I understand completely. Because, honestly, I don't think that I would be able to offer her forgiveness right now. However, I would want some kind of closure. I know you want answers to questions that you have about the whole situation."

"I do, but I'm not ready to have any kind of correspondence with her, because I don't trust anyone who could look me in the face after doing something like that. I would honestly have respected her more if she had shown some type of remorse by telling me and turning herself in," I said truthfully.

"Facts, but listen to me. When Qua gets home, please remember that if you're upset, angry, and stressed, the baby will be too," she told me.

"Okay, April. And thanks for listening. I'll call you later," I told her, then ended the call.

I couldn't for the life of me just lie back and relax. Even though I tried not to be, I was upset, and it showed. If my feet weren't as swollen as they were, I would have left and gone to my mother's house. That's the only way that I could promise that I was not going to go off upon seeing Qua. I had to rub my belly, as my little baby was in there playing kickball. I tried to calm my nerves and forced myself to lie back and relax.

When Qua finally made it home and walked into the room, he knew something was wrong just by the look on my face. His smile disappeared quickly. "What did I do now?" he joked, but I didn't find shit funny.

"Qua, you've known me long enough to know that I have trust issues and I don't like being lied to. I've told you time and time again that no matter how I'm going to take something, I would rather be told the truth," I said, tearing up.

"Jakiyah, what the hell are you talking about?" he asked nervously, which in my book equaled guilty.

"How did Keem know our address to convey it to Yessenia?" I asked him.

I watched his facial expression, which told me he dreaded answering my question. He knew this conversation was probably going to end up as an argument.

"Keem has been my friend for, like, forever, so I'm sure he knows my address. But as far as my giving him permission to use it, that I didn't do," he answered.

"So, have you been speaking to him?" I asked him.

"Like I said, he's my best friend."

"So, after what they did, you could still be his friend?" I asked, in disbelief.

"Jakiyah, the only thing Keem is guilty of is cheating on his girlfriend," he had the nerve to say.

"What? You can't be serious! His actions cost my sister her life!" I yelled at him.

"He's not responsible for Yessenia's reaction to him cheating, so let's be real here and place that blame where it belongs, and on the person who is serving time for it," he said, sounding as if I was agitating him.

"Wow," I said, because I was really taken aback by his response.

"Wow what? You can't blame him for what happened, but you can stop speaking to him, like you chose to do. He's my best friend. I'm not going to stop speaking to him over something he had no control over," he spat.

"So why the fuck was it a secret, then?" I shouted.

"It was a secret for this very reason. We could never have a conversation without you getting like this. That's why some things I just keep to myself," he said, then walked out of the room.

After thinking about the conversation, I felt that I could have handled it better. I wanted to get up and apologize, but my damn feet were hurting. But after an hour passed and he didn't come to see if I was okay, I got angry all over again. I got up, no longer caring about my swollen feet, and went into the bathroom to take a shower.

The hell with him and his attitude, I thought.

Chapter Forty-Nine

Qua

Jakiyah had been giving me the silent treatment for the past few days, and I was just sick of it, so I decided to go meet Keem at the bar after work. I knew it was early in the afternoon, but I wasn't ready to go home, just to be ignored. I hoped she got her attitude in check before her doctor's appointment tomorrow.

"It's a little too early to be throwing back shots," Keem joked, taking a seat next to me at the bar.

"Nigga, your ass the reason I'm in the bar this damn early," I told his ass.

"I apologized. My bad. How many times do you need me to say it?" he said after ordering a shot.

"I need for you to say it, and don't stop saying it until my girl starts talking to my ass again."

"Nah. But on some real shit, at the time I wasn't thinking that it would cause a problem between you two, being that she was writing Jakiyah to apologize. If you need me to tell her that you didn't give me permission, I will, but you know she's not trying to talk to me."

"It's all good. She'll come around. But, anyway, what's going on with you, being that I haven't heard from your ass in a few weeks?" I asked him.

"I just been stressing lately because this shit with Yessenia has been taking a toll on me, man. I really feel like bailing, but I kind of blame myself for her being in this predicament," he said, then ordered another shot.

"It's not your fault, Keem, and you need to stop blaming yourself for her decision to take a life," I told him, keeping it real with him.

"I know, man, but it doesn't stop me from feeling just as guilty as she is," he stressed.

He had been stressing since it all happened, and had even been depressed. What kind of friend would I have been if I had turned my back on him? I needed Jakiyah to understand that it wasn't fair to ask me not to be friends with my best friend anymore. If she decided to forgive Yessenia, I wouldn't judge her. I wouldn't tell her that I thought that she shouldn't write or visit Yessenia. Instead, I would be supportive. The woman whom I want to spend the rest of my life with was that woman who could tell me when I was wrong but could support me while I righted that wrong. That was the woman who Jakiyah *was*, but I didn't know what the hell had been going on with her lately. I wanted to believe that the pregnancy was to blame for her being so argumentative and not conversational, like she used to be. I needed her to have this baby so that I could get my baby back.

"Fuck!" I mumbled under my breath when I caught sight of Kim and a few of my other coworkers walking in the bar.

Kim then walked right over in my direction. I honestly wasn't in the mood for her bullshit. I was tired of telling her that I didn't want anything to do with her.

"So, I got all your messages to leave you the hell alone, and I haven't contacted you since, so why the hell did you report me? That's some punk shit, acting like someone is obsessed with your ass. Trust when I say the dick wasn't all that, and payback is a bitch," she said before walking back out of the bar.

"Whoa. What the fuck was that about?" Keem laughed.

"That shit is not funny, man. This chick was harassing me after I kept telling her ass that I had a girl," I told him.

"Well, did you tell her before or after you smashed that you had a girl?" he asked.

"Before *and* after, I think. Shit, I was drunk."

"I can't believe you cheated on Jakiyah after that shit Tamara put you through. I guess you just attract crazy broads." He laughed.

"Whatever, man. Let me get my ass out of here, before I need a cab," I told him.

When I got home, Jakiyah was in the kitchen, cooking dinner, and she seemed to be in a good mood. I wasn't going to spoil it by saying anything to her. So I forced myself not to address her, but I wanted to. I was tired of this shit, because she really had no reason to be upset with me. I went upstairs, stripped out of my clothes, and took a shower to try to clear my damn head. While I stood under the streaming water, I decided I would go back downstairs to talk to her and see if we could get back to how it was before she received that damn letter. When I got back downstairs, I saw Jakiyah sitting on the couch, crying. She was looking at some papers in her hand, and all I could think was, *What now?*

"Are you okay?" I asked, figuring she must have received another letter from Yessenia that had her upset.

"You bastard, how could you?" she cried, throwing the papers at me. She raced upstairs.

I couldn't believe what I was looking at. That bitch Kim had set me up. She must have follo-wed me from the bar. I had thought I heard the doorbell when I was in the shower, but I wasn't sure, but indeed, I had. That bitch had given her a printout of all our text messages, minus the ones with me telling her ass that I was involved with someone and it couldn't happen again, because I had made a mistake while drunk. I went upstairs to try to talk to Jakiyah. She was packing a bag to leave, and my heart dropped at the thought of her leaving me.

"Jakiyah, don't do this please. Let's just sit down and talk about this," I pleaded.

She didn't respond. She just walked over to the dresser, took off her engagement ring, and left it on the dresser. She walked back over to the bed, grabbed her bag, and left the room. As much as I wanted to follow and beg her, I just figured I would let her go and cool off. I made sure to call Ty to let him know what had happened and to ask him to give me a call and let me know that she had made it safely to his mom's house. I didn't know what to do with myself at this point. I knew that I had fucked up and might have lost her for good for one night of some not so good sex.

Chapter Fifty

Jakiyah

When I left the home I shared with Qua, I was pissed off, and I'd just known that I was done with his ass. Two days had passed, and I hadn't heard from him. He hadn't been blowing up my phone with calls or text messages, and I had started to think that he was with that bitch, and I'd started to worry that he was done with me too. I had talked so much shit the night I got to my mother's house, so I couldn't even beg Ty to call him to see what was up with him. That would just make me look stupid.

I'd been having some cramping all day, and I just wanted to call Qua to tell him that I wasn't feeling well. Then I realized I had lost that privilege, as he was probably hurt that I had taken my ring off. I had every right to be upset with him, but I should have at least heard him out—even if nothing he said would have changed how I felt about him sticking his dick into another woman. I simply should have handled the situation better. Did he deserve another chance? Probably not. And he should have been kissing my ass right now. Still, I honestly thought that he was fed up, that my ass had probably pushed his ass into the arms of that bitch.

"You need to stop wobbling around here, sulking, and call that man, before that girl lay it on his ass so good, you not going to have to worry about walking down the aisle with that man," my mother said after walking into the kitchen.

"Mom, I'm not calling him. He cheated on me, remember?" I said to her, knowing I wanted to call him.

"I didn't say that he didn't, but I heard you for two days around here talking about how you were done with him and you didn't want nothing to do with him. But let me be the first to tell you that your actions are speaking much louder than those words of yours," she said.

She went on. "You expected that man to be here, kissing your ass, didn't you? Since you been pregnant, I have watched you push that man away and argue with him about just about anything. Again, I'll be the first to tell you that without communication, the relationship isn't going to work. I don't condone cheating, but you have to take responsibility for the part you played in it. And with that being said, go and call that man." She laughed as she walked out of the kitchen.

I wanted to call him so bad, but something in me just wouldn't allow me to make that call. He was the one who had cheated on me, so I just couldn't do it. It bothered me that he wasn't begging for me to come back, when he was in the wrong. And I swear, it caused me to have so many thoughts going through my head right now. I went up the back stairs to take my ass to my old room, where I had been sleeping for the past few days, because I was starting to feel pressure from this damn baby. I decided to lie down and to try to take a nap. Just as I was about to doze off, Qua walked in, looking sexy as hell, knowing his ass wouldn't be denied, since he was looking that damn good. I was trying to pretend that I was still mad at him, when all I wanted to do was smile. He was standing there, and now I didn't have to call him.

"Jakiyah, I know you probably dislike me right now, but I came here to say that I'm sorry. I don't want to give no explanation as to why I did it. No excuse is going to make you feel any better, because the fact remains that I cheated on you. I waited a few days before coming to ask for your forgiveness and to promise you that it will never happen again. I want to be your husband, and I want you to be my wife. So I was wondering if you could put this ring back on and make me a happy man again," he said. Then he got down on one knee, with the ring in his hand, and reached for my hand.

"Jakiyah, the way your ass been around here, sulking, you better take that damn ring and put it on your finger," my mom said as she stood in the doorway. Ty stood next to her, shaking his head.

I wanted to scream from the top of my lungs that I forgave him and that I was going to marry him, but I took a few minutes and pretended that I was thinking about it. He turned around, took a bag that Ty had in his hand, and handed it to me, saying it was a peace offering to help with my decision to forgive him. I opened the bag and couldn't help but smile when I saw the vanilla-bean ice cream and a bag of party mix.

"Yes, Qua, I will put the ring back on, but we still have some things that we need to talk about," I told him.

"I agree that we have to talk. So you go ahead and eat that nasty-ass concoction of yours, and we can talk after," he said.

Qua and I had a very long talk, and I agreed that I would stop lashing out at him and would talk to him instead. We even talked about the Keem situation and his continuing to be friends with him. Although I wasn't ready to be friends with Keem again, I agreed that he could be Qua's best man, like he wanted, when we got married. I let Qua know that if he ever pulled a punk move again and cheated on me because we got into it, I was going to stop his ass from breathing, and I meant it. I packed up my little overnight bag, and I followed him back to our house, smiling all the way that he had come to me and had proved that he had made a mistake but that his heart was with me and only me.

I had forgotten to call April back. I had snapped at her earlier because it had seemed like she was taking Qua's side, and I didn't want to hear what she was saying about me, as it was the truth. She was the only friend that I had left, besides Chanel and Desi, and I loved her like a sister, so I didn't want to lose her.

When I got home, all I wanted to do was soak in a tub of water, but I knew that Qua wasn't going to allow it. So I took a shower and waited for him to finish his. Then he ordered out, and we found a movie we wanted to watch and sat and ate dinner in front of the television.

Once Qua started massaging my feet, the movie started watching me. I fell asleep with my foot still in his hand. I woke up, like, three times that night to use the bathroom, because the baby was sitting on my bladder. After the last time, I couldn't go back to sleep, so I turned the television back on and watched *Flashpoint* until I eventually fell asleep again.

Chapter Fifty-One

Qua

As promised, my mother was flying in today. I was getting ready so I could pick her up at the airport, as her plane was landing at noon. Jakiyah had been having contractions for a few days now. When she went to the doctor yesterday, she was already dilated one centimeter, so she'd been trying her best to walk the baby down, because she said she was ready. I had told her to let me dick her ass down, but she was all scared that I might hurt the baby, so I'd told her ass to keep walking then.

Once I picked my mom up from the airport, I had to break the news to her that my dad and his wife, Emily, were flying in tomorrow and would be here until Jakiyah had the baby. She was cool with it: she said that she didn't have any problems with him or his wife and felt that the wife didn't care for her. I just hoped that they got along. Even though my dad and his wife would be staying at the hotel, I still wanted them to come by the house to have dinner and to spend some time with us.

When we got back to the house, Jakiyah was attempting to make lunch for us, but I could tell that she was in a lot of pain. My mother told her to sit down and handed her a bottle of water. I wanted to take her to the hospital, but she said that her contractions were too far apart and that she didn't want to go to hospital, just to sit on a bed, in pain. I grabbed a Corona from the fridge and joined her on the couch. I put her feet on my lap, and I rubbed her belly. I was nervous as hell, but I wasn't going to let her or my mom know it. I'd grabbed the Corona to try to calm my nerves. I couldn't believe how calm Jakiyah was being. This was her first child too, but I couldn't tell.

"Babe, you sure you don't want to go to the hospital?" I asked her again nervously.

"No, I'm going to wait it out. My doctor said that I shouldn't go to the hospital until the contractions were at least five minutes apart," she said, but I really didn't care what the doctor had to say, because her ass was in pain.

"Jakiyah, I really don't care what the doctor said. If you're in pain, I think that we should go. I'd rather we be safe than sorry," I told her.

My mom stepped into the room just then. "Qua, she's fine. Come on and get some lunch. And if it makes you feel better, after we finish lunch, we could pack a bag for Jakiyah and the baby, just in case it happens tonight," she said, then went back into the kitchen to set the table for lunch.

After lunch, I followed Jakiyah to the bedroom so that she could pack a bag. Once again, I stood back in awe: she was a pro at this. She smiled when she saw that I was holding Pampers and, like, five outfits for the baby in my hands.

"Silly, we are not taking those to the hospital. The Pampers are fine, but just grab a few onesies, some socks, receiving blankets, and that green and yellow sleeper right there," she said, coaching me as I put the other things back and got what she wanted to go in the bag.

I was a newbie for real and needed to learn, and quickly, because my li'l man or li'l princess was going to be here soon.

"Babe, do you need these too?" I joked, holding up a pair of her thongs, which her ass had stopped wearing when she became pregnant.

"Stop playing, Qua. You know you love these," she said and laughed as she showed me her granny panties.

I grabbed her and pulled her into my arms, being gentle. I held her and whispered thank you in her ear for having my baby. She was about to make me the happiest man in the world, because she was making me a daddy. And I was going to be the best daddy, even though I didn't know how. I figured I would follow in my dad's footsteps, because he was a great dad.

"Come on. Let's go downstairs before your mom thinks we abandoned her to do naughty things." She laughed as she pulled me out the door.

Later, we were all sitting on the couch, watching *Madea's Family Reunion*, when Jakiyah yelled out in pain. I jumped up, in panic mode, and panicked even more when she screamed that her water had broken. My ass was losing it, and my mother had to tell me to calm the hell down, and she didn't even curse. I rushed up the stairs to get the bag Jakiyah had packed, then rushed back downstairs to help Jakiyah to the car. My mom followed right behind us.

"Qua, stop pulling me and wait a second," she said, bent over, trying to wait for another contraction to pass.

"I'm sorry, bae," I told her, rubbing her back, as we all waited for the contraction to pass.

We couldn't get to the hospital fast enough. I tried to be sympathetic toward her because she was in pain, but I wasn't going to take too much more of her telling me to shut up. At a red light, I looked back at my mom, and she basically gave me that look that warned me not to say a word. So instead of talking, I grabbed Jakiyah's hand, like I had seen done in so many movies, and tried to soothe her as best I could. When we pulled up to the hospital, I parked the car and helped her out, while my mom grabbed the bag. At one point, we had to stop again to let another contraction pass.

As soon as we got to the emergency entrance, they put Jakiyah in a wheelchair and wheeled her up to labor and delivery. I started to get excited, because it was happening. I stepped out for a second to call Jakiyah's mother and Ty. I had honestly forgot to call sooner and let them know that we were on our way to the hospital. Her mom said that Ty was at her house and that they were on the way.

After I got off the phone, I stepped back into the room, and they were just putting Jakiyah on the monitor. Last month she had said that she didn't want any medication during childbirth, but she was in a lot of pain, and I thought that she was going to need something, because she was banging her head against the pillow. The nurse told her to do her breathing exercises, but she wasn't trying to hear the nurse. So I stepped closer to the bed, took her hand again, and told her to do the breathing exercises, but she cursed me out.

Chapter Fifty-Two

Jakiyah

I was in so much pain that I wanted to rip the damn IV out of my arm and slap the shit out of this nurse and Qua's fucking ass. I knew this shit was going to hurt, but I had had no idea that the pain was going to rip through my ass the way it was doing, and as much as I didn't want medication, my ass was singing the medication song. When I saw my mother come into the room, I let go of Qua's hand and started balling my eyes out for my mother. But another misconception that I had was that I thought Mama could make it feel better. I cursed, I screamed, and I cried for them to just take this damn baby out of me, because I couldn't take the pain anymore. I heard my mother ask the nurse if they could give me anything, and she said that I had to wait until the doctor came and examined me. I lost it.

"I been here over thirty minutes now, so where the hell is the doctor?" I yelled at her ass.

"Babe, calm down," Qua felt the need to say, and I gave him a look that shut his ass up quick.

Another doctor walked his ass in like he didn't want to be there, and I was pissed off that my doctor couldn't be here for the delivery. He told me to relax my legs so that he could do a vaginal examination, but I had to wait, because the contractions were really coming, like, seconds apart. When he said that I was dilated ten centimeters and I was ready to push, I was pissed. I wasn't ready to push. I wanted something to make the pain go away, but he said pain medication couldn't be given now. I swear, if I didn't want this baby out of me, I would have closed my legs tight and told him to get out of my face.

Fifteen minutes later, I swear, I felt like I had been pushing forever, and his ass saying, "Just one more push," was starting to get on my damn nerves. I had already given his ass at least six pushes. After one more big push, the baby was out, and it was a little boy. Once they removed him from my chest, I passed out. That was how tired I was, but I was proud of myself for getting his ass out. When I woke up, I was out of the recovery room and was now in a private room, and all my guests had gone, except for my baby daddy, who was sitting in the chair, admiring his son. He looked up at me with a smile so big, it warmed my heart, and I knew I needed to apologize to him for how I had treated his ass, because most women didn't get this lucky.

"Hey, do you want to hold him?" he asked me.

"Yes, I want to hold him." I beamed.

"You feel asleep as soon as the nurse laid him on your chest, so let me fill you in. At birth he weighed seven pounds and five ounces, and he was nineteen inches long," he said, handing him to me.

He was perfect, I thought as I counted his little fingers and toes. He had a head full of curly hair, and I wasn't trying to toot my own horn, but he looked just like his mommy.

"He's perfect, Qua," I said, then kissed his little cheeks.

Qua didn't want to name the baby after himself, so we had picked the name Chase Jamar Moore, but let me go on the record by saying his daddy named him. If it had been left up to me, I would have named him Quameek, after his damn daddy. I still felt some pain, so I handed the baby back to Qua, and he placed him in the bassinet so the nurse could come and get him. Being that Qua's mom was staying at the house,

Qua wasn't going to stay the night with me at the hospital, so I had requested that the baby sleep in the nursery. I was still tired and didn't want to drop him. After Qua left for the night, I called April and spoke to her for a while, giving her all the info on her godson and sending her a picture. Then I nodded off.

The nurse came into my room at 8:00 a.m. the next morning to tell me that Chase was being circumcised this morning and she would bring him to me for feeding as soon as he was done. I tried to get a few more hours of sleep in. I knew I was going to get a lot of visitors today, because Chanel and Desi didn't make it to the hospital yesterday. Ty's scary ass had stayed in the lobby during the delivery, so he had called me last night and had said that he would be back up here today to see his bigheaded nephew. I'd told him he held the title of bighead, so he could not pass it on to my son. I wished my dad was here to see my li'l man, but I knew he was looking down and smiling at his baby girl for bringing such a handsome baby into the world.

I enjoyed all the visits that day, but after visiting hours ended, I was beat again. Chase was cranky after being circumcised, so Qua decided to stay the night. I was being discharged in the morning, so he dropped his mother back off at the house and came back with the clothes I needed to go home in. I had worn my slippers to the hospital, so he brought me my sneakers, as well as a sweat suit.

Chapter Fifty-Three

Jakiyah

I'd been home from the hospital for two weeks, and when I tell you Qua and I were worn out, you wouldn't even believe me. Who would think that a two-week-old would be so much work? But it was true. My baby was a big ole crybaby. If I didn't know any better, I would think he didn't like me or Qua, since all his little ass did was cry, no matter how many attempts were made to quiet him down. I had expected motherhood to resemble the time I'd spent caring for baby Andrea, but nope, he was giving me hell.

I was upstairs getting dressed. I had already dressed him for his two-week checkup, and he was downstairs, giving Qua the business. I swear, I was going to miss Qua when he went back to work next week. I was going to be stuck with the little nightmare all by myself. I had tried to tell Qua to tell his mother not to sit and hold the baby when he was sleeping and not to pick him up every time he cried, because now she was gone, and we were left to deal with this spoiled little boy who never wanted to be put down. When I got downstairs, I saw Qua struggling with him. Chase was having a fit right now, screaming at the top of his lungs. It made me laugh.

"Don't just stand there. Take your damn son," he said, then handed him to me.

"So now he's my son, but when I was telling you to tell your mom not to spoil him, you paid my ass no mind."

"I'll be in the car," he barked. He grabbed the baby bag and his car seat before leaving.

I didn't know why he was upset with me because we had a little demon baby who was giving both of us the business. I wrapped Chase in his blanket and headed out the door, giving myself a pep talk not to go off on his ass for being rude.

The doctor said that Chase was fine, and it pissed me off that this little boy didn't cry one time at the doctor's office, making it look like we were exaggerating about our baby's behavior, given that we were new parents. I swear, I wanted to pinch his ass now that he was sleeping so peacefully, basically making us look like liars.

When we got back to the car, Qua took him from me to put him into the car seat, and I got in the car, thankful that he was sleeping.

"Babe, I'm sorry for snapping at you earlier," Qua said, apologizing, once he was in the car.

"Qua, Chase is driving me crazy too, but we can't take it out on each other," I told him.

"I know, babe, but his little ass had me tight." He laughed.

"But did you see how he played us and didn't cry one time in front of the doctor?"

We laughed.

Once we got back to the house, Chase was still sleeping, so I went into the kitchen to take something out for dinner and fix us some lunch. Qua said that he needed to talk to me about something, and I just hoped that it didn't end up with us arguing. I took a deep breath as I sat down at the table after fixing our plates. I prayed that I took whatever he needed to say in stride.

"So, what's up?" I asked him.

"Keem wants to come and see the baby," he blurted out.

I had to take a few minutes because I didn't want whatever I said to come out the wrong way, and I had to think about the conversation that we had recently had. I mean, if Keem were to come over, I could stay upstairs, in my bedroom, since I was not ready to talk to him or see him right now.

"Qua, if you want him to come and see Chase, I'm okay with it," I said, not believing the words that were coming out of my mouth.

"Are you serious?" he asked in disbelief.

I knew he didn't expect me to say that it would be okay, because I was stuck on blaming Keem, but after our last argument, Qua had made me realize that I couldn't blame him for how Yessenia had chosen to handle the situation. I never agreed with Qua, but he was right when he said that Keem was guilty only of cheating on her. He didn't put the gun in her hand.

"I'm serious, Qua, but I don't know if I'm ready to be in his presence right now. I could stay upstairs when he comes by," I said, being truthful.

"I understand, and thank you for doing this, and if you're not ready to see him, I'm sure he'll understand," he said.

After we finished eating, I went to tend to Chase, who had just woken up. I was in the kitchen, fixing him a bottle, when someone rang the doorbell. I didn't think that Qua had meant that Keem was coming over today, as in now. I was stuck in the damn kitchen, which meant I would have to see him to get back upstairs to

Chase. I wished Qua had back stairs like my mother had at her house, as that would work perfectly right now.

I tried to listen to see who entered the house. Maybe it wasn't Keem, I thought, but then I heard his deep voice. So now I was standing against the refrigerator, trying to figure out how the hell I was going to get out of here without having to see him. I promise you, I was ready for this awkward moment and would force myself to respond to him if he said anything to me. I wished I had my phone with me. I would have called Qua to tell him that I was stuck in the kitchen. I heard him go upstairs to get the baby, so I had to put my big girl panties on and come out of the kitchen. I walked out of the kitchen, and Keem was sitting on the couch, his back to me. I thought about sneaking by him, but then, that would be petty and childish, so I made my presence known.

"How are you doing, Keem?" I asked, causing him to turn around. He was shocked that I had spoken to him, and it showed on his face.

"I'm good, Jakiyah. Thanks for having me over," he said.

"No problem," I said before walking up the stairs, leaving it at that.

But it was a start, and I was proud of myself.

Chapter Fifty-Four

Qua

"Yo, I ain't never been so damn nervous in my life. Your damn girl scares me," Keem joked.

"It's all love. You know she'll come around sooner or later," I told him.

"Nah. I didn't expect her to even speak to my ass, so it's all good."

I just hoped that she came around, because now that Keem was going to be a part of the wedding, he was going to be around quite a bit. We had decided that we were going to get married on January 15, which was, like, a month and a half away, so we had to get on the ball with the planning. I heard Chase upstairs, having a fit again, and I was about to tell Jakiyah to bring him to me, but nothing I did stopped him from crying. I chilled with Keem for about another hour, before he headed out. Then I got right on the phone and called my mother to tell her what was going on with Chase, that no matter what we tried, it didn't work. I wanted to tell her that Jakiyah had said that she needed to come back, because she was the one who had spoiled his little behind, but I didn't. All she would have said was that there was no such thing as a spoiled baby.

My mother told me that when he got the way he'd been getting, I should lay him on my chest and rub his back, and that should work. She also said that if that didn't work, I should lay him on his stomach and rub his behind or his back until he quieted down. I was starting to really think that my baby had colic, because when I googled "a crying baby" some of the symptoms fit, but the doctor had said that he was fine and that if he had colic, there wouldn't be no in-between crying.

After I hung up with my mother, I went upstairs and took Chase from Jakiyah, who looked frustrated. I lay on my back and put the baby on my chest and started to rub his back, and I'd be damned if he didn't stop crying. Jakiyah looked at me with a smile on her face. I whispered to her to thank my mom, as she was the one who had told me to do this. I lay there for about ten minutes, and when I noticed that Chase was asleep, I gently got up off the bed with him and took him to his room and placed him in the crib. I waited a few minutes, just to make sure that he didn't wake up, before rejoining Jakiyah in the bedroom.

"Some peace and quiet, and it feels good," I said, plopping down on the bed, next to her. "Thanks for not treating Keem the way I thought you would upon seeing him," I added, then kissed her on the lips.

"I just wish that you had told me that he was going to come to the house today," she said.

"Yeah, when I asked you, he had already said that he wanted to stop by when he got off work. So when you said it was okay, I sent him a text letting him know that it was okay. You know, we have to start planning this wedding. We don't have that much time to plan."

"I know. That's why I let Chanel and Desi know that they need to come by one day this week so that we can start with the planning. I also want to hire a planner. I don't think that the three of us will be able to pull it off on our own in the short time that we have."

"Once you come up with the color scheme, that's when I'll get my dudes on board as far as our tuxedos are concerned, because we don't have much to do. The biggest thing for us is them planning my bachelor's party. I can't wait to get my freak on with the strippers," I joked.

"Yeah, okay. Die before you even walk down the aisle, if you want to," she said, cutting her eyes at me.

I scooped her up, pulled her into my arms, hugged her, and kissed her on her lips as I whispered in her ear, asking her if she was ready to be my wife.

"I'm more than ready," she said, kissing me on the lips and slipping her tongue in my mouth.

"Girl, you about to start something you know your ass can't finish, so I'm going to need you to fall back," I told her because she had my dick hard as hell knowing I can't tap that ass.

"No, you can't tap this ass, but there is something that I could do to take care of all of this," she said, reaching inside of my shorts and boxers pulling my dick out and putting it in her mouth.

I laid back and let her do her thing as my toes curled, causing me to grab the back of her head as I pumped in and out of her mouth. Chase must have known some shit was going down because once again he was screaming at the top of his lungs stopping my damn action as Jakiyah rushed into the bathroom and I went to pick his ass up. Fucking around with Chase ass I was going to keep a damn dry dick I thought as I picked his little crying ass up.

Chapter Fifty-Five

Qua

I was home alone today with the baby because Jakiyah, Chanel, and Desi were out picking up their dresses. Me and my dudes had got our tuxedos last weekend. Jakiyah had decided that she wanted the men in white tuxedos with turquoise shirts. At first I wasn't feeling it, but then I tried the shit on, and a nigga looked good. The bridesmaids were going to be in turquoise dresses, and Jakiyah was sticking with traditional white. To be honest, I didn't care what she walked down the aisle wearing, just as long as she was going to be my wife. I really couldn't believe how fast this day was coming: I really couldn't believe that next Saturday I was going to be a married man with a son. When we first met, I knew that Jakiyah was the woman that I wanted to marry. Although we had separated, our fate couldn't be denied, and Saturday would be the proof of that.

I was still a little upset with my father, although I didn't speak about it. The fact that he had not shown up when Jakiyah had the baby really bothered me. I knew it had had something to do with his wife, but I just felt as a man, he should have taken a stand, and if still she hadn't wanted to come, he should have been here. I had still extended to him an invitation to my wedding, and if he chose not to come, then he didn't ever have to worry about me inviting him to anything else of mine. He had assured me that he would be here, but only time would tell. I wasn't going to stress myself out about this.

Anyway, my mother and Donavon were going to be there without a doubt. If my mom and my brother showed up, I was good, because we needed my mother to be there for the demon baby. I prayed that Chase would be good at the wedding. I'm not going to lie. he had gotten much better. He didn't cry as much. However, he always wanted to be in either my arms or Jakiyah's arms, like the spoiled little baby he was. He didn't give Jakiyah's mom any problems, so I didn't know what his deal was with me and Jakiyah. Chase had to know somehow that Jakiyah and I were new at this parent thing: if he did not give her mother or my mother any problems, he must be trying to play us.

Jakiyah got back to the house later, all smiles as she came to sit next to me on the couch.

"What you smiling about?" I asked her.

"Today was a great day. I can't wait for you to see my dress. I'm so excited right now and can't believe that this is really about to happen." She was beaming even more now.

"Well, let's not wait. Let me see the dress now," I told her.

"Why, I knew you was going to say some shit like that. That's why I'm keeping my dress at my mother's house." She laughed. "So how was Chase today?" she asked.

"He was a good boy for his daddy, only flipping out on me one time, but I laid the spank down on his Pamper, and he got his act right," I joked.

"Yeah, okay. He knows he's the boss up in here," she said, getting up, probably to go wake his little ass up.

The next night we packed Chase's bag with everything he would need to be with his grandmother for the night. He was staying over at his grandmother's because tonight was the night I was hanging out with my dudes and Jakiyah was hanging out with the ladies. April was here, and she had planned something for Jakiyah tonight, but she wasn't telling me what that was. I had joked about crashing her little get-together, but I had only been bullshitting. I had let her know that me and the guys were going to Cheetahs Gentlemen's Club, thinking she was going to tell me what they had planned, but it had backfired and she hadn't told me anything.

After dropping the baby off and returning home, Jakiyah and I hugged and told each other to behave tonight. Then I left and headed over to Keem's spot, where we were all meeting up. When we got to the club, Keem had shit looking right. We sat around drinking and enjoying ourselves, and I was praying that he didn't have no damn special dance set up. That thinking right there let me know that I was ready to be married. But knowing Keem, I should have known that he was up to no good.

At some point two females approached and asked who the lucky man was who was getting married. I'm not going to lie. Both of them were some bad bitches. I sat back and let them do their thing, keeping my hands to myself. The Dominican chick was a bold one as she gyrated her body up and down mine and whispered in my ear, asking if I wanted a private dance. I kindly declined. She wasn't about to get my ass caught up, because I had plans to marry Jakiyah, and nothing was going to mess that up. I was tipsy, but I wasn't that damn tipsy. And I didn't go overboard with the liquor, because so many dudes drank too much and fucked around and got drunk and had that one last fuck. But it wasn't going to be happening to my ass.

We left the club at closing, which was at 4:00 a.m., and my ass was staggering just a little. When Keem dropped me off at home and I went inside, I discovered that my boo was waiting on me to make it home. Let's just say that my ass wasn't that tipsy, because I made love to her and couldn't wait until we were husband and wife. After we showered, we both collapsed. We had to go to pick Chase up in a few hours, so that was enough to warrant some sleep.

Our marriage ceremony was tomorrow, and I was really on edge now. I had no idea why, because I knew that this was the woman whom I wanted to spend the rest of my life with. But I could not shake my damn nerves. My mom was already here with her husband, and they were staying in a hotel this time. I was on my way to meet up with them, because they were going with me to do the finishing touches on Jakiyah's wedding gift from me. I just couldn't wait to see her face when I gave her my gift, as a whole lot of love had gone into doing this for her.

My mom telling me how proud she was of me was one of the best feelings in the world. I had really thought that our relationship was going to be strained after I found out that she had kept from me the fact that I had a twin brother, but it had just made it stronger. My father was the one who was acting all brand new with this wife of his. I really didn't understand why that was, but like I said, if he wasn't in attendance tomorrow, I was done. Once I had done everything with regard to Jakiyah's wedding gift, I told my mother that I would see her at the church tomorrow. Then I headed to the hotel where I was staying until I saw my beautiful bride at the church tomorrow.

Chapter Fifty-Six

Jakiyah

I stood at the entrance to the church, feeling nervous as I held on to Ty's arm and trying to calm myself as we waited for the music to start playing, our cue to move down the aisle.

"Are you ready?" Ty asked me as "You Are," by Charlie Wilson, began to play.

I tried hard not to cry and mess up my makeup before Qua saw me, but it was hard not to cry when I saw him as he stood up there, looking so handsome. As soon as his eyes met mine, I knew this was the man whom I was supposed to spend the rest of my life with. I swear, I was in a daze throughout the entire ceremony, until I heard the pastor say that we were now husband and wife and that Qua could kiss his bride. I was so lost in the kiss that I didn't even realize that everyone was clapping and waiting to snap pictures of the now married couple.

When we left the church, I thought that we were going to go to take pictures with the wedding party, but the limo pulled up to a house instead.

The house was beautiful. It was a two-story brownstone, the kind that I had always dreamed about owning one day. When I got out of the limo and saw Qua holding a SOLD sign in his arms, the tears fell. He put the sign down and picked me up and carried me into the house. When he put me down, I was in awe, because the downstairs was already furnished. It had a big sign that read WELCOME TO YOUR NEW HOME. I couldn't stop my tears from falling. *This man right here is truly amazing*, I thought as I took it all in.

"Do you like your wedding gift?" he asked me.

"No, I *love* my wedding gift. And to think I got you only a gift card to Macy's," I joked.

After Qua gave me a tour of the house, we left to take pictures and then headed to the reception to get our party on. Besides having my son, this was the most amazing feeling in the world, and I couldn't help but wish that my father was here to share my special day. Qua tried to act as if he didn't care if his father was here or not, but I knew it was a front, because he was so happy that his dad had made it to share this day with him. As the night came to an end, we thanked everyone for being here to share this day with us and for their gifts.

We then kissed Chase good night, because he was going back to the house with my mother. Qua and I weren't going on a honeymoon, but we were going to spend the night at the Peninsula Hotel. There we were going to enjoy each other and end our wedding night by making love as husband and wife.